# BURN HOT BURN LONG

## BRYAN CASSIDAY

BRYAN CASSIDAY

Bryan Cassiday
Los Angeles
ISBN 9798988189510
Published in the United States of America
First Edition: October 30, 2023

BOOKS BY BRYAN CASSIDAY

Hotbed (Apocalypse City Book 1)
Zombie Apocalypse: The Chad Halverson Series 1–7
Cutthroat Express (Zombie Apocalypse: The Chad Halverson Series Book 7)
Knot of Fear (Scott Brody Thriller 5)
Threads (Scott Brody Thriller 4)
Electric Green Mambas (Scott Brody Thriller 3)
Horde (Zombie Apocalypse: The Chad Halverson Series Book 6)
Ice in the Blood
Crime Blotter USA
Murder LLC (Scott Brody Thriller 2)
Bolt (Scott Brody Thriller 1)
Riptide of Fear
The Payout
Force of Impact (Ethan Carr Thriller 3)
Dying to Breathe (Ethan Carr Thriller 2)
Countdown to Death (Ethan Carr Thriller 1)
The Bus Stops Here—and Other Zombie Tales
Two Moons Rising
Alien Assault
Comes a Chopper
Zombie Apocalypse: The Chad Halverson Series 1–5
Helter Skelter
The Anaconda Complex
The Kill Option
Blood Moon: Thrillers and Tales of Terror
Fete of Death

Mere anarchy is loosed upon the world,
The blood-dimmed tide is loosed, and everywhere
The ceremony of innocence is drowned;
The best lack all conviction, while the worst
Are full of passionate intensity.
  –William Butler Yeats

Chapter 1

Phoebe kept jogging down the sidewalk away from the flame-engulfed Strip. She had to get as far away from the death trap as possible.

She didn't understand how her life had declined to such an abysmal state.

It wasn't like she had a choice. You couldn't choose what happened to you. You could only make your choices and deal with the results. You couldn't know for certain what the results would be. You just had to take your chances. She couldn't know Jason would cheat on her when she had decided to marry him.

You couldn't live without making choices unless you were a slave, Phoebe decided. If you didn't make a choice, someone else would make it for you, and you would lose your freedom. Meredith had been right about that. Poor Meredith. Her best friend. Murdered by government homicidal maniacs in choppers in cold blood.

How much did you have to bleed before the world left you alone? Phoebe wondered. Until you had no drops of blood left, it looked like. It was a never-ending battle you could never win. All you could do was survive to live one more day in the jungle, to fight one more day to stay alive as the world buffeted you with crippling blows.

Staying alive was hard enough with a killer virus on the loose. It was going to get much harder with the government targeting her. She didn't know what they wanted with her, but she knew they weren't planning to pin a medal on her chest. Maybe they wanted her because she had witnessed the murders of innocent citizens by government shooters. For sure, they wouldn't want her eyewitness account of the debacle on the Strip to see the light of day.

Phoebe had to find her husband Jason to see what he knew about the virus that drove its victims mad and turned them into cannibals. If that wasn't bad enough, it also turned them into zombies. The only cure was a bullet to the head and cremation. Or, like Margaret, you could kill yourself before the virus infected you. At least that way, you avoided the need for cremation. Phoebe wasn't going to take Margaret's route—not yet anyway.

No matter how hopeless her prospects were, she felt the urge to keep fighting in futility both a fatal virus and a government that committed wanton murder to wipe it out. At this point, Phoebe didn't know which was worse—the disease or the cure. She could do without both.

The government was after her.

They must think she was infected, because she was on the Strip when the virus broke out. Therefore, they wanted to "cure" her, government-speak for "kill" her.

She needed to get off the street and go into hiding. The problem was she didn't have a car. The cops had set it on fire on the Strip.

She had to find Jason. If anyone would know what was going on, he, as the mayor, would. He might even know why the cops had put out a bulletin for her arrest.

She produced her cell phone. The battery was down to 20 percent, but it should still work. She speed-dialed his number. It went straight to voicemail.

She couldn't understand why he wasn't answering. Was he deliberately cutting himself off from her? Or was something or someone preventing him from answering his phone?

She had nothing going for her. She was one person alone. How could she hope to resist the all-powerful government? If Jason couldn't help her, who could?

She didn't want to hitch another ride. Somebody might recognize her and report her to the cops. She kept walking down the sidewalk.

Wearing khaki Bermudas and a bright green and yellow aloha shirt, a middle-aged bald man with tattoos of monkeys on his forearms was jogging on the grassy median strip when he spotted her. He glowered at her and, foaming at the mouth, commenced drooling. He bolted toward her.

He must be infected, she decided. He must have escaped the Strip before the choppers had rendered it a napalm inferno. She broke into a run.

The man charged into onrushing traffic to cross the street to reach her on the sidewalk.

Unable to stop in time, the thirtysomething Hispanic driver of a stake truck crashed into him and mowed him down. The driver slammed on his brakes—too late. His stake truck juddered over the bald man's head and pancaked it.

The blood drained from the driver's face as he realized what he had done when he felt his tires bounce over the man's head. He froze in his seat in shock.

How many other infected had escaped the Strip? wondered Phoebe, accelerating her gait. The firebombing of the Strip had not been successful in wiping out the virus. Did that mean the government would torch other parts of the city to complete their mission?

She heard a loud rumble behind her. She craned around. A bus was approaching. She faced forward and saw a bus stop. She waved at the bus to slow down, so she could board. The bus would bring her anonymity. She could fade into the crowd of passengers. Just another face. A nonentity.

Not that anyone cared who she was. They had their own problems.

She forgot she didn't have her purse. She became pale as her heart sank. How could she get on the bus without money?

As the bus slowed down to pick her up, she dug frantically into her jeans pocket to find loose change. She sighed with relief when her fingers felt coins. She fished them out. She had enough quarters to pay the fare.

The bus pulled over and stopped. Its door opened with a pneumatic whoosh. She climbed the metal steps and deposited her quarters in the coin slot near the bus driver.

She walked down the aisle. The passengers paid little attention to her. Some of them sniffed the air as she passed. She smelled wood smoke. She wondered if it was coming from her, a memento of the burning Strip.

She found an empty seat and sat in it.

She didn't know where this bus was going—just as long as it was heading away from the Strip.

She saw the Burger King up ahead. She felt hungry. Her stomach growled in agreement. Without her pocketbook, she realized she didn't have enough money to buy food. She had had barely enough to pay for the bus. Food would have to wait. When she got back to her house, she could get one of Jason's credit cards. Except—

The cops might be waiting for her at her house. It was the logical place for them to look for her. They would be staking out her house awaiting her return.

She slouched her shoulders in despair. She couldn't go home.

She would have to meet Jason elsewhere. He would give her cash or a credit card to use. She was going to need money whatever she decided to do to escape the authorities.

She pulled her phone out of her jeans front pocket and speed-dialed Jason again. Again, he didn't answer. Was he in danger? she wondered, her pulse accelerating. Was that the reason he wasn't answering?

Her world was collapsing around her. Somehow she had to hang on.

She used to have it all. She was the mayor's wife. She had a beautiful house. A glamorous life. Now she had nothing. No car. No house where she could feel safe. No money. A wanted woman on the lam.

She had to find Jason. Maybe he was in his office. She hoped the cops didn't have his office staked out. There was only one way to find out.

From across the aisle, her large purse in her lap, a middle-aged woman with henna hair and a wrinkled face like a walnut was looking at her.

Phoebe turned quickly away from her and stared out the window on her left. Had the woman recognized her? Phoebe wondered.

She withdrew her cell from her trouser pocket, tapped on the camera app, reversed the view, and saw the image of her face on the screen with the woman's face behind her. The woman wasn't looking in this direction anymore.

Maybe she hadn't recognized her, decided Phoebe. After all, what would the mayor's wife be doing riding a municipal bus? Everybody knew wealthy pols rode limos.

Phoebe laughed to herself. What a joke. She didn't even have enough money to buy a burger.

Chapter 2

Phoebe decided to get off the bus the better part of a mile from Jason's office. She could tell from the bus's posted route that the bus wouldn't get any closer to her destination.

She made a point of looking away from the henna-haired woman as she made for the door in the middle of the bus, which wheezed open as the bus came to a halt. She darted down the steps and out of the bus onto the sidewalk.

She would have to walk the remaining mile.

At least the weather was nice with a clear blue sky above. The smoke from the Strip hadn't drifted in this direction, since she was upwind of the fire. The few pedestrians on the sidewalks didn't look concerned about contracting the lethal virus that had decimated the Strip.

The existence of the virus must not have been broadcast on the news yet, decided Phoebe. She wondered if it was Jason's idea. As mayor he could be keeping the news of the virus under wraps—for a while anyway. The media was bound to find out eventually.

As well, the incineration of the Strip couldn't be concealed from the media indefinitely. But news of a fire wouldn't panic citizens like that of a killer virus would.

Despite her tired legs, Phoebe kept walking toward Jason's high-rise office at city hall. She didn't know who else to turn to for help. She was also worried about him. Why wasn't he answering his cell phone?

She tried calling him again. It went straight to voicemail. Granted, her phone battery was all but dead. But she could hear ringing when she dialed his number. Which meant the call must be going through.

After she crossed the next block, she could see his high-rise looming in the distance dwarfing the shorter buildings surrounding it.

Her pulse picked up speed. Jason would know what to do, she decided. He was smart, and he had power as a politician. Maybe he could get the authorities off her back. She wasn't the one who had shot innocent victims on the Strip. It was the cops in choppers.

She kept walking.

She could see the high-rise several blocks away from her. She could also see ambulances with flashing red lights parked in front of it. Police cruisers were blocking the traffic on the street, redirecting it.

Scanning the high-rise she could see a broken window on one of the higher floors.

Adrenaline coursed through her system. What had happened? she wondered. She picked up on the cops standing in the street and froze. She couldn't let them see her. They would be on the lookout for her.

The EMTs were transporting somebody on a gurney toward their ambulance.

A crime scene or maybe an accident? she wondered. She counted the floors to the broken window. Jason's office was on that floor. She gasped. Had something happened to him? It would explain why he wasn't answering his phone.

It didn't look like an accident, she decided. How could someone accidentally break a window and fall out of a building? The victim either was pushed or jumped through the window. Hence the presence of the cops.

The victim might be Jason. It might just as easily be someone else, she decided.

She couldn't tell if the broken window belonged to Jason's office. Even if that office was on his floor, it could belong to someone else. It could be a member of his staff who had fallen. She didn't want to jump to conclusions.

Jason wasn't the type of person who would commit suicide. And who would push him out his window? The populace loved him. He was their incorruptible mayor.

She ached to know what had happened, but if she went over to the building, she risked being recognized and busted by the cops on the scene. There was no way she could get past the cops into the building. The street was crawling with them.

If something had happened to Jason, why hadn't someone notified her? she wondered. As his wife she was the person to contact in case of an emergency.

She checked her cell phone to see if she had received any e-mails or phone calls regarding Jason. The battery was dead.

Chapter 3

Phoebe spotted one of her bank's branches two blocks away. She was going to head for it when she remembered she didn't have her ATM card, which was in her purse. Her purse must still be in her would-be kidnaper Hardy's wrecked car.

She thought about telling a bank cashier that she had lost her ATM card and wanted a new one. To do that, she would need to tell them who she was. The cashier might notify the police. Forget it.

She would have to lie low. Whatever she decided to do, she needed money.

She pondered her next move.

She would head to her mother's house.

She returned to the bus stop and studied the map of the bus route. She found out at which stop she had to get off to catch the bus to her mother's. She had enough change in her trouser pocket to pay for a couple more bus rides.

She sat down on the bus bench and looked down at the sidewalk so nobody noticed her. She waited and listened for the next bus to arrive.

She desperately wanted to find out who had fallen out of Jason's high-rise, but she dared not go over to the building lest cops spot her. Sitting at the bus stop, she felt exposed and vulnerable.

At last the bus arrived.

As she walked down the aisle, a seated, middle-aged, burly guy wearing jeans and a sweatshirt said, "Hey, Mrs. Mayor."

He waved at her with dirty fingers.

She didn't acknowledge him. Maybe if she ignored him, he would leave her alone.

She found a seat and gazed out the window.

She cast a furtive glance in his direction to see if he was using his cell phone to call the cops. He didn't have his cell out, but he was looking in her direction. His ridged yellow hardhat hung on the back of his seat. His hair cropped, he had a large equine face and a squat, sunburned neck.

"Are you too good for us smelly Walmart types who drink beer and eat Cheetos at tailgate parties at football games?" he said, his visage surly.

"I don't know what you're talking about," she said.

"I got a Dodge Charger up on blocks in my front yard too. You uppity types wouldn't want to be caught dead near my house."

"There must be some mistake."

"Yeah, my mistake. I voted for your husband."

"You must have me confused with someone else."

He paused, staring at her in bemusement.

"I dunno. You sure look like the mayor's wife."

Phoebe had to think fast. She couldn't afford to draw attention to herself. She had to get out of this mess.

"Why would the mayor's wife be riding a bus?" she said.

The guy shrugged. "You're the mirror image of her."

"Oh, I get that all the time," she said, smiling. "I guess I should be flattered."

"I thought we had a celebrity with us," he said, disappointed.

"I wish."

The guy grunted and looked away from her.

She didn't know if she had convinced him she was someone else. He didn't look completely satisfied with her answer. On the other hand, he wasn't pursuing the conversation either.

At least he wasn't reaching for his cell phone. If he started talking on his cell, it would mean he didn't believe her and he was telling a friend, or worse, he was telling the cops of the whereabouts of the mayor's wife. He scratched his chin with his grimy, callused fingers.

She looked away from him. She didn't want him to notice her looking in his direction. It would make him suspicious of her lies.

Chapter 4

A half hour later, Phoebe found herself in front of her mother's house, a white clapboard affair with a freshly mown pocket lawn. Phoebe enjoyed the scent of fresh-cut grass.

She wished she had good news to tell her mother. Not today.

She walked down the cement path to the front door. Several flame-colored birds-of-paradise burst under the front picture window on her right looking like they wanted to peck her hands with their beaks. On her left, grew an aromatic rosemary bush that smelled like mint.

Standing on the cement stoop, she opened the screen door and tried to open the front door. It was locked. She rapped on it.

Moments later, her mother Lila appeared at the door.

Middle-aged with a perm, Lila stood in the doorway. Since she didn't know who had knocked, she wore a no-nonsense expression on her face, the same expression she wore for the classroom where she taught, decided Phoebe.

Lila had an aquiline nose, which, combined with her icy blue eyes, gave her countenance a dour aspect. She was wearing a subdued peach organdy shift.

"Phoebe. I wasn't expecting you," said Lila, her visage melting into a smile.

"I need help, Mom."

"What?" said Lila with concern. "Come in. What happened?"

Phoebe entered the sparsely furnished living room. Her mother never spent money on fancy furniture. She and Dad spent the bulk of their money on books, which filled a plethora of shellacked pine shelves fastened with metal L-shaped shelf brackets to the surrounding walls. The only rooms that didn't have any shelves of books were the kitchen and the bathrooms.

Anxious, Phoebe felt her stomach twisting into a knot. She saw no way out of it. She had to tell her mother. Dad wouldn't be buying any more books.

"I have bad news," said Phoebe.

"Go on."

"Maybe you should sit down."

"I don't want to sit down."

"OK, I'll cut to the chase. Dad—uh, Dad is dead."

"What?" said Lila, aghast. "What are you talking about?"

"It's true, I'm afraid. I saw it."

"But he wasn't even sick. How could he be dead?"

Phoebe decided to tell her the truth, no matter how implausible it sounded.

"Cops in a helicopter shot him," said Phoebe, recalling with horror the ghastly image of his murder.

Lila widened her eyes. "I don't believe it. Why would cops shoot him? He's not a criminal. Not Sam. He never even got a parking ticket."

"They shot a lot of people on the Strip."

Lila shook her head in befuddlement. "You're coming at me from left field. Why was Sam on the Strip?"

"He was working on a story for his paper."

"That doesn't give cops the right to shoot him," said Lila, her voice cracking.

Feeling her legs giving out, she sat on the emerald green linen sofa.

"They thought he was infected with a virus," said Phoebe.

"So they shot him?" said Lila, her voice ringing with disbelief.

"I know it's hard to believe, but that's how the cops are treating the infected."

"Where's his body?" said Lila, face grim.

"They burned it."

Unable to get her head around it, Lila stared into space.

"It's true," said Phoebe. "I saw it happen."

"Not Sam. This can't be true."

"Do you think I would make something like this up?" said Phoebe, feeling guilty for Sam's death.

After all, she was the one who had asked him to investigate the hooker Val Lewton on the Strip to find out if she had committed murder. Otherwise, Sam would have been nowhere near the Strip when the cops had started massacring people.

"Have you reported this to the police?" said Lila.

"How can I? The police are the ones that shot him."

"Then you need to report the police who did it."

"To who? The cops protect their own. They're not gonna do anything."

She sounded like the hooker Courtney with her cynical outlook, Phoebe realized.

"Report it to the state cops," said Lila.

"The state cops were involved in the murder."

Lila began sobbing. "Not Sam. He never hurt a soul. He can't be dead."

Phoebe sat beside her. "I know."

"Have you heard any updates on Jason?" said Lila, her eyes mournful.

"Updates? What are you talking about?"

"Didn't anybody tell you?"

"Tell me what?" said Phoebe, her body tense.

"I can't believe nobody told you."

"My cell phone's dead. What happened?"

"Jason's in the hospital—"

"Hospital?"

"He's in a coma."

"No. That's impossible."

It would explain why he hadn't answered any of her calls, decided Phoebe, distraught.

"The police notified me as his next of kin that he fell out of his office window onto the street," said Lila. "I guess they couldn't reach you."

"How could he fall out of his office window? That window doesn't open."

Lila shook her head, her face glum. "Why is everything happening to us?"

Chapter 5

"It sounds fishy to me," said Phoebe. "Something's going on."

"Maybe you should go to the police," said Lila.

"I can't. They put out an arrest warrant for me. I heard about it on the radio."

Lila widened her eyes. "For what? What did you do?"

"I think it has to do with what's going on at the Strip. I saw the cops murder people, including Dad."

"What crime did you commit?"

"None. They don't want me to tell anyone about the murders they committed."

"They can't arrest you for being a witness to a crime. That's illegal."

"If it's legal to shoot people who are infected, it's legal for the shooters to arrest me for anything they want."

"That doesn't sound like America."

"Haven't you been listening to the news?"

"I haven't had a chance. I've been grading my students' tests," said Lila, glancing at a wooden desk in the living room cluttered with papers.

"The Strip burned down. Helicopters set it on fire to eradicate the new virus. A lot of people on the Strip died."

"*That* was on the news?"

"No. The news says it was an accidental fire that burned down the Strip."

"Then why do you say it was deliberate?"

"Because I saw the choppers napalm the Strip."

"That's not how we do things in this country. Why would Jason tell them to burn the Strip?"

"I can't believe he told them. Someone else must've given the order."

Then again, maybe Jason was afraid of his liaison with Val Lewton getting out, decided Phoebe, so he ordered the Strip wasted, hoping Val would be killed. Phoebe couldn't believe Jason

18

would give the order to kill innocent people just to cover up his illicit affair. Somebody else must have given the order. But not to cover up an illicit affair. To kill the infected.

"You must be right," said Lila.

"And I don't believe for one instant that Jason fell out of his office window. Someone must have thrown him out."

Lila gasped. "Do you know what you're saying?"

"It's the only explanation that makes sense."

"Who would do such a thing? You're talking about an assassination attempt."

"The cops don't want anyone to tell the public that they're killing innocent people. Maybe Jason found out what the cops were doing, and they were afraid he'd go public with it. So they threw him out his window."

"Are things really that bad?"

"I'm afraid so."

Phoebe cringed as she heard the whump-whump of a chopper flying over the house. Her eyes bulging, she looked up at the ceiling like it would cave in any minute.

"What's the matter?" said Lila.

"Choppers. Every time I hear a chopper I think of them shooting people."

The chopper could be looking for her, decided Phoebe with dismay. It would make sense for the authorities to send someone to check Lila's house to see if her daughter was hiding there.

"I better not stay here," said Phoebe. "I don't want to get you into trouble."

"You're my own flesh and blood. Why can't you stay here?"

"Because the cops want to arrest me. They'll arrest you for harboring a suspect."

Lila clutched her forehead. "This isn't the country I grew up in. I don't recognize it anymore. Cops shooting infected people from choppers? No."

"I better leave."

Lila removed her hand from her lugubrious face. "Where will you go?"

"I'll have to think of somewhere." Phoebe paused in thought. "Maybe I should leave the city."

"Let me help you."

"I told you I don't want them to arrest you."

"At least let me loan you my car."

"Yeah. OK. But how will you get around without your car?"

"I'll use Sam's. He's not gonna—uh—not gonna be needing it, from what you say," said Lila, standing up, looking exhausted.

Phoebe hugged her mother. "Thanks, Mom."

Lila retrieved her car keys from her purse and handed them to Phoebe.

"Be careful," said Lila. "I don't want to lose you too."

"I'll be in touch as soon as I find somewhere safe to hide."

"I can't get my head around losing Sam," said Lila, dazed.

"Stay away from the Strip—what's left of it anyway."

"What do you mean?"

"The only thing left is ashes."

"I don't understand why you were over there in the first place."

"I—um—it's a long story. I better be going."

Phoebe angled to the front door. She didn't want to tell her mother Jason had been cheating on her with Val Lewton. Phoebe wondered what had happened to Val. Were the authorities holding her in captivity? If so, why?

Phoebe halted in front of the door.

"By the way, Mom, if you see anyone frothing at the mouth and moving really fast, stay away from them. Get away from them as far as possible."

"Why would I see someone like that? It sounds awful."

"It means they're infected with a virus that turns them into raging cannibals. I hope you don't see anyone like that. The napalm fire at the Strip was supposed to wipe out the virus and kill the infected."

Lila's face looked more drawn than ever as she digested Phoebe's words.

"Unconscionable," muttered Lila. Her eyes brightened. "Maybe we should report this to the FBI. They would know what to do."

"I believe they're involved in the containment of the virus."

"Who *isn't* involved in it?" said Lila, flabbergasted.

"The government is in charge of the program. Anyone with ties to the government is suspect," said Phoebe, latching onto the doorknob, preparing to leave.

She needed to be going. She knew her presence jeopardized her mother's safety.

"If we can't tell the FBI, who can we tell?" said Lila, bewildered.

Phoebe had no answer.

"I'll be in touch when I find a hideout," she said, and departed.

Chapter 6

Phoebe could hear another chopper approaching overhead.

She bopped to the garage, lifted open its folding wooden door, and unlocked Lila's unwashed 2015 silver Ford Fiesta, which had a dented left front fender. The tire under the fender looked like it needed air, but it would have to do. She would fill it with air after she left the city limits. She clambered into the driver's seat.

She doubted the chopper pilot had seen her. The chopper hadn't been in view when she had made her run.

Was she being paranoid hiding from the chopper? she wondered. Maybe the pilot wasn't even looking for her. He could have been on an altogether different assignment that had nothing to do with finding her. Maybe it wasn't a police helo. It could be a commercial helo.

The less choppers in the sky, the better, as far as she was concerned. They were the harbingers of death. The cacophony of their rotor blades would forever jangle her nerves after her blood-soaked nightmare on the Strip.

Maybe she was paranoid, she decided once again. So what? Nobody ever died from paranoia.

On the other hand, you could die from trusting too many people. They could turn you into the cops or, worse, kill you. Or the cops could kill you. Hell, she was a wanted woman, and she had witnessed cops murdering innocent people.

There might be a reward on her head, for all she knew. Bounty hunters could be searching for her. She told herself to stop thinking about it or she would go nuts.

She didn't know what the cops were going to charge her with. Maybe it wouldn't get to that point. Maybe they had orders to shoot her on sight. Without a trial, she couldn't expose their murders during her testimony.

She flicked on the car radio. Her mother had been listening to Rush Limbaugh. Phoebe switched to a local all-news station. It didn't take her long to find out the charge against her. Five minutes after she had turned on the news, the newscaster said they were charging her with murder and she was considered armed and dangerous.

In other words, the cops would shoot her on sight, she decided. The cops couldn't risk a trial, because she had not committed murder and they knew it. *They* were the murderers, and they had the full support of the government behind them.

As she had told her mother, her best bet was to leave town.

She would take Main Street to the border and keep on going before she found a place to hole up in another town. She had no real destination in mind. All she knew was she had to get out of town.

Staying here any longer was hazardous to her health.

"We interrupt this newscast to bring you an important bulletin," said the radio newscaster. "All roads leading in and out of Costaguana are closed. By order of Governor Vitti, nobody is allowed to enter or leave the city. The city is locked down to halt the spread of a lethal virus. Stay tuned for further developments."

"What?" said Phoebe in alarm. "No. They can't do that."

She hammered the top of the steering wheel with her fist in frustration as she felt the noose tightening around her throat.

Chapter 7

CDC medical officer Vincent Zandorf entered Jason Albright's room at St. Luke's Hospital in downtown Costaguana. He ran his fingers through his receding widow's peak and adjusted his black plastic glasses with thick bows.

He approached Jason's bed.

Jason was hooked to a wheezing ventilator, which helped him breathe. An electronic monitor recording his blood pressure, oxygen level, and heartbeat stood next to his bed, blinking green, pale blue, and white digital numbers on its screen, accompanied by fitful beeps.

"How is the mayor, Doctor?" Zandorf asked a fortysomething surgeon in scrubs standing beside Jason's bed with a clipboard in his hand.

"Not good, I'm afraid," said Dr. Raspail, lowering his blue surgeon's mask. "And who do I have the pleasure of speaking to? Are you related to Mayor Albright?"

"I'm Vincent Zandorf, a medical officer at the CDC. I'm spearheading the investigation into the new virus that was reported on the Strip."

Raspail nodded. "The mayor is still in a coma."

Zandorf eyeballed Jason with concern. Virtually Jason's entire body was swathed in bandages or encased in casts as he lay in bed.

"What's the prognosis?" said Zandorf.

"As you can see, he has sustained multiple fractures, including a broken spine. He also has internal injuries to his spleen, liver, lungs—"

"Will he live?" Zandorf cut in.

"He fell five stories. The human body wasn't designed to fall from such a great height."

"Does that mean no?"

"I'm not in the fortune-telling business—"

"You're a professional doctor. Surely you can tell me if he's going to live."

"If he lives, he will be bedridden for many years, perhaps his whole life."

"I need to talk to him."

"What's this about?" said Raspail, growing weary of the third degree.

"It's about the new virus going around. We need to know if he's infected."

"He's not gonna be able to tell you anything."

"Why not? This is urgent. The future of our great country could depend on it. The future of the world, for that matter."

"Can't you see? The mayor's in a coma."

"When do you expect him to come out of it?" said Zandorf, studying Jason as he lay motionless with his eyes shut, the ventilator tube in his mouth.

"Impossible to tell. As a fellow medical professional, you must know comas can last many years."

Zandorf nodded his grim face. "Not good."

"He has life-threatening injuries. He's lucky to be alive."

"The human race will lucky to be alive if he doesn't come out of that coma soon and tell us what we need to know about the virus."

"What could he possibly tell you?"

"How he got infected. We need to establish patient zero for the virus. We think it was a hooker called Val Lewton. She kept repeating the mayor's name before she died. We need to find out if they knew each other. If they met recently, he could be infected."

Raspail eyed Jason with commiseration. "He won't be telling anybody anything for quite some time. We could lose him any minute."

Zandorf scowled. "I can't impress upon you enough that finding out if he's infected is of the utmost importance to the future of mankind. We will have no future if this lethal virus continues to spread."

"The mayor is barely clinging to life. I'm only a doctor. I can't raise the dead."

Zandorf looked nonplussed.

"Are you OK?" said Raspail, remarking the pallor of Zandorf's complexion.

"You said, 'raise the dead.'"

"Yes . . ."

"The infected victims are returning to life," said Zandorf, his voice hoarse.

"Impossible," said Raspail, taken aback.

"It's true." Zandorf paused. "We'll need samples of the mayor's blood for analysis.'

"Of course."

Zandorf stroked his chin. "Somehow we must find out who he had contact with this week. If he's infected, he could have infected others. As a public figure, he could have infected hundreds."

"Maybe his wife could help you."

"Instead of Val Lewton, *he* might be patient zero."

"As I understand it, this virus kills very quickly. If the mayor is patient zero, wouldn't he have died by now?"

Zandorf raised his eyebrows. "Could be. But as far as this virus is concerned, we know very little about it. All we have is speculation. We need facts. We need to know if Albright's infected. If he is, he could be an immune carrier, since he's showing no symptoms of the virus."

"His wife might know who he has met recently."

Zandorf snorted in frustration, fluttering his nostril hairs.

"We can't find his wife," he said. "She was sighted on the Strip, but has since disappeared."

"I can't help you. He hasn't said a word since entering the hospital." Raspail's face clouded. "Do you think he's infected?"

"That's what we need to find out. Hopefully, there's a clue in his blood. The fact is we know very little about this virus. It has no precedent. We're feeling our way."

"Is he infectious in his current state?"

"If he has the virus, he could be. It's highly contagious."

Raspail furrowed his brow with worry and slipped his mask back on.

"I'll tell the nurses to wear their masks when they treat him," he said.

"Masks aren't very effective against this virus."

"We have state-of-the-art N95s left over from Covid."

"Masks aren't gonna prevent him from biting you," said Zandorf, and left the room before Raspail's jaw dropped.

Chapter 8

Maybe it was propaganda, decided Phoebe, continuing her drive down Main Street toward the city border. Many believed the mainstream news media was hand in glove with the current government administration. The news just said what the government told them to say to help the current administration stay in power. Her journalist father had wanted to tell the truth about the massacre on the Strip, and look what they had done to him. They had murdered him.

Phoebe felt her throat tighten at the thought of her father's cold-blooded murder.

The announced lockdown could be disinformation, she decided.

On the other hand, it *was* true that traffic was becoming slower and more congested as she drove closer to the city limits.

Maybe Main Street really was closed, she decided. The problem was there weren't any alternative routes out of town. Costaguana was surrounded by desert, which had no roads through it other than Main. She would need a four-by-four to drive onto the desert if she wanted to risk it. The Fiesta wouldn't last five minutes traveling across the undeveloped desert. The bumpy terrain could break an axle or the driveshaft, or damage the chassis.

She didn't want to risk coming in sight of the cops blocking the road. Maybe it was time to turn back, she decided.

She started when she heard a chopper approaching overhead. The flight crew was no doubt helping the roadblock up ahead.

She needed to drive elsewhere, but first she needed to make sure Main Street was blocked. She couldn't see a roadblock from here.

She kept driving toward the border.

Traffic was barely moving now.

She didn't want to get stuck in traffic. She would need to exit Main soon.

She tensed behind the wheel as she picked up on a commotion up ahead. She heard yells and screams. A mob of angry people was congregating, venting their frustration and wrath at cops who were blocking the road with their parked cruisers.

Some members of the mob were hurling rocks and beer bottles at the cops and their cruisers.

A full-blown riot, decided Phoebe. She had no desire to become stuck in the middle of a riot. She would turn off the road at the next right.

She heard sirens approaching in the distance. Reinforcements for the cops, she decided. A cop up front was using a bullhorn to order people to disperse. Incensed by the cop's orders, the agitated mob increased their hubbub and flung more objects in the direction of the cops.

"I'm losing money if I can't drive out of town," cried a bearded thirtysomething man wearing coveralls with a white button-down shirt. "I have a family to feed."

The mob roared, cheering him on.

"You're taking the food out of my family's mouth," he yelled.

"Highway robbery," cried a guy in a red gimme cap, pumping his fist above his head, his face twisted with fury. "Let us out."

The cops weren't budging, continuing to snarl traffic.

"You are ordered to disperse," said the cop with the bullhorn. "Go home. By order of the governor, under the rules of the lockdown nobody is allowed to leave town."

"You can't do this," hollered Gimme Cap.

"This is a health mandate. You are ordered to obey the mandate."

The crowd started muttering among themselves, looking puzzled.

"Return to your homes and shelter in place," the cop went on.

A fleet of clattering police choppers arrived on scene, adding to the tumult.

"It's for your own good to return to your homes and shelter in place," said the cop. "A lethal virus is on the loose."

Phoebe didn't need convincing. She wanted out of here. If a cop saw her, she was dead. She was sure these choppers carried snipers like those that had decimated the Strip. The snipers would open fire if the crowd didn't disperse.

Her car was stuck in gridlock. She couldn't reach the nearest crossroad to turn off Main. She couldn't back up either because of the half mile of traffic that stretched behind her.

She wished the cars ahead of her would turn off and go home.

She had no idea where to go. She only knew she had to get out of here. With this many cops around, one of them was bound to spot and bust her. Or shoot her—which she figured was more likely, since her death would prevent her from testifying against their murderous rampage on the Strip.

Where could she hide from the all-powerful government that was out to destroy her? she wondered. They had a full array of resources at their disposal. She had none.

She didn't like her chances. It didn't bear thinking about.

She would never surrender, though. She must expose their corruption—somehow. It was the only way she could think of to free herself from their persecution.

Would anyone believe the cops had murdered everybody on the Strip? she wondered. Somebody had to believe her. She needed to think positive. But who would believe her? And who could she trust? The FBI? How did she know they weren't involved in the slaughter? The state cops were. She had seen Highway Patrol cruisers blockading the Strip when the cops had razed it to the ground with napalm.

How far did the tentacles of corruption extend into the government? Did the killers have the blessing of the president when they committed their atrocities to wipe out the new virus? It was chilling to think so, she decided.

In the creeping traffic, she inched her mom's Fiesta forward, desperate to reach the upcoming intersection, where she could turn before reaching the blockade. She lowered the car's sun visor, hiding her face from the cops who were swaggering around the better part of a mile up ahead inspecting cars.

She considered abandoning the car and making a mad dash for safety. However, she thought a cop might spot her, though she doubted it, because they were barely in view at this point. It was the choppers that worried her the most. They were hovering closer to her, and their crewmen could spot her abandoning her car. It would arouse their suspicions, and they would give chase.

Best to wait for the intersection up ahead, she decided, grinding her teeth with apprehension. Spotting a car turning away from the roadblock wouldn't arouse the cops' suspicion, since they had given the order to disperse and return home. By turning away she was following their instructions.

If only she could reach the intersection.

Chapter 9

Jason's father, real-estate tycoon Jackson Albright, thought his son was getting a bum rap for triggering the upheaval in Costaguana. Sure, Jason was the mayor, but you couldn't blame everything that was wrong in town on the mayor, decided Jackson, clad in a grey suit as he strutted around his office desk, circling it like a great white going in for the kill.

Even in his eighties, he had a military bearing and walked with determination and purpose.

No matter what Jackson did, he gave the impression he was out to take someone's scalp. His acquisitive dark blue eyes signaled he wouldn't let anybody stand in the way of his object of desire.

Even when he laughed, people didn't warm to him. It was the laugh of a bloodthirsty hyena. His smiles, like feral grins, silenced people and raised the hackles on their necks.

Jackson would not stand for his son's reputation as incorruptible being trashed. He wasn't going to let the government timeserver Zandorf bruit it around that Jason was responsible for wrecking the town. In the injured state Jason was in, he couldn't defend himself from scurrilous charges. It was all too easy to take a guy down a peg when he was lying comatose in a hospital bed. Jackson wasn't going to stand idly by and let that happen.

Jackson had enough power, money, and connections to find out what was really going on in this town. He didn't believe for one moment the news report that his son had fallen out of his office window, a window that couldn't be opened. Someone had tried to assassinate him by defenestrating him, decided Jackson. No other conclusion could be reached.

The question was, who? Did it have anything to do with this killer virus that was spreading through Costaguana? Had somebody blamed Jason for the virus because he was the mayor and, as a result, had tried to kill him?

The value of real estate in town was going to hit the skids if this virus wasn't contained and eradicated on a dime. His company would suffer irrevocable financial losses if the lockdown continued much longer.

With his son comatose and a new mayor in charge, how could he influence the government? wondered Jackson. Jason had been his direct line to the seat of power. Jackson didn't know the deputy mayor who was assuming Jason's job. He didn't even know the guy's name. Whoever it was had better open up the city fast.

Shutting the city's borders was an egregious error, decided Jackson. Residents would be moving out en masse if the city was locked down for any length of time. The bottom would fall out of the real estate market.

He had already taken a disastrous hit on the Strip, where he owned multiple buildings that had burned to the ground. He couldn't sustain any more losses in his real-estate empire. How could the entire Strip have burned? It was impossible to get his head around it. Was the fire department taking a siesta when it happened?

Who the hell was in charge at the time of the fire? The deputy mayor?

Maybe the deputy mayor was a mere figurehead. According to the media, it was Governor Vitti who had ordered Costaguana's lockdown. What was the idiot thinking? Jackson had to get the guy to open up the city posthaste.

Jackson also needed to talk to Jason's wife Phoebe. He couldn't understand why there was an arrest warrant out for her. She might know who had killed Jason. She was his closest confidante. How was he going to find her while she was running from the police? The news bulletins had said she was armed and dangerous. Phoebe? Were they talking about the same Phoebe he knew? No matter how hard he tried, he couldn't imagine Phoebe armed and dangerous.

Jackson produced his cell phone. He had a direct line to the governor.

"Hello, Governor. This is Jackson Albright."

"Hello, Mr. Albright. Sorry to hear about your son's accident."

*Accident, my ass.*

"Thank you," said Jackson.

"How can I be of service to you?"

"You can tell me why you've locked down our fair city."

Using the remote, Jackson flicked on the HDTV bolted to his office wall. The news was showing a riot on Main Street. Jackson watched the scene with concern.

"It's a health mandate," said Vitti. "I had no choice but to issue it to curtail an outbreak of a lethal virus in your city."

"Isn't that a bit draconian?"

"There are no survivors of the virus. It kills everybody it infects, without exception."

Jackson hiked his eyebrows. "You can't punish a city and its inhabitants because of a virus."

"I'm not punishing anyone," said Vitti, raising his voice. "I'm saving lives by containing the spread of this dreadful disease."

"Haven't you been watching the news? Your blockade of the street out of our town is inciting riots."

"It's news to me."

"Turn on your TV set."

"I don't have time to watch TV. Anyway, this is probably an altercation of some sort. I doubt it's a full-blown riot."

Jackson watched the mob on TV throwing beer bottles and rocks at the riot police who were blocking the street with their squad cars. The police were wearing riot gear, including Plexiglas face shields. They were also holding up polyethylene ballistic shields to protect them from projectiles flung by rioters.

"You're strangling our city with your blockades," said Jackson. "This must stop."

"I'm concerned about the health and welfare of the entire state of California. This outbreak must be contained before it spreads beyond your borders."

"That gives you the right to kill our city?" said Jackson, fit to be tied.

"It if means saving California and the rest of this great country, the answer is yes."

"I'm not gonna stand for it. I supported your campaign the last time you ran. I'm one of your principal donors. Do you want my support for your reelection or not?"

"I will not be blackmailed, sir."

Vitti hung up.

Jackson stood smoldering with his phone in his hand.

Chapter 10

Farther up the road, Phoebe could see angry, frustrated people getting out of their cars and joining in the melee near the police barricade.

She was almost at the intersection where she could turn off Main Street and head elsewhere. She hoped the drivers directly in front of her weren't going to abandon their cars in the road and walk to the riot. For sure they wouldn't reach it soon if they were planning on driving the whole way.

Several people had the same idea she had. They turned off Main, giving up their plans to leave town.

Rackety choppers continued hovering overhead, inflaming the tempers of protesters. A crewman on a bullhorn told the mob to disperse or get arrested.

This was getting too much like the Strip, where they had shot and burned everybody who was in the street, decided Phoebe, feeling her pulse accelerate. As far as she knew, nobody in their cars was infected with the virus. The cops couldn't claim they were containing the virus by shooting drivers.

She doubted the cops would open fire here. But the helos were scaring her. These might be the very same helos that had murdered innocent pedestrians on the Strip when she was there, she decided.

All she knew for sure was she would feel a whole lot better when she drove as far from the choppers as she could get.

Ten more feet and she could turn at the intersection coming up.

If the guy driving the white Land Rover in front of her would turn, she could follow him out. It looked like he couldn't make up his mind whether to turn or keep going straight. She could see him through his rear window scratching his head in confusion.

Why would anyone want to get involved in the riot up ahead? Phoebe wondered. Rocks and bottles were continuing to fly through the air in the direction of the cops manning the roadblock.

One good thing about the riot, she decided. It was keeping the cops preoccupied so they couldn't go around checking cars to see if Phoebe was in any of them. She wondered if the cops had a description of her mother's car. Had they talked to her mother since Phoebe had left? They were going to check with her mother sooner or later to see if she knew where her daughter was. Checking with her relatives was the logical thing for them to do.

Phoebe decided she couldn't go back to her mother's home. Cops might be lying in wait for her to show up.

She started when she heard gunfire up ahead. Cops were shooting riot guns discharging rubber bullets at the screaming protesters.

This was getting worse by the second, she decided, willing the driver in the Land Rover to move forward so she could turn at the intersection.

"Come on, come on," she said, drumming a nervous tattoo on the Fiesta steering wheel with her fingers.

It was only five more feet to the intersection. The Land Rover wasn't budging. She could hear sirens behind her. The cops had sent for reinforcements. She didn't know how the approaching squad cars were going to get past the gridlock of traffic to reach the blockade.

She saw three additional choppers converging near the blockade. Cops began rappelling down from the hovering choppers to reinforce the cops managing the riot on the ground.

The cops were hemming her in, coming at her from front and behind—and even from above, decided Phoebe, listening to the sirens becoming louder behind her.

Chapter 11

Phoebe couldn't wait any longer.

She drove onto the sidewalk on her right, cutting the corner so she could turn at the next intersection. The Fiesta's front tires slammed hard into the curb, jerking her head forward. She had to get over the curb. She accelerated, bumping onto the deserted sidewalk, the car juddering and bouncing.

She felt another hard bump as the rear tires crashed into the curb. Her head lurched forward. She hit the gas, giving the car enough momentum for the rear tires to roll onto the sidewalk.

The Fiesta rocked and shuddered across the sidewalk. Phoebe cut across the sidewalk that led to the intersection. She proceeded to drive toward the empty road on her right.

The car thudded and jounced as it flew off the sidewalk and hit the tarmac. Phoebe felt her neck whipping to and fro. And she felt it again as the rear wheels crashed off the sidewalk onto the tarmac. She heard the rear bumper scraping across the curb as the car dropped eight inches onto the tarmac.

Phoebe felt dizzy from all the bouncing and jerking of the Fiesta. She managed to collect herself and drive down the road, obeying the posted speed limit, wishing to avoid drawing the attention of nearby cops. She probably didn't have to worry. They had their hands full with the violence of the riot escalating as a response to the unpopular blockade.

Incensed rioters were, in fact, commencing to rock blocked cars in front of them, trying in futility to move the vehicles out of the way, frustrated at their inability to drive out of town. The cops peppered the mob with rubber bullets, further infuriating the rioters.

A black Dodge Challenger caught fire and exploded the better part of a hundred feet from the police blockade, agitating the melee. Ink black smoke plumed from the flaming Challenger and billowed over Main Street. Screams of rage near the burning wreck rent the air. The Challenger exploded again.

Phoebe figured somebody had abandoned the car in the gridlock and somebody else had torched it because it was in their way.

Phoebe drove in the opposite direction.

She had no idea where she would go. She had to find a hidey-hole where she could lie low until the cops opened Main Street and she could leave town. She had a feeling it might be a long while before they opened up Costaguana again.

She couldn't stay in her mother's car much longer. She had to ditch it as soon as she got the chance. There must be a police BOLO out for it by now. If the cops pulled her over because she was driving the Fiesta, they would bust her. Luckily, most of the cops were busy at the blockade quelling the riot. Which gave her time to find a place to abandon the car.

She couldn't go very far on her feet. Where was she going to go anyway in a city that was locked down?

She saw a middle-aged man clad in green trousers and a beige button-down shirt standing on the sidewalk with a twisted face and a foaming mouth watching her, a grey linen flat cap askew on his head.

Growling, he bolted toward her. His hat flew off his head.

Feeling an adrenaline rush she accelerated. Even so, he was catching up to her. Terrified, she floored the gas. He was inhumanly fast. She hit forty-five miles an hour, and he was closing ground on her.

*Impossible.*

She hit fifty, not believing her eyes as he pursued her. The cops were going to pull her over at this speed.

She managed to put some distance between him and her. The guy was breathing hard as he pumped his fists and legs, giving chase. Why was he chasing her of all people? she wondered. Because she had looked at him?

She gasped, realizing she had to stop for a red light. She slowed down.

He was gaining on her, his gaping mouth lathering.

She accelerated and ran the light, her head snapping backward.

The young driver of a pickup slammed on his brakes in order to avoid T-boning her in the intersection. He blasted his horn and gave her the finger, his face irate under his blue Dodgers baseball cap.

She tore through the intersection, glancing into her rearview mirror.

A silver SUV skidded to a halt, burning rubber, to avoid striking the berserk man, who was running in the middle of the intersection. Angered at the vehicle for nearly hitting him, he approached the driver, a fortyish woman sporting a pair of designer sunglasses, and yanked open her door.

She screamed in panic.

He latched onto her arm and tried to wrench her out of the driver's seat. Her seat belt prevented it. Ticked off, he took a bite out of her wrist, severing an artery. The driver shrieked in agony. Arterial blood shot into the air, soaking the man's face.

He had to be infected, Phoebe decided. The chopper cops hadn't wiped out the virus on the Strip with their napalm. The virus was spreading, she thought with horror.

The Dodger fan clambered out of his pickup, clutching a tire iron in his hand. He approached the berserk man and bashed in the back of the guy's skull with the tire iron just as the guy was tearing a blood-soaked, pear-sized chunk of flesh out of the SUV driver's forearm with his teeth.

The infected assailant collapsed on the shrieking woman and slid down her body and down the SUV rocker panel into a lifeless heap on the tarmac.

Phoebe kept driving.

She wanted to be long gone when the maniac rose from the dead.

Chapter 12

A helicopter hovered over St. Luke's Hospital and descended onto the helipad on the roof. A man of average height in a white hazmat uniform descended from the chopper after it landed.

Several hospital officials in suits greeted him and escorted him to the entrance to the building's stairwell, bowing and squinting under the downdraft from the whirling rotor blades. The officials led the man down the stairs from the roof to the elevator on the top floor. The elevator descended one story to the seventh floor, where the passengers exited.

Standing in the hallway, dressed in green scrubs, Zandorf greeted the man.

"Hello, Governor," said Zandorf. "You don't need to wear a hazmat uniform in the hospital."

"I'm wearing it everywhere in this cursed city," said Vitti through his Plexiglas face mask. "I'm not taking any chances, and I don't plan on staying here."

"I'm glad you could come."

"I need firsthand knowledge of what's going on. Have you contained the virus?"

"We believe we contained it when we razed the Strip, which was the breeding ground of the outbreak."

"Can we risk opening the city or do we continue the lockdown?"

Zandorf thought about it. "To be safe, we should keep the lockdown in effect until we're certain the virus has been brought under control and neutralized."

"Let me be clear. I don't want this virus spreading beyond Costaguana's borders," said Vitti, his face stern.

"The president doesn't want that, and the CDC doesn't want that. Nobody wants that."

"At least we're on the same page."

A thin fortyish man wearing a navy blue suit approached them. He adjusted the horn-rimmed glasses on his hatchet face. Smiling, he extended his hand.

"Hello, Governor," he said. "I'm glad to meet you. I'm Luis Strus, the deputy mayor. I'm the acting mayor of Costaguana on account of the mayor's illness."

Vitti extended his gloved hand to shake Strus's. "How is Albright?"

"He's in a coma, I'm afraid."

"How unfortunate."

"With all due respect, Mr. Governor, we need to reopen our city. Local businesses are going broke. The city can't survive a prolonged lockdown."

"I understand, but you must see it from my point of view. I can't risk letting infected people in your city infect the rest of California. It would be a debacle of biblical proportions."

"The thing is, our citizens are rioting in the streets on account of the police blockades."

"I'm on your side. I can send more state troopers here to handle the riots and reinstate law and order."

Strus shook his head, dejected. "Having a bigger police presence isn't gonna raise the morale of the locals."

"The state troopers will be able to quell the riots. I'll even send the National Guard here to help out."

"Our citizens don't want to live in a police state."

"Tell them it's temporary until the virus is annihilated."

"The only thing that's gonna satisfy them is reopening the city for business. Turning the city into a prison camp isn't the answer."

"It *is* the answer to save the great state of California. There must be no more infections here. Understand? Until that day comes, the lockdown continues."

"You're turning my city into a ghost town. Everybody is gonna move out."

"Nobody is moving out until this city is declared free of the killer virus that started here. Your city is ground zero. I will not allow the virus to spread. If it spreads beyond your city, it will be on your head. Your name will be mud. You will be the most hated man in California. I repeat, I will not allow the virus to spread beyond your city. I will do everything in my power to stop the virus dead in its tracks. If you're not with me, resign immediately."

"We haven't discovered any infected citizens since we razed the Strip," chimed in Zandorf. "That's a good sign."

"Before declaring this city virus free, make sure there isn't a single infected victim here," said Vitti. He paused a beat. "Do you have any of the infected in captivity?"

"We have a victim in the biolab at the end of the hall. Follow me, if you please."

Chapter 13

Zandorf led them to the biolab, whose room was locked.

"Is it safe to be in the same room as a victim?" said Vitti, worried.

"You have no need to fear in your hazmat uniform."

Zandorf latched onto a key that was hanging from a lanyard draped around his neck and hanging inside his scrubs. He inserted the key in the biolab's door and led the way into an anteroom where hazmat uniforms were hanging.

"The rest of us will need to put on hazmat uniforms," he said, lifting one off a hanger.

He put on the uniform and the face mask that went with it. Strus followed suit.

Zandorf opened a door that led to the biolab.

The three men entered the biolab. In front of them stood a Plexiglas picture window, which separated them from the infected victim's cell.

A thirtyish disheveled blonde clad in black leggings was suspended from chains bolted to the ceiling and secured to her wrists. Thrusting her legs up and down as if running in place, she hung the best part of six feet off the floor. Her grimacing face was foaming at the mouth as she continued to run, sweating profusely.

"Good God," said Vitti, aghast. "What are you doing to her?"

"The virus has accelerated her metabolism. She needs to expend energy. It's impossible for her to stand still. Hanging her in chains is the best way to let her burn off energy without her harming herself or anyone else."

"What do you mean, she's not harming herself? Her face is twisted with agony. Look at her."

"The virus's parasitic worms in her brain are eating her alive. The pain is unbearable. There's nothing we can do about it. She finds some relief by burning off energy like she's doing now by running in place."

A threadlike stream of blood was leaking out of both of the victim's ear canals.

"Why are her ears bleeding?" said Vitti.

"The virus worms are burrowing tunnels in her brain and eating the cells," said Zandorf.

Vitti grimaced in disgust.

"Whatever you do, don't let the media find out about this," he said. "It looks like you're torturing the poor woman. The optics would end all of our careers."

"This is why we keep the biolab locked at all times."

Letting loose unearthly screams, the woman writhed in her chains and ran faster in place.

"The virus worms gouging out her brain reproduce with unbelievable speed," said Zandorf, his deep-set eyes focused like lasers on the woman's face. "It's quite amazing."

"How do you feed her in that contraption?"

"We don't. She only eats living human flesh.

"You're kidding," said Vitti, taken aback.

"I wish I was."

"Then we can assume she will die of starvation."

"Naturally, we want her to live as long as possible in order to study her, but we'd have to be barbarians to mutilate people in order to feed her."

"I hope this is the last known victim," said Strus, eyeballing the woman with consternation.

"As far as we know, she is," said Zandorf. "I have men continuing to search the rubble on the fire-gutted Strip for any infected survivors."

"Are you going to put this poor woman out of her misery soon?" asked Vitti.

"We need to keep her alive as long as possible to find out how the virus spreads."

"I've seen enough," said Vitti, his face ashen, and headed for the exit. "This godawful disease must be nipped in the bud. If it spreads, you're toast, Struts—"

"Strus," said Strus.

"I don't like being interrupted. I'll personally see to it that your career in politics is kaput."

"It's not gonna spread," said Strus, following him. "Not under my watch."

"If it does, you won't be able to get a job as a eunuch in a harem when I'm done mopping the floor with you. You hear what I'm saying?"

"The situation is under control."

"Now get me out of this goddamn city."

Chapter 14

Phoebe pulled into a crowded Ralphs supermarket parking lot. She could ditch the Fiesta here, where it would be inconspicuous amid the hundreds of parked cars. Days, or maybe weeks, could pass without anyone noticing it, she decided. As long as she was long gone, it didn't matter when or if the cops found it.

She sat in the car and watched unhappy shoppers pushing their loaded carts across the lot to their cars, getting through their dead-end lives as best they could, waiting to take out their frustrations during their next incident of road rage.

At least they didn't have the cops chasing them with the intent to kill, she decided.

Where could she go to hide from the cops? she wondered. She couldn't stay here. A supermarket security guard would notice her if she never got out of the car, especially if she stayed overnight.

Alone, broke with nowhere to go, and wanted by the cops. How much lower could she get?

She didn't want to find out.

She would have to keep moving, hoping things would get better. You could only fall so far. Then things would pick up. Or was she kidding herself? Why did things have to pick up?

How could she get out of town if the road that led out was blocked? she wondered. The only way out was by air. The problem was Costaguana didn't have its own airport. What was she going to do? Hijack a police chopper? As soon as the cops saw her anywhere near their choppers, they would bust her. They wouldn't even bother to bust her. They would blow her away.

Maybe she could escape by walking. Yeah, straight into the miles of desert that surrounded the city, where she would die of thirst or heat prostration on her long trek. Before the heat got to her, the cops in choppers surveilling the desert on the lookout for walkers trying to leave town would have no problem spotting her. There was no place to hide in a desert. Ask Saddam Hussein. At least he had a hole to hide in, the little good it did him.

She didn't want to live a life on the run. It wasn't like she had a choice. Play the hand you're dealt. She knew too much. She had witnessed police executions of innocent people on the Strip. The murderous cops would see to it that she paid for it. What chance did she have against the whole police force, including the state police and the FBI?

The more she thought about it, the more depressed she became. Her chances for survival were nonexistent.

She had to do something. She couldn't just sit here and wait to be arrested when the cops spotted her mother's car and searched it.

She needed to disguise her face to prevent passersby from recognizing her. Flipping open the glove compartment she rummaged around and found a pair of her mother's sunglasses. She withdrew them and wiped off their dust-mantled lenses with a tissue from a small package of Kleenex in the compartment. Dust motes flew all over the place.

She put on the sunglasses and looked at herself in the rearview mirror. It would have to do, she decided.

She climbed out of the Fiesta and cut across the parking lot to the sidewalk that skirted the street. She strode onto the sidewalk. It would be nice if she knew where she was going. For sure, she wasn't going to the nearest police station. If she couldn't go to the cops for help, who could she go to?

Maybe she should go to the *Courier*, where her dad used to work. They would be interested to know if cops were killing innocent citizens and cremating their remains. A sob caught in her throat as she recalled the cops in the chopper shooting her dad dead on the Strip without giving any explanation. She felt anger superseding her sadness. They had no right . . .

She walked the better part of a mile.

She was heading in the appropriate direction for the *Courier* office. She had been there several times to see her father. She was walking past a bowling alley on her right. The parking lot looked almost deserted. Probably because it was a weekday, she decided.

She passed by an eightyish man walking in front of her heading in the same direction as her. She turned her face away from him to avoid being recognized.

"Howdy," he said, smiling. "Are we the only ones who walk in this city?"

"It looks that way," she said, trying to be amiable.

"I can walk for a mile without seeing another pedestrian."

"You must do a lot of walking."

"I do. It keeps me healthy. And it gives me something to do. I'm Wally, by the way."

Wearing round-lensed spectacles he had sparse white hair. He wore blue jeans, a coral polo, and fluorescent orange sneakers.

"I'm Phoebe."

Two blocks away Phoebe picked up on a thirtysomething man running toward them, his eyes on fire. He was wearing jeans and a black hoodie that had a silkscreen of a skull and crossbones on its chest. The wind flipped his hood off his head and down onto the nape of his neck as he picked up speed. Blowing out his cheeks he charged Phoebe and Wally.

Chapter 15

Phoebe's pulse raced as she felt adrenaline course through her body. She glanced at the bowling alley. A place to hide.

She sprang toward the building and came to an abrupt stop. She turned back to face Wally.

"We have to go," she said.

"Go? I *am* going. I'm on my daily walk."

"I mean we have to *run*," she said, glancing at the attacking running man.

She could make out the foam on his mouth and knew she was right when she had surmised he was infected.

"Let's go to the bowling alley," she said. "We'll be safe inside if we lock the door."

"Safe? Safe from what?"

"That man ahead of us is infected with a lethal virus."

Wally widened his eyes as he stared at the man. "I never saw anyone run that fast."

Phoebe glommed onto Wally's arm. "We have to go inside."

"I don't know anything about no virus."

"You have to believe me," she pleaded. "Let's go."

"Something's wrong with him. That's for sure. Look at his eyes. A crackhead, I bet."

"We're not safe out here."

Wally nodded yes. "Not with drooling crackheads running amok. That's for sure."

She pulled Wally toward the bowling alley. He didn't need any more prodding. She let go of his arm and ran for the alley. He jogged after her.

He moved fast for his age, she decided. It was a good thing he did.

Grimacing and panting, the infected maniac was closing in on them fast.

Phoebe yanked open the plate-glass door to the bowling alley and waited for Wally to catch up to her. He darted past her with no time to spare.

She slammed the door shut in the infected maniac's face and twisted the lock to keep him out.

Driven into a frenzy by their escape, he jerked on the door handle, trying to get in.

"My heart's beating like crazy," said Wally, hunching over and gasping for breath. "I hope it's not a heart attack."

"Maybe you should sit down."

Agreeing, holding his chest, he trudged to a chair in the nearby food court.

She hoped he was going to be OK. The stress brought on by the attack might end up killing him.

His face working, the infected maniac banged his fists on the plate-glass door, fit to be tied that they had locked him out.

Phoebe wondered how long the plate glass would hold.

"Hey," cried a five-nine bald man standing behind the main desk of the bowling alley. "Don't lock the door. I'm losing customers. We're open for business."

Wally sat down on a chair and looked like he was about to drop dead with exhaustion.

"That man outside is infected with a lethal virus," said Phoebe.

Clad in green chinos and a white polo with an alligator logo on its chest, the stocky bald man emerged from behind the main desk and approached the front door.

"What virus?" he said.

"Look at his face," said Phoebe, pointing at the berserk attacker. "He's foaming at the mouth."

"That's because he's mad because you won't let him in. He wants to bowl."

"He wants to kill us."

Chapter 16

"What are you? Crazy?" said the alley manager. "Why would he want to kill us?"

"He's infected with a virus that drives him to kill and consume his victims," said Phoebe.

Growling and salivating, the infected maniac banged his fist on the door again.

"He's angry because he can't bowl," said the manager. "Unlock that door and let him in."

"Look at his face. Does he look normal to you? He's in agony. The virus is killing him."

"I don't know about you, but I don't want that maniac in here," Wally told the manager.

"He'll calm down after we let him in," said the manager, eyeballing the infected, not sounding sure of himself.

"Want to bet your life on it?" said Phoebe.

"I'm calling the cops if you don't let him in."

"No cops."

"Who put you in charge?" said the manager, and retreated to the main desk to use his phone.

She couldn't be here if cops showed up, decided Phoebe. On the other hand, where could she go with the infected maniac standing out there waiting to attack? The authorities thought they had contained the virus on the Strip by incinerating it. Despite their brutal tactics, the virus was spreading.

She watched with apprehension as the manager lifted the landline handset to his ear behind the main desk. He was making good on his promise to call the cops. She envisaged her life coming to an end with the arrival of the cops. They would recognize her and bust her or, more likely, kill her to prevent her from reporting the murders she had witnessed the cops commit on the Strip.

She watched the manager hang up in irritation and produce his cell phone.

"You lucked out," he said. "You must have someone watching over you. The phone's not working." He tried his cell phone and shook his head. "Neither is my cell phone."

"Oh no," she said.

*It begins again.*

Before the police murders started on the Strip, the phones went out, she remembered.

"You should be happy I can't call the cops," said the manager.

"You have no idea how bad things are gonna get."

"How did I get into this?" said Wally. "I was just taking a walk. Is it a crime to go for a walk these days? I never in my life saw that crazy guy out there. Why did he attack me?"

"Maybe he didn't like your sneakers," said the manager with half a grin.

"What about my sneakers?"

The manager shook his head.

"We can't let him in," said Phoebe.

The manager approached her. "How am I supposed to make a living if you don't let anybody in?"

"I'm doing you a favor by locking that guy out."

"A favor? How am I supposed to pay the rent with no income from my job? I'm gonna open that door, and you can't stop me."

"Don't," said Phoebe. "You must understand. If he gets inside, he'll kill all of us."

The manager eyed the bellicose man outside, not sure what to do.

"Will you calm down if I let you in?" he asked the guy through the plate-glass door.

Grimacing, the infected maniac growled and frothed at the mouth.

"I'm not letting you inside, buddy, unless you settle down," said the manager. "I'll even let you bowl a game for free. I want bowlers. That's what the alley's open for. What do you say?"

The maniac grunted and tried to yank the door open.

"Watch it there, buddy," said the manager. "I didn't unlock it yet. Don't bust the door. You break it, you pay for it."

Snarling, the maniac continued yanking on the door handle, rattling the door in its frame.

"I'm not kidding, buddy," said the manager. "That door ain't cheap. It's gonna come out of your bank account if you bust it."

The maniac roared at him.

The manager turned to Phoebe. "What's with people these days? You try to do them a favor, and they want to bite your head off."

"He doesn't know what he's doing. The virus is killing him."

"That's no cause for him to take it out on us."

"Don't let him in, whatever you do."

The manager stared at the maniac, who contorted his face in agony.

"I'm thinking you're right," said the manager. "I don't know what his problem is, but I don't want him coming inside and trashing my place. I'll get Babette."

The manager retreated behind the main desk and returned, gripping a baseball bat.

"I better have Babette ready in case he tears down the door," he said.

"What's wrong with my sneakers?" said Wally, eying his fluorescent orange sneakers.

Chapter 17

"Look at that guy," said the manager, wiping his cheek with his hand. "He doesn't even wipe the crud off his face. He's drooling like an animal."

"Bad news," said Wally.

"I'm trying to run a decent place," said the manager. "The name's Bud, by the way."

"Wally."

"Phoebe."

"I don't want pigs like him getting in," said Bud. "I don't allow bums near the lanes. They make the customers uncomfortable. I have the right to refuse to allow anyone into my private establishment. It's the law."

"That's the trouble these days," said Wally. "They allow bums, psychos, drug addicts, and gangs of violent shoplifters to walk the streets, and everybody else is afraid to go outside without getting mugged."

"Wait till the helicopters come," said Phoebe, widening her eyes with anxiety.

"Helicopters?" said Bud, scratching his head. "What do helicopters have to do with anything?"

"You'll find out."

"You've been eating too many LSD burritos, lady. Hey, don't I know you?"

"No," said Phoebe, not wanting to admit she was the mayor's wife. "I never met you."

"You look familiar."

"I get mistaken for other people all the time."

"Maybe. Anyway, you're spreading bad vibes in my establishment, so I'm gonna ask you to leave as soon as that maniac hightails it."

"It doesn't look like he's going anywhere soon," said Phoebe, watching the infected maniac marching back and forth in front of the door like he was guarding it, his froth-covered jaw set.

"If he doesn't get the hell out of here pretty quick, I'm gonna go out there and bash his brains in," said Bud, flourishing his bat.

"Bad idea. If he bites you, you'll become infected."

"He's not gonna bite anyone with his brains leaking on the pavement."

"Look how fast he moves. You won't have a chance against him with a bat in your hands. He'll take a bite out of you before you take your first swing."

A seventyish woman with blue rinse hair and a hunched back was walking down the sidewalk with ski poles in her hands to keep her from falling. When the infected caught sight of her, he bolted after her.

Seeing him charge, the woman's eyes popped out of her head in fear. She gawked at him.

The maniac reached her in no time.

Horrified, the woman jammed one of her ski poles into his chest. He pulled the ski pole out, wrestled it out of her hand, and tossed it fifty yards away. He sank his teeth into her throat and ripped out her jugular. She screamed in pain and shoved him away. She flailed her other ski pole at him, trying to jab its point into his eye as a stream of blood shot out of her throat.

"We gotta help her," said Bud, watching in horror from behind the plate-glass door.

"Don't go out there," said Phoebe. "Nobody can help her now. She's already dead."

The infected took another bite of the old woman's throat. Blood sprayed his face.

Bud started to unlock the front door to go outside and succor the woman.

"Don't," said Phoebe, grabbing his forearm.

"I'd listen to her if I was you," said Wally. "She seems to know what's going on. I never seen anything like this."

"I got Babette with me," said Bud.

Phoebe shook her head no.

The woman dropped her remaining ski pole and toppled to the sidewalk, where the maniac leapt on her and chewed off her face with rapid bites.

"Jesus," said Bud, consternated.

"We can't help her," said Phoebe, her face chalk white as she watched the horror unfold on the sidewalk.

Bud removed his hand from the door lock, having trouble believing his eyes.

"That guy has gotta be stopped," he said.

"I'd shoot him if I had my gun with me," said Wally.

"There'll be two of them soon," said Phoebe.

Baffled, Bud looked at her. "Two of what?"

"Two infected maniacs."

"You're not making sense. Where's the other one? The woman he attacked is dead. That leaves only him."

"You'll see."

Chapter 18

Her face mauled and raw with strips of ragged flesh dangling from it, her throat covered with blood, the old woman sat up on the sidewalk.

"What?" gasped Bud. "It can't be. How could she still be alive?"

"She's reanimated," said Phoebe.

"Bullshit. You're talking zombie movies."

"Except this isn't a movie. The infected come back to life to kill and eat humans."

Her face missing, the old woman stood up and shambled down the sidewalk.

"Somehow she's alive," said Bud, amazed.

"If you call that living," said Phoebe. "She's infected with the virus like the guy that killed her."

Wearing black jeans and a turquoise down jacket, a slender blonde in her thirties pelted toward the bowling alley's front door, her ponytail flapping behind her. With big brown eyes and muscular arms, she was five six and Hispanic.

"Help," she cried.

She reached the door and pleaded to be let in.

Bud didn't know what to do.

"There's a homicidal maniac out here," she said, her eyes bulging with fear. "Please let me in."

Grimacing, his face smeared with the old woman's blood, the infected maniac barreled toward the blonde.

She grabbed the door handle and tried to enter the bowling alley. The door was locked.

At a loss, Bud looked at Phoebe. "Is she one of these infected you're talking about?"

Phoebe studied the situation, trying to figure out the answer, knowing she had no time to spare.

"He's gonna attack her," she said. "She must be OK. They don't attack each other."

The infected tore across the parking lot toward the blonde, yammering, his blood-smeared face knotted.

Terrified, the blonde pounded on the door.

"Help," she cried. "He's gonna kill me."

"Are you sure she's OK?" Bud asked Phoebe.

"I—I—think so. I'm not an expert. She's not frothing at the mouth. The infected foam at the mouth, and they can run inhumanly fast."

"Let the poor woman in," said Wally. "Can't you see she's scared out of her wits?"

Bud stood motionless, unable to make up his mind. He watched the maniac charge the blonde, who screamed with horror.

Bud unlocked and opened the door.

The woman burst inside, gasping for breath, struggling to inhale on account of her panic.

Six feet away, the infected maniac stormed toward the open door and closed fast.

Bud slammed the door shut in the maniac's face and twisted the lock. The maniac slammed his face into the plate glass, which held.

"That glass must be strong," said Phoebe, surprised it didn't shatter on impact.

"I had it reinforced," said Bud. "I used to get a lot of break-ins. Kids trying to rob the place, so I invested in bulletproof glass." He held up his bat. "I also bought Babette to keep me company."

"That—maniac—murdered a woman on the sidewalk," said the blonde, between gasps.

"We saw it," said Phoebe, placing her hand on the blonde's back, trying to soothe her. "You can relax now. You're safe here. I'm Phoebe."

"I'm—uh—I can barely talk, I'm so out—of—ugh—breath. I'm Crystal."

"What's all the excitement?" said a portly eighteen-year-old guy wearing a Raiders black ball cap backwards on his head as he approached from the rear of the building. His shaggy brown locks curled out from the bottom of his cap like excelsior. He hitched up his jeans. "I was in the restroom."

"Smoking weed and stuffing your face with Twinkies, Herman?" said Bud.

"Weed's legal in California, in case you haven't heard."

Bud stalked over to Herman and bitch-slapped him.

"Hey, what'd you do that for?" said Herman, seeing red.

"For stinking up my restrooms with weed. Customers complain and never come back. This is a family bowling alley."

"Somebody got murdered outside," said Crystal, her face flushed from her hairbreadth escape from death.

Grimacing as his victim's blood dripped from his face, the maniac pounded on the front door.

"Holy shit," said Herman, forgetting Bud and staring at the maniac. "Why do I always miss all the excitement?"

"This ain't some stupid horror slasher about Jason Voorhees," said Bud. "That nutbag out there killed a lady in the flesh—with his teeth."

"Yeah. Whatever."

"You wanna go outside and shake hands with him?"

"Is he a movie star?"

"Get your head out of your ass and wake up. That maniac wants to chew on your face."

"He's not an actor?"

"I'm an actor," said Crystal, starting to breathe normally, now that she was out of harm's way.

"Is this a movie?" said Herman, wide-eyed.

"No." Crystal took a deep breath to calm down. "I'm an actor, but I'm not acting now."

"What movies were you in?"

"I was in *Green Hell Alive* shot in Colombia."

"Wow. I didn't see that one. Sounds cool."

"It's an Italian production about a tribe of cannibals that nobody ever heard of. They protect their village from being found by selling cocaine dirt cheap to a cartel. In return the cartel works for them as bodyguards."

"It sounds like Umberto Lenzi's *Cannibal Ferox*. I saw the uncut version. Heinous."

"Is that the one where they tortured real animals on camera?" said Crystal with repulsion.

"There was a sensational murder trial connected to that movie. Lenzi told his actors to disappear after the movie. Nobody could find them. The authorities thought it was because Lenzi had murdered them, because they had been murdered in the flick. A snuff movie, you see. They actually put him on trial for murder."

"Not true."

"What do you mean, not true?" said Herman, annoyed at being contradicted. "Lenzi didn't want to be found guilty, so he told his actors to reappear. They reported to the court. Otherwise, he would've been found guilty."

"That wasn't Lenzi. You're thinking of Ruggero Deodato."

"It *was* Lenzi."

"Deodato. He was put on trial for the murder of cast members in his movie *Cannibal Holocaust*. He made the actors sign a contract that they would disappear and not do any interviews after they finished the movie. People thought Deodato had murdered them, because they all died in the movie. The murder trial was in Italy. Then the actors came out of hiding, and Deodato was found not guilty."

"It was Lenzi," said Herman, becoming animated.

Crystal shook her head no, her expression firm. "Deodato. Look it up on the Internet."

"We can do your filmography some other time," said Bud. "We need to deal with the infected guy right now."

"Call the cops," said Herman. "They'll take care of him."

"Our phones aren't working, dumb ass."

"What are we gonna do?"

"I can call my agent," said Crystal.

"Call your agent?" said Herman. "What's he gonna do?"

"This has movie written all over it. He's gonna love it for a script. I can hear him now: 'You're meshuga. Let's do business.'"

"Haven't you been listening?" said Bud. "The phones don't work."

"Mine might," said Crystal.

Chapter 19

Crystal rummaged through her pocketbook and fished out her cell phone. She tapped her agent's name on her list of contacts.

"Tell him to call the cops," said Bud, watching her expectantly.

Crystal shook her head. "The call's not going through. I don't get it. The battery's OK. Why isn't it working?"

"The cops are jamming the phones," said Phoebe.

"Why would they do that?"

"To cover up the truth. They don't want anyone to know what's really happening in this town."

Bud glared at Phoebe. "My phone worked fine till you got here."

"It's not me. It's the infected guy at your door. Somebody must've reported him to the cops. Now they're gonna close down this part of town. Then the helicopters will come."

"Helicopters?" said Bud, shaking his head and frowning. "Is this supposed to make any kind of sense?"

"You'll see."

"Is this a movie stunt? I didn't sign on for a movie. If this is a movie, I wanna get paid."

"It's not a movie. A virus is killing people."

"This isn't a movie," said Crystal. "That guy outside killed that woman and would've killed me if you didn't let me in."

"Except the woman isn't dead," said Bud, squinting his eye with suspicion. "We saw her get up and walk. That only happens in the movies."

"This isn't a movie," said Phoebe. "The infected maniac out there is real. If you let him inside, he'll kill all of us."

"There's more of us than him," said Wally. "We could gang-tackle him and beat the crap out of him."

"You don't understand. If he bites us, he'll infect us with a fatal virus. We can't take the chance of letting him inside."

"Isn't there some antidote we can take?" said Herman. "There's always an antidote, a vaccine, or something."

"There is no cure," said Phoebe.

"Then how do the cops deal with it?"

"You don't want to know," said Phoebe with a grim visage, remembering the chopper crew shooting her father and her best friend.

"Wait a minute," said Herman. "That doesn't sound good."

"I used to be a fireman before I retired," said Wally. "I'm still pretty strong. We had to carry people out of burning buildings some days. We outnumber that psycho. We could take him, I'm telling you."

"It's too risky," said Phoebe.

"Let me finish. I could bushwhack the psycho and pin his arms behind his back after you let him inside. Then you guys kick the living shit out of him."

"Man, what are you? Eighty years old?" said Herman. "The maniac's half your age."

"And he has superhuman strength," said Phoebe. "Did you see how fast he can run? Adrenaline is shooting through his system thanks to the virus, doubling his normal strength."

"Ahh," said Wally, waving her off. "Five against one. We could take him."

"I don't want him coming in here and trashing my place," said Bud. "My insurance doesn't cover vandalism by a psycho."

Phoebe sat beside Wally, giving her legs a rest.

"What do you do for a living?" said Wally.

"I'm—uh—trying to find my way in life," she said, not wanting to reveal her true identity as the mayor's wife, fearing the others might blame her for the spread of the virus.

"I know how you feel. I'm eighty, and I'm still trying to find my way." Wally paused. "I was a fireman most of my life, but I never felt satisfied. I felt like I was missing something. I still do." He shrugged. "I guess I'll have to keep looking, just like you. It doesn't get any easier when you get older. Not for me."

With a shudder Phoebe heard a helicopter approaching.

"Here they come," she said, looking at the ceiling with dread.

"It's a chopper," said Bud. "They fly over all the time."

"Whatever you do, don't go outside with that chopper out there."

"I just want to reopen my alley, so I can make a living. Is that OK?"

"The chopper crew isn't gonna allow it."

"The choppers are part of the movie, I bet," said Herman, his eyes lighting up.

"This isn't a movie," said Phoebe.

"That's what you're saying to get us to act naturally. I never thought I'd be in a movie—even if I'm only an extra. My dream come true. This is awesome," said Herman, beaming.

Phoebe heard knocking at the front door. She gazed at the door and picked up on the old woman without a face striking her knuckles against the plate glass. The other infected was standing the better part of three feet away from her, grunting and drooling, waiting for the door to open.

"Where's my copy of the script?" said Herman. "How do I know what to say without a script?"

Bud looked at him and shook his head.

"Get it through your head, this isn't a movie," said Crystal. "If this is a movie, where's the director? Do you see John Carpenter anywhere?"

Herman surveyed the bowling alley. "No. Is it a found footage movie? I know. It's a remake of *The Thing*."

"Where's the camera?"

Herman cast around the alley. He stroked his chin in thought.

"It must be hidden," he said. "This is cinema verité. We're not supposed to know where the camera is, because the director is going for candid realism."

"Think for a moment," said Bud. "Why would anyone want to make a movie about you? You're a crackhead nobody."

"Don't say that," said Crystal.

"Well, he is."

"I dunno," said Herman. "They make movies about all sorts of people these days. Why not me? And you. You're in it too."

"He's tripping on weed," Bud told Phoebe. "There's no getting through to him."

"As long as he doesn't let any of the infected in," said Phoebe. "This is a life or death situation. No fooling around."

"Tell *him*, not me."

"I get it," said Herman. "You want me to believe those are zombies outside."

"I want you to shut up," said Bud.

Chapter 20

Herman looked at Crystal. "You're an actor in horror movies, you said. What's your stage name?"

"The same as my real name. Crystal Morena."

"Crystal Morena, movie star. How cool. I wish I was you."

"No, you don't," said Crystal. "I was a sex slave for the Jalisco New Generation Cartel in Tamaulipas. They held me captive for years. I lifted weights, because I was locked up all the time. That's how I got these arms." She flexed her muscular arms.

"Gosh," said Herman, widening his eyes.

"I poisoned my prison guard with some of the fentanyl the cartel cranked out. I made my way to TJ. Then I escaped across the border to California."

"How did you get across?"

"I hid in a drum in a Mexican oil tanker that crossed from TJ into San Ysidro. I thought I would die from the fumes in the back of that eighteen wheeler. I got a job as a maid in a movie producer's house in the Hollywood Hills. He suggested I try out for a part. Of course, I had to have sex with him first or he couldn't recommend me. That's how I got the role in the movie. They haven't paid me yet."

"Assholes."

"They're not half as bad as the cartel. Whenever I tried to escape the cartel, they used to hold my head under water in a full bathtub till I almost drowned. They kept doing it over and over. I thought I was gonna die."

"Jesus."

"I'm used to it. I've been living off crumbs most of my life, trying to get by. I've met the worst people in my life. They're all liars, crooks, shakedown artists, and sicarios. If I make it through the day, I figure I'm lucky."

"I thought actors led glamorous lives. That producer sounds like a sleazeball."

Crystal shrugged. "Not a whole lot better than the drug cartel. But other producers might hire me for a movie after they see me in *Green Hell Alive*. I hope, anyway. They can't all be crooks."

"I guess not."

"The thing is, I really want to be an actor now. I developed a rich imagination when I was in the cartel prison. I couldn't go anywhere or do anything behind bars, so I imagined I was elsewhere. What I imagined became very real to me, realer than reality. I believe I can be a great actor. All I need are chances to show my stuff."

"I really want to see your horror movie. What's the name of it? *Green Jungle Hell*?"

"*Green Hell Alive*. My character gets captured by the cannibals. They lock her in chains in a dungeon cell. When they're ready to eat, they cut off pieces of her body while she's still alive and eat them."

"The cartel did that?" said Herman, wincing in dread.

"No. It was in the movie I made."

"Don't cannibals cook the meat before they eat it?"

"Oh, yeah. They take the body part somewhere else, cook it, and eat it."

"I don't get it. Why do they keep her alive?"

"Because they like only fresh meat from a living person. They don't eat dead people."

"The infected don't eat corpses either," said Phoebe.

"Which parts of her body do they cut off first?" Herman asked Crystal.

"Her toes and fingers," answered Crystal. "They want to keep her alive as long as possible, so they cut off the nonessential parts of her body first."

Herman shivered. "I get the creeps just thinking about it. How can she stand it, knowing every time they come to her cell they're gonna cut off another piece of her?"

"Doesn't she bleed out when they cut off her body parts?" said Bud.

"They stanch the bleeding and patch her up," said Crystal.

"Doesn't it terrify her whenever she hears them opening her cell?" said Herman, hanging on her every word.

"She doesn't have a choice. I've been treated like dirt and tortured all of my life. I know what it's like, so I could feel what she was going through. She makes believe she's somewhere else, like at Cannes in France attending a movie premiere."

"Wow. I gotta see it. Can you get me a DVD?"

"The producers didn't give me one."

"Maybe when they pay you, they'll give you one."

"I'm beginning to think they'll never pay me. Just another way of getting screwed in my life."

"Horror movies are the best. I saw this one about Nazi zombies—"

"My life is a horror movie. Maybe that's why they want me to act in them."

"If we get infected, you won't be starring in any more movies," chimed in Phoebe.

"It was called *Dead Snow*, I think," said Herman. "A Norwegian flick. I read they're gonna make a sequel called *Dead Snow 3* in South America, because a lot of Nazis fled to Argentina after they lost the war. Maybe you could get a part in that one."

"I'll tell my agent when my phone works," said Crystal.

"And tell him we need help out of this mess," said Bud.

Crystal glowered at him. "Is that supposed to be funny? He's an agent, not a miracle worker."

Chapter 21

"I'm losing business," said Bud. "Is anybody listening?"

Bat in hand, he strutted to the plate-glass door and frowned at the two infected who were growling and drooling outside. The faceless woman stuck her tongue at him. Her beefy cohort snagged the door handle and tried to jerk open the door.

"Don't they have anything better to do?" said Bud.

"Don't stand too close to the door," said Phoebe.

"Why not? They can't break through."

"The chopper could open fire on them any minute."

"Great. I wish they would. I told you before, the door is bulletproof."

"Is it fireproof too?"

Bud gave her a look. "What's that got to do with anything?"

"They incinerate the infected with flamethrowers after they shoot them."

"This is sounding more and more preposterous. How do we know you're not making this stuff up?"

"Yeah," said Wally. "If there's a deadly virus going around, why hasn't it been announced on the TV news?"

"You saw what the maniac did to that woman," said Phoebe. "Look at her."

The old woman without a face growled at them beyond the door, snapping her bloody jawbones beside her murderer, who was contorting his face in the white heat of rage, chomping at the bit to tear apart another victim as he stared through the door into the bowling alley.

"This can't be real," said Bud.

"If you open that door and the infected kill you, will you believe me, then?" said Phoebe.

"I saw this movie called *The Game*," said Herman.

"Not another movie," said Bud.

Herman ignored him. "Horrible things happen to Michael Douglas, but it turns out none of it is real. It's just a game they're playing with him for his birthday."

"Is that all you do all day is watch movies?" said Bud. "We have a situation here. It's serious."

"Michael Douglas thought it was serious, because he didn't know it was a game."

"There you go again, talking about movies. This is real."

"It's not that bad," said Herman, his face smug. "Those clowns can't get inside."

"I'm losing business," said Bud, pounding the end of his bat against the floor, startling Herman. "Haven't you been listening? Going broke is bad. Real bad. People kill themselves when they go broke."

"They're not gonna be out there forever," said Herman, nodding at the infected.

"I hate to tell you this, but there could be even more of them soon," said Phoebe.

"That's just what I want to hear," said Bud.

"The virus is spreading. They thought they had it contained on the Strip, but they were wrong."

A rangy six-seven guy belted from the sidewalk to the front door of the bowling alley and hammered on the door with the bottom of his fist, screwing up his face and snarling, his mouth smeared with foam. He was wearing blue jeans, hiking boots, and a red and black flannel lumberjack shirt.

"Great," said Bud. "Now Dinty Moore's here. This can't be real. I bet if I open that door, those guys will burst into laughter. This has to be a put-on."

"This isn't a joke," said Phoebe, becoming angry. "I lost my father and my best friend to the cops."

"There you go. Those guys out there aren't cops. They won't harm us."

"What do *you* know?" said Crystal. "You weren't out there with them like I was. They were gonna kill me."

"The cops will start shooting any minute at anybody who's outside," said Phoebe.

"Why should we believe you?" Bud asked Phoebe. "How do we know you're not an escapee from a loony bin?"

Feeling miserable, Phoebe rubbed her hand across her forehead.

"I wish I was making it up," she said. "But I'm not. You have to believe me. *We are in danger.*"

"You sound like that stupid robot on *Lost in Space*," said Herman. "Danger, danger, Will Robinson."

Phoebe shook her head in dismay. "This is real. Your lives depend on believing me."

"Who made you all-powerful?" said Bud. "Our lives depend on what you say? Talk about egomaniacs."

"This isn't about power. It's about the truth. I've been through this before. I know what's gonna happen next. Bullets are gonna fly."

"How come you're the only one who knows the 'truth,'" said Bud, making air quotes, "and the rest of us don't?"

"I wish I was wrong, but I'm not."

"But why you? Why are you the great knower of truth?"

"Lucky, I guess," said Phoebe dryly.

"I have yet to see anybody with a piece," said Bud, scanning the parking lot.

The chopper hovering overhead became louder.

"Why's that thing flying so low?" he said.

"I don't know what's going on," said Crystal, "but this isn't a movie. I don't see a single camera anywhere. Not even a food truck or a rent-a-cop guarding a trailer."

"Because the filmmakers want you to believe this is real," said Herman.

"It's as real as death," said Phoebe, her face glum.

"Let's look at the bright side," said Wally. "After the cops waste those creeps at the door, we'll be able to go outside."

"No, you won't."

"Why not? If they're dead, why should we fear them?"

"Because the cops in the chopper will waste you next."

"Why the hell would they do that?"

"Because they're gonna think everyone in this area must be infected, since they found infected victims here."

"That's their idea of a cure?" said Bud, outraged. "Murder?"

"There is no cure."

Chapter 22

"We're not infected," said Bud. "So why do they have to kill us?"

"I can only speculate," said Phoebe. "They kill everyone in a zone where the virus has spread. That's what happened at the Strip."

"That's not science. It's wholesale slaughter."

"I heard on the news about the fire on the Strip," said Wally. "I didn't hear anything about a virus there."

"It's a cover-up," said Phoebe. "They don't want to panic anyone."

"They don't want to panic anyone, so they shoot innocent people?" said Bud. "What kind of sense does that make?"

"That's why this has to be a movie," said Herman. "Because it makes no sense. The government would never murder everyone they suspected of contracting a virus. This is the USA. What you're describing sounds like Nazi Germany."

"That's what I thought till I saw it with my own eyes," said Phoebe. "I saw the cops shoot innocent people on the Strip."

"We can't trust her," Bud told the others, indicating Phoebe.

"We saw that maniac kill that old woman on the sidewalk," said Wally.

"The old woman is standing outside. She's still alive."

"And she's as crazy as the maniac that killed her."

"You're missing the point. It means he didn't really kill her."

"Because it's a movie," said Herman. "If we realize we're in the middle of a horror movie, everything makes sense because horror movies defy belief." He chewed it over. "Is this the *Saw* franchise? If this is a *Saw* movie, we'll be released from our captivity if we find a clue hidden by the serial killer John 'Jigsaw' Kramer."

"What if we don't?" said Crystal.

"We'll all be killed."

"How? I saw a bunch of *Saw* movies. The victims all died differently."

"I dunno. It'll be heinous, though. They don't call those movies torture porn for nothing." Animated, Herman paced around the bowling alley, gesturing with his hands. "He kills his victims with torture devices. And he gives them a choice. Like, do you want to dissolve your hand in sulfuric acid or cut it off with a hacksaw? Maybe this new sequel we're in is about him using psychological torture."

"Jigsaw died in the third film," said Crystal. "He can't be doing this."

"One of his acolytes is doing it. He had a lot of followers."

"This is nuts," said Wally. "I can't believe we're in a movie. I almost got killed out there. I don't know about any virus, but those are homicidal maniacs at our door. I do believe it, because I can see them standing there, dying to rip us apart."

"The virus is driving them insane," said Phoebe. "It's driving them to kill."

"How do we know Jigsaw didn't send them here as part of the movie?" said Herman.

"Because it's not a movie. How many times do I have to tell you?"

"Would they risk killing somebody just to film a movie?" said Wally. "I barely escaped that maniac."

"People really do die in movies," said Herman. "Vic Morrow died while they were shooting the movie *Twilight Zone*. A helicopter decapitated him."

"That was an accident."

"The point is it *did* happen."

The blood drained from Phoebe's face. "Don't talk to me about helicopters. They're death machines. I saw them in action on the Strip."

Hearing the chopper hovering overhead, she looked upward.

Frowning in thought, Herman surveyed the bowling alley.

"Where would Jigsaw hide the clue that will get us out of this mess?" he said.

"You're wasting your time," said Phoebe, exasperated.

"We need to be on the same page," said Wally. "Otherwise, we won't be able to accomplish anything."

Bud pounded the crown of his bat on the floor twice to get attention.

"Listen up, everyone," he said. "I don't believe we're in a movie. The filmmakers would have to get a permit to shoot inside my business. Nobody asked me for a permit or got one from me."

"If their cameras are outside, the producers wouldn't need a permit from you," said Herman.

"I don't see any cameras outside."

"They're hiding them so you won't look at them." Herman looked outside. "They're probably in a van in the parking lot. You're not supposed to look at a camera while you're acting in a movie. Everybody knows that."

"I'm not acting in a movie."

"You can't be sure of that. You gotta admit things that are happening to us seem like they belong in a horror movie. Cannibals. People rising from the dead like zombies and attacking living humans."

"I can tell you right now, I'm not acting. I already got a job and I want to keep it. So I need to reopen for business."

Herman stared at the three maniacs standing outside.

"How do we know those three maniacs aren't actors?" he said.

"Because they're not acting," said Phoebe, tired of arguing. "They're infected with a virus that drives them insane and makes them want to feed on living human flesh."

"How do we know you're not working for the movie producers? Your job could be to convince us this movie is actually real."

"Show me your proof."

"If you think those three outside are actors, go out there and talk to them," said Bud.

"Uh—that's not in the script," said Herman. "I'd ruin the movie."

"Ahh," said Bud, shaking his head. "You're making this up on the fly."

"Everybody knows there are rules in horror movies. If you violate the rules, you ruin the movie. Going outside and talking to the three maniacs would violate the rules. It would be out of character for me."

Phoebe heard yelling outside.

Chapter 23

It was overcast outside, grey like cadaver flesh.

Phoebe gazed through the plate-glass door and saw with horror a dozen-odd howling individuals charge after a 2019 Volkswagen Beetle that was turning into the bowling-alley parking lot. Foaming at the mouth and growling, the mob converged on the car, forcing it to stop.

The horrified fortysomething male driver with three day's growth fought them off. He punched the first attacker, a peroxide-blonde fiftyish, stocky woman with thick legs sticking out of her auburn dress. The blow to her face didn't faze her. She kept coming at him, clawing at him with her meaty arms.

Two middle-aged guys clad in business suits latched onto the VW passenger, a brunette in her late twenties wearing a black halter and flamingo pink shorts, and hauled her out of the passenger-side window, dislodging her shorts, which slid all the way down her legs and revealed her lavender thong. Terrified, she screamed and tried to fight the maniacs off to no avail.

The bespectacled suit gnawed on her face, ripping her cheeks off and devouring them as he swung her onto the asphalt and crouched over her body. The short, tonsured suit tried to grab onto her legs and chew her calves, but she kicked off her shorts and kept kicking him away. Frustrated, he snagged one of her arms and yanked it out of its socket, blood fountaining out of the wound.

The victim screamed and fainted as she bled out.

The tonsured suit commenced chewing the arm in his hand with gusto.

Panicking at the gruesome sight of his girlfriend, the driver hit the gas.

The VW lurched forward with the stocky blonde grasping the steering wheel, which she cut toward her. The car crashed into another car in the parking lot and came to a halt.

Six other maniacs mobbed the VW. A teenager listening to headphones flung open the passenger-side door, crawled into the car, and chewed on the driver's arm, ripping flesh out in large bloody chunks and gobbling them down.

Writhing in his seat the driver screamed in pain even as the stocky blonde kept trying to pull him out the window. Another maniac, a twentyish, mustached guy wearing a grey service station uniform, joined her in her efforts, shoving his grease-stained hands through the open window to grab the driver.

"Do you still think this is a movie, Herman?" Bud asked, turning away in revulsion and dread from the hellish scene taking place in the parking lot.

"It could be," said Herman, his face pallid as he watched the blood-drenched massacre. "The only way we can know for sure is for us to go outside and inspect the bodies to make sure they're not pretending to be dead. That could be fake blood in the parking lot."

"It's not over yet," said Phoebe.

The helo approached the maniacs and descended directly over them, its swirling rotor blades tousling their hair. They looked up from their meals at the whirlybird.

An AR-15 protruded from the cockpit and opened fire on the bloodthirsty mob. A hail of automatic rifle fire cut down the fiends. They collapsed on the asphalt, their bodies riddled with bullets, blood streaming from their wounds.

"That rifle could be firing blanks," said Herman. "We can't know for sure."

"Then why are they bleeding?" said Bud.

"Blood squibs. That's what they use in Hollywood to imitate bullet wounds."

"Looks like a real massacre to me," said Wally, awestruck at the mass carnage.

"One of us needs to go outside and inspect the bodies."

"Any volunteers?"

"I nominate you, Herman," said Bud. "You're the expert on movies."

When the blood-soaked bodies stopped squirming on the asphalt, a flamethrower protruded from the chopper cockpit. Flame leapt from the weapon's muzzle and torched the bullet-shredded flesh eaters as well as the VW driver and his girlfriend.

Chapter 24

The three maniacs standing at the plate-glass door to the bowling alley watched the holocaust with stupefaction. The chopper continued to hover overhead, ginning up a racket.

"Why don't they shoot these three over here?" said Bud, nodding at the three.

"Maybe they're not sure they're infected," said Phoebe.

"They sure ain't acting normally."

"Or the cops might want these three as prisoners for the CDC to examine."

"With the bodies burnt, we can't examine them to see if they're really dead or actors playing dead," said Herman in frustration.

"How can actors fake being torched skeletons?" said Bud.

"Haven't you heard of FX?"

"FX?"

"Special effects. Horror movies are supposed to scare us, and this one's scaring the pants off me."

"It's even scarier if it's real."

The VW exploded as its fuel tank caught fire. Golden flames and clouds of black smoke shot up into the sky. The smoke unfurled upward like a tornado.

"You say those are cops in the chopper?" Bud asked Phoebe, one eye cocked in skepticism.

"That's right," answered Phoebe. "The cops will start blockading the road any minute as they seal this virus-infected area off."

"What happens to us?"

"They napalm the entire area to eradicate the virus," said Phoebe in a monotonic voice, her expression blank.

"And you know this how?"

"I saw it done on the Strip."

"I heard on the news about a big fire on the Strip," said Wally. "The cops are looking for the mayor's wife. They say she had something to do with it."

Phoebe tensed. Were the cops blaming the Strip fire on her? she wondered.

Regardless, thanks to Wally, everybody in the alley knew she was a wanted woman. Her only advantage—nobody recognized her. She thanked her lucky stars that nobody in the alley cared about politics. Otherwise, who knew what they would do to her?

She planned on keeping her identity secret.

She took in the bombed-out wasteland of the parking lot.

Pieces of charred human flesh flung from the exploding VW hung from eucalyptus limbs like ornaments on a Christmas tree and dripped blood.

Two more choppers appeared in the sky, striking fear in her.

Wally walked up to her. "You look like you just saw a ghost."

"This is how I lost my father and my best friend."

"All life is risk. Sometimes we win and sometimes we lose. Sometimes we lose everything, including our family and even our own lives. I was a fireman. I've seen scores of people die in fires. They were good people. But they still died. I tried to save them, but I failed."

"What's your point?"

"My point is if we want to live, we have to take risks. When you take risks, you can't be sure what's gonna happen. A lot of the time you will fail. It's called life."

"It bugs me that I might have been able to save my dad if I was more persistent about persuading him not to go outside and confront the chopper on the Strip," said Phoebe, staring at the floor in a funk.

"You can't be sure of that. Your dad did what he thought was right. He probably wouldn't have listened to you no matter how much you hounded him to do otherwise."

"I have a history of making wrong decisions."

"You know what I do when I make a bad decision?"

"What?" said Phoebe, looking at him.

"I make another decision—and I keep making more decisions."

"I'd feel a lot better if I made a right decision once in a while."

"I dunno," said Wally, shaking his head, looking weary. "I'm just an old man trying to get through the day. What do I know? I don't dwell on all the bad decisions I've made, though." He smiled. "I'd never get any sleep that way."

"I wish I could make a good decision. Why's it so hard for me?"

"There was a nine-year-old kid in a fire," said Wally. "I was trying to save him while I was standing in a cherry picker near a flaming apartment house. I was reaching for him as the fire burned all around him on the balcony he was standing on. I felt sure I was gonna save him. He reached out to me. I told him to walk toward me. He took one step, and the balcony floor collapsed on account of the fire. He fell to his death. I still have nightmares of that day, seeing his screaming face as he fell into the flames, continuing to reach out to me."

"You didn't know the floor would collapse."

"And you didn't know the chopper would kill your dad."

"I thought it would."

"And I thought the balcony might collapse. Every time we do anything, we take our chances. You can't get away from that if you want to go on living. Life isn't about reliving the past. It's about living the present."

Phoebe heard another helicopter join the fleet congregating over the bowling alley. She knew this was going to end badly.

Chapter 25

Clad in a white lab coat, Zandorf was standing with the acting mayor Steve Strus in Jason Albright's hospital room.

Jason was lying on his back in bed, his eyes staring out of his head, as he breathed with the help of the respirator.

"We need to know where your wife Phoebe is," said Zandorf. "Can you help us?"

Jason's face remained blank.

"Why do we need her?" said Strus, wearing a charcoal grey suit with an aqua rep necktie.

"She might be infected," said Zandorf. "We had reports that she was seen on the Strip before it burned down. The police haven't been able to locate her."

"Why do you think she's infected?"

"Since she was on the Strip when the virus broke out, we can't give her a clean bill of health till we examine her. Also . . ."

"Also what?"

"Her husband might have infected her."

Strus backed away from Jason's bed with apprehension. "The mayor's infected?"

"We can't be sure yet. We're doing his bloodwork, but it's not clear whether he was infected by Val Lewton."

"Who's Val Lewton?"

"She's the hooker who we think might be patient zero. We believe the mayor was patronizing her at the Strip."

"Why do you think that?"

"Because she kept calling out his name before she died. Which is why we believe he could be infected."

"Why can't you be sure?"

Zandorf adjusted his black plastic-framed glasses as he studied Jason's face.

"It might be because he's in a coma, which has affected his brain—shut it down, if you will," he said. "The virus spreads inside the brain with lightning speed. However, if the brain is nonfunctional as in a coma, perhaps the virus cannot spread—if it's present. We're not sure it's present. Maybe it becomes dormant if the brain is comatose. Maybe it can't feed on a comatose brain. We just don't know."

"Can't you see the worms in his brain?"

"We cannot. The CAT scan didn't detect any worms. So we can't tell if he's infected."

"When will you know?"

Zandorf fetched a noisy sigh. "Impossible to tell. This is a virus the likes of which we've never seen before. We don't know enough about it to be certain of anything regarding it."

"We can't let it wipe out every citizen in Costaguana."

Ignoring Strus, Zandorf kept scrutinizing Jason's motionless face.

"If infected, he could have infected his wife," said Zandorf. "Or she could've gotten infected while she was on the Strip just before it burned down. It is of vital importance that we find her, examine her, and question her."

"The police have a BOLO out for her," said Strus, flicking his thumb under his upper front teeth in a nervous gesture. "I don't know what more they can do."

"This isn't a huge town. Where can she hide?"

"We'll find her. It's only a matter of time. Her face is all over the TV. Somebody's bound to recognize her."

"She's the mayor's wife. How can nobody not recognize her?" said Zandorf, incredulous.

Strus shrugged. "It just goes to show people aren't informed about their government."

"She could hold the key to the virus."

"What do you mean?"

"If she's not infected, it could mean she's immune. If that's the case, we need to study her ASAP."

"Aren't you jumping to conclusions?"

"She could be a carrier."

"Someone who—?"

"Someone who's infected and contagious but shows no symptoms of the virus."

"Then we have to get her off the streets before she infects everybody."

"Exactly. Have the cops figured out how Jason ended up sprawled in the middle of the street next to his office building?"

"They're investigating it. They found a broken chair near his body on the tarmac. They theorize that the chair was used to break the window, since the window can't be opened."

"Is that the best they can do—a theory?"

"They're actually pretty sure of it. The chair was identified as one from the mayor's office."

"The question is, who threw the chair through the window?" Zandorf did a double take. "Are they calling it attempted murder? Did somebody push him?"

"His secretary said the mayor was alone in his office at the time of the fall."

"Then they must think he tried to kill himself. Why else would he throw a chair through his office window?"

"The only problem with that explanation is they can't find a suicide note."

"Lack of a suicide note doesn't prove anything."

"The thing is, nobody can understand why he would want to jump. He wasn't having problems that anyone knew of. At least, ahem, he hadn't told anyone about any."

"No financial problems?"

"The cops haven't uncovered any."

Zandorf mulled it over, worry creasing his brow.

"I can think of a reason he might want to kill himself, but I hope I'm wrong," he said.

"Then you're a step ahead of the cops. They can't find any evidence to suggest suicide."

"He might have thought he had become infected with the virus thanks to his association with the infected hooker Val Lewton. The pain from the infection is unbearable. If he was suffering from the pain, he could have opted for suicide instead."

"Then he's infected," said Strus, glancing at Jason with apprehension.

"Or he *thought* he was," said Zandorf, crossing his arms over his chest. "I'm no psychiatrist, but maybe he mistook the pangs of a guilty conscience for cheating on his wife as proof he was infected with the virus. After all, he *is* married."

"If he tried to kill himself, he's damned to hell—no matter what his motivation."

"We might all be damned to hell before this is over," said Zandorf under his breath.

Strus's cell phone chimed.

Chapter 26

Strus took the call and listened, all ears. He terminated the call.

"Who was it?" said Zandorf.

"The police," said Strus, his face grave. "They've located a fresh outbreak of the virus at the bowling alley."

"Hell. I thought we had it under control when we burned the Strip. It's more important than ever that we find Phoebe Albright. We might be able to fashion a vaccine by studying her blood—*if* she is indeed immune from the disease. That's a big *if*." Knitting his brow, Zandorf adjusted his glasses. "We can't come to any conclusion without studying her. In any case, we must not let this virus pass beyond the city limits."

"I gave the order for the police to blockade the road leading out of town. The governor has given the same order to the state police. I understand he's sending the National Guard down here too."

"The FBI is also sending men here. I requested the president to send them because of the severity of the situation."

"Then we can contain this, I'm sure," said Strus, inflating his chest with self-confidence.

Zandorf stared out the window of the hospital high-rise at the clearing sky.

"We might have to burn the entire city to the ground," he said, brooding.

"Out of the question," said Strus, taken aback.

"I don't like it any more than you, but the fate of the nation is at stake. This virus has a hundred percent fatality ratio. You get it, you die. And you die in excruciating agony as the virus worms eat your brain."

"Jesus."

"It has to be stopped here and eradicated from the face of the earth before it can spread," said Zandorf with a determined visage.

"I'm sure we can stop it."

"Until then we need to lock down this town tighter than a flea's ass."

"No problem."

"You better be right."

"We always have hope. Where there's no hope, there's horror."

"We need more than hope. That's why we have science."

Jason groaned, startling them.

Zandorf looked expectantly at Jason, as though he might be coming to—no matter how improbable it seemed.

"Jason?" he said.

Jason's face remained motionless and unresponsive.

Chapter 27

A California bear flag hanging behind him on a pole, Governor Vitti sat behind his impressive desk in his Sacramento office and called the director of the FBI, Bryce Friedlow in Washington, DC.

Vitti could see the five-eight, forty-five-year-old Friedlow in his mind's eye with his Princeton cut and off-the-rack navy blue suit. Hunched over his desk, phone in hand, Friedow was a miser who horded everybody's secrets like they were gold ingots. Indeed, the secrets he harbored could make or break a person's career.

"Hello, Director Friedlow. This is Governor Vitti of California."

"Hello, sir."

"I need your help. The president told me I should contact you because I want to shut down all communications in the city of Costaguana. He said you would know what to do. First of all, can it be done?"

"The president told me to expect your call. Exactly what do you want shut down?"

"Everything. Phones, cell-phones, e-mails, the postal service, texting, radios, live TV broadcasts. Everything leaving and entering Costaguana. You know the drill."

"POTUS didn't go into the details why you want this done."

"We're trying to put a lid on what's happening in Costaguana. If citizens find out what's going on there, it would cause widespread panic. We can't let that happen. We need to get the situation under control before we allow communications in and out of the city."

"I can relay your request to the NSA. I'm sure they will be able to help. I need to ask you a question first."

"By all means. Shoot."

"Does this situation you're describing have anything to do with a terrorist act on our soil?"

"As far as we know, the answer to your question is no."

"If you find out otherwise, let me know posthaste."

"Of course."

"Then what's the problem, if not terrorism?"

Vitti fidgeted in his seat. "The president wants me to limit the amount of people who know the exact nature of the situation."

"Why?"

"Again, we're concerned about panic. The less people who know, the better. Under no circumstances must the media find out what's going on in Costaguana."

"I would never tell the media."

"No, sir. I'm sure you wouldn't. But there are leaks in your office. We—uh—we can't take the chance. Whether we like it or not, DC is full of leaks. It's what keeps the papers in business."

"Is the nation's security at stake?"

"Yes."

"Then I must insist. I have to be aware of all threats against this great country."

Vitti hesitated. "Will you agree to have Costaguana's comms shut down?"

"You have my word."

Vitti lowered his voice. "Can I count on you to keep what I'm about to tell you secret?"

"You can."

Vitti cleared his throat and continued to keep his voice low.

"We're dealing with the most lethal virus ever discovered," he said. "No one must find out about its existence. So soon after Covid, the resulting panic from the disclosure would trigger a massive revolt in the populace. If not controlled and eradicated, the virus will wipe out this country in a matter of weeks. No one must find out about it." He paused a beat. "Do you agree to keep this information secret?"

Silence on the line.

"Mr. Director?" said Vitti.

"I'm—uh—coming to grips with this."

"I know. Now you understand why the NSA must shut down comms in the infected city."

"We're gonna make that city a graveyard of silence when the NSA gets done with it."

Vitti didn't appreciate the analogy, but decided the city could very well end up a graveyard. Though he didn't want to think about it, he would kill everyone in town to stop the spread of the virus if he had to. His actions now could pave his way to the White House as the next president. If he had to kill everyone in Costaguana, nobody but nobody must find out about it, or it would doom his career and his presidential ambitions. Discretion was essential from here on in.

Which was why he had reservations about telling Friedlow about the virus. But he needed the fed's cooperation. He could only hope Friedlow would keep his damn mouth shut. Vitti could trust a director like Herbert Hoover, but Friedlow was no Hoover. Times had changed since Hoover's days as director.

In the end, people must be led to believe that any deaths in Costaguana were caused by the virus, decided Vitti. But for now it suited his purposes to keep everyone ignorant about the existence of the virus. Its very existence needed to be covered up until it was eradicated.

Of course, the citizens of Costaguana weren't going to be happy when the NSA shut down their comms. Too bad for them, decided Vitti. They would have to suffer in silence.

Chapter 28

Jackson Albright, Jason's father, met the bald, bowlegged fixer Declan Hardy at an aromatic, dim-lit steakhouse. They sat at an isolated table in the back of the restaurant. Hardy had a bandage on his forehead.

"I've heard you've done work for my son Jason," said Jackson, nursing a Coors as he waited for his meal.

Hardy nodded yes. "How is he, by the way? I heard he met with an accident."

"He's still in a coma."

"Sorry to hear it. What's the prognosis?"

Hardy reached for a slice of heated sourdough bread from a warm dish in the middle of the table. A white cloth napkin folded over the sliced baguette was keeping the bread warm. He unfolded the napkin and selected a piece of bread.

"The doctors aren't sure," said Jackson.

Hardy chewed on the sourdough. "They keep this bread warm. That's a plus in my book."

"As I said on the phone, I need your services."

"I'm available if you can afford me."

Jackson unleashed a wrinkled smile. "I can afford anyone."

"What's the nature of the problem that needs to be fixed?"

"Don't you put butter on your bread?"

"Never. Occasionally, I use marmalade. Otherwise, nothing."

"I need you to find Jason's wife Phoebe."

"You're not the only one looking for her."

"I know the cops want her. I want you to find her for me before they get her. I need to talk to her."

"It will cost you extra, because she's on the lam. It's gonna make her harder to find."

"I understand."

"I have a score to settle with her."

"You know her?" said Jackson in surprise.

"She caused an accident I was in."

"Is that how you got the bandage on your forehead?"

"Yeah." Hardy paused and nibbled on his slice of sourdough bread. "If you want me to remove her, it will cost you even more, though I would be glad to do it."

"At this point, I just want to talk to her. She might know how my son got injured."

"I doubt she was anywhere near him when he fell."

"How would you know that?"

"Because I was with her."

Jackson looked hopeful. "Then you must know where she is."

"Not at the moment. But I can find her. Don't worry. I can find anyone."

"I also want to know why the cops want her."

"I can ask her when I find her."

"I want to ask her in person."

"Fine," said Hardy, and polished off his slice of sourdough bread.

"I have a feeling she knows what's going on in this town. There's something rotten in the state of Denmark."

"I get your drift. These road closures are just the beginning."

"I need to know exactly what's going down. My son used to be my pipeline for information. Now I'm shut out of the loop. My real-estate business is losing money hand over fist thanks to the lockdown."

"There's something about this virus they're not telling us. Hell, they burned down the Strip to wipe it out."

"They did what?" said Jackson, flummoxed.

"You heard me."

"The TV news said the fire on the Strip was an accident."

"It was no accident. I was there. I saw it. They used napalm fired from choppers."

"They?"

"The cops. The state cops. Whoever was in the choppers."

"Why in the world would anyone burn down the Strip on purpose? I lost millions of dollars' worth of real estate. I'll sue the cops, goddammit."

"They're trying to stop the spread of this new virus that's infecting the town."

"By burning down part of the city?" said Jackson, aghast.

"What can I say? I saw them do it."

"What kind of a nitwit would give such a half-assed order? My son would never do it."

"I dunno. I only know what I saw," said Hardy, reaching for another slice of bread from under the napkin.

"This is outrageous."

Hardy took a pull on his Corona longneck. "I couldn't believe it when I saw it."

"That clown Vitti is the only one foolhardy enough to pull a stunt like this. After all, he's the one locking down our city. But to deliberately burn down the Strip? He should be thrown out of office on his ass."

"I'm lucky I didn't end up dead there."

"How many people burned to death because of him?"

"A lot."

"If I can prove he had something to do with the Strip fire, I'll do everything in my power to have him removed from office."

"I could remove him from office if you want."

"No, no, no. I was thinking out loud."

"Suit yourself. I can't wait for my filet mignon," said Hardy, gazing toward the kitchen with longing.

"I need to talk to Phoebe," said Jackson, preoccupied. "She might be able to shed light on what's going on. Why else would the cops want her?"

Chapter 29

Phoebe stood inside the bowling alley and watched the VW Bug continue to burn in the parking lot as three choppers hovered over the wreckage.

The three remaining infected maniacs knocked on the lobby front door, frustrated that nobody was letting them inside.

Phoebe wondered why the choppers hadn't shot them.

"Maybe now we should let them in," said Herman.

"No," said Phoebe. "They're infected. They'll kill us."

"Then why didn't the cops shoot them?" said Herman, taking in the choppers that had mowed down the maniacs that had attacked the VW. "They shot the other maniacs."

As if they had overheard him, the three choppers flew toward the three infected.

Ignoring them the three infected pounded more furiously on the bowling alley plate-glass door.

An AR-15 barrel protruded from the lead chopper's cockpit. The automatic rifle ripped apart the three infected. They jittered as if dancing to rock and roll then crumpled in front of the bowling alley door, their bodies leaking blood.

"Satisfied?" said Phoebe.

"That this isn't a movie?" said Herman. "No, I'm not satisfied. Those guys outside could all be actors playing dead."

"Now that the infected are all dead, can we go outside?" said Bud.

"You go outside, they'll shoot you," said Phoebe.

"Why? I'm not infected."

"It doesn't matter. They're gonna shoot everyone in this vicinity."

"Why should we believe you?" said Herman. "You could be working for the movie producers."

"Can't you get it through your head?" said Phoebe. "Those are real bullets flying out there."

"This type of thing doesn't happen in real life. This has to be a horror movie."

"I wish you were right," said Phoebe as if to herself, recalling the cold-blooded murder of her father at the hands of the cops in the chopper at the Strip.

Bud approached the front door. "I'm going out there to tell the cops we're not infected."

"The worst thing you can do."

"Why?" said Bud, confused.

"Because they won't believe you."

"I gotta open up for business. People want to bowl," said Bud, grasping the door handle, preparing to undo the dead-bolt lock.

"Don't," said Phoebe, her eyes bugging out. "I'm trying to save your life."

"This mess started when you arrived. *You* brought these maniacs here."

"Yeah," said Herman. "You and your movie people."

"She helped save my life," said Wally, sitting at a table near a vending machine in the food court.

"Maybe you're in this with her," said Bud.

"If you movie people don't want us in the movie, why did you come here?" said Herman.

"Don't go outside until the choppers leave," said Phoebe, knowing the choppers weren't going anywhere after this new outbreak of the virus.

"Easy for you to say," said Bud. "You're not running a bowling alley to make a living."

"Just wait a little longer."

Bud stood at the door, debating whether to unlock it, bat in hand.

"I think she's right," said Crystal, standing near Wally. "Let's wait a while. What's the big rush?"

"Can I have your autograph while we wait?" said Herman, angling toward her.

"Sure."

"How are we doing?"

"What?" said Crystal, bewildered.

"Our acting. Are we believable?"

Crystal decided to humor him instead of continuing to argue.

"Yeah," she said. "Sure."

"Don't encourage him," said Bud.

"What'd I say?" said Crystal, looking innocent.

"Don't mind him," said Herman.

"I'm gonna tell you the best acting advice I ever got."

"Great. What is it?" said Herman, eager to know.

"If you're acting in a movie, act like you're *not* in a movie."

Herman mulled it over for a few moments. "Oh, I get it. That's smart. I really gotta see that movie you were in. I bet you were good."

"Can you stop drooling over her?" said Bud. "I'm the one that has to clean the floor."

Herman waved him off with distaste. "Whatever." He turned back to Crystal. "Now where were we before we were so rudely interrupted?"

Chapter 30

Hardy drove his rented black Honda Accord to Lila Spillane's house. He was using it to replace his previous Honda which he had wrapped around a coral tree near the Strip—with the help of Phoebe. He figured Phoebe's mother's house was the best place to start his search for Phoebe.

He had two incentives to find Phoebe. Not only had Jackson hired him to find her, but Hardy also had unfinished business with her. She was the one who had wrecked his car and tried to kill him in an accident she caused. He wanted payback.

Hardy parked in the driveway and walked to the front door. The air was mild and bore the scent of rosemary, which he could see planted in Lila's front yard, flanking the front stoop.

He opened the screen door and knocked on the wooden door.

Wearing jeans and a lilac blouse Lila opened the door.

"Hello," she said, not recognizing him, not sure she wanted to keep the door open.

"Hi. I'm looking for your daughter Phoebe. Is she here?" he said, smiling politely.

"No," she said, starting to close the door.

He kicked open the door and shoved his way inside, knocking her backward.

Lila didn't scream.

"Get out of here before I call the police," she yelled, recovering her balance, furious at his break-in.

"Where is she?" said Hardy, casting around the small house.

"She's not here. What business is it of yours anyway?"

"I need to talk to her."

"You're wasting your time. Now leave."

She stepped toward her cell phone that lay on the sideboard a few feet from where she stood.

Hardy whipped out a Beretta 92 Compact concealed in a shoulder rig beneath his jacket.

"Don't move," he said, training the muzzle on her.

She halted.

"Sit on that sofa," he said, waving toward it with the Beretta barrel.

Grudgingly, Lila walked to the indicated sofa and sat.

"You'll never get away with this," she said.

"Tell me where she is and save yourself some grief."

"Who the hell are you? You come barging in my house like you own it—"

"Shut up."

"Get out of here this minute and maybe I won't call the police."

Keeping her in sight, Hardy retreated from her and peeked into the different rooms, searching for Phoebe.

"OK, where is she?" he said, returning to her.

"Stop aiming that gun at me."

He reached for a sound suppressor in his trouser pocket and screwed it onto the Beretta muzzle.

"Start talking," he said.

"I don't know where she is," she said, widening her eyes with apprehension.

"You must know. You're the only one she could go to. Her father's dead. Her husband's in a coma. Where else could she go?"

"How do you know so much about her?"

"I'm the one asking the questions," he said, losing his patience. "Tell me where she is, or I'll blow out your kneecap."

"I don't—"

"I'll put you on crutches for the rest of your life."

"You wouldn't—"

Hardy squeezed the Beretta trigger and kneecapped her.

Lila screamed in shock and pain as blood blossomed out of the hole ripped in her jeans and in her knee by the bullet. The denim turned dark with blood.

"Tell me," said Hardy. "Or I'll do your other knee."

"I gave her my car," said Lila, whimpering in agony, gripping her wound.

"What kind of car?"

She groaned. "A silver Ford Fiesta."

"License plate number?"

She told him, her voice shaky.

"Where did she go?" said Hardy.

"I dunno."

Hardy trained the Beretta on her other knee. "I'll do it."

"She didn't tell me," Lila cried, wide-eyed, her hands covered with blood as she grasped her wound.

Hardy weighed her answer, searching her face to see if she was lying.

He believed her. He unscrewed the silencer from his Beretta muzzle and pocketed it. He holstered the Beretta.

"Don't call the cops, or I'll come back and whack you," he said.

White-faced from loss of blood, she glanced at her cell phone on the sideboard and nodded.

"After I whack your daughter."

Hardy snagged her cell phone on the sideboard and took it with him as he cut across the living room to the front door.

"I need my cell phone to call the hospital," said Lila.

"Use your landline."

"I can't reach it. It's in the kitchen."

"Learn how to limp. You're gonna be doing it for the rest of your life."

Hardy wasn't going to lose any sleep if she bled out.

He shut the door behind him as he exited. He flung her cell phone into the street, where passing motor vehicle tires would smash it to bits.

Chapter 31

Governor Vitti was sitting in his office when his secretary buzzed him on the intercom.

"What is it, Mabel?" he said.

"I have a Mr. Manuel Picasso on the phone. He wants to talk to you about Costaguana."

Vitti pricked up his ears. Costaguana. How could anyone know about Costaguana? he wondered. He had the entire city locked down.

"What does he want?"

"He said he has medical information for Costaguana."

"Where is he calling from?"

"Matamoros, Mexico."

"Which line?"

"Line three."

Vitti snapped up his handset and punched line three. "This is Governor Vitti speaking."

"This is Manuel Picasso in Matamoros, Mr. Governor."

The only thing Vitti knew about Matamoros was that it was controlled by the Gulf Cartel.

"I'm a busy man, Mr. Picasso. I must admit I don't recognize your name."

"I'm an associate of Rick Muldoon in Costaguana."

The late Rick Muldoon, decided Vitti. White slaver and drug dealer on the now-defunct Strip. An associate of the Gulf Cartel in Matomoros. Not surprising. The gangster also contributed money to his reelection campaign. A lot of money.

"I don't know any Rick Muldoon," lied Vitti, not wanting to be associated with the thug. "I don't understand why you're calling me."

Lowering his handset Vitti prepared to hang up.

"I think you do," said Picasso. "Anyway, he told me about your virus outbreak in Costaguana. We had a similar outbreak in Matamoros."

Vitti brought his handset to his ear again. "I never heard anything about a virus outbreak in Matamoros in the news."

"Some things are better left out of the news as you well know. We have more control of our news in Matamoros than you do in your country."

*Because the Gulf Cartel whacks out all the journalists if they tell the truth,* thought Vitti.

"Are you listening, Governor?"

"Go on."

"We believe we can help you with your outbreak."

"I doubt it. But I'm listening."

"My company, Cobygenex Pharmaceuticals, has developed a vaccine to stop the spread of the virus."

Taken aback, Vitti pressed his handset hard against his ear.

"You what?" he said.

"You heard right. We have a vaccine. And we are willing to sell you thirty thousand doses for thirty million US dollars."

Vitti looked skeptical. "How could you create a vaccine so quickly."

"We used the same mRNA technology that was used for the Covid virus."

Costaguana was turning into a black spot on his record as governor, decided Vitti. If he could vaccinate everyone in Costaguana and wipe out the killer virus, it would be a load off his mind and leave his path to the White House clear of obstacles. The longer Costaguana festered with the virus, the slimmer his chances of becoming president.

The best of all possible worlds would be for him to wipe out the virus here and now before anyone got wind of its existence and of all the deaths it had caused, decided Vitti.

"Are you interested in saving your citizens, Governor?"

Vitti knew the Mexican cartels could manufacture drugs quickly and distribute them just as quickly. Was he clutching at straws? Perhaps. But his career depended on taking care of the Costaguana crisis chop-chop.

"How do I know this isn't a scam?" he said.

"If it is, you will have us arrested. Why do we want to risk being busted by the US government?" Picasso laughed. "Your federal prisons are a lot more secure than ours."

Vitti had his back to the wall. He knew he had to act decisively on Costaguana and wipe out the virus. Hell, it wasn't his personal thirty million. It was the government's, the taxpayers'. And this was a good investment to save the people of California. No one could fault him for significant expenditures on vaccines.

"Are you a scientist?" asked Vitti.

"No. I'm in the pharmaceutical business."

"How fast can you get these vaccines to California?"

"In a matter of hours."

Impressed, Vitti raised his eyebrows. "How can you get them here so fast?"

"Like I said, we used the vaccines to end an epidemic here. We have some left over and ready to ship at a moment's notice. We're equipped to produce more of the vaccine, and we can produce it—how do you say—ah, I know—in a New York minute."

Ordinarily, Vitti wouldn't have jumped at this deal. There were too many unknowns. But these weren't ordinary times. Despite all his precautions, the outbreak in Costaguana was spreading. If it spread beyond the city limits, he was convinced he would never be able to stop it.

He didn't want to have to torch the entire city. The people would be in up in arms. Nobody in California would vote for him if they found out he had razed Costaguana to the ground with fires, killing all of the residents in the process.

He wasn't going to have time to test the vaccine. He would have to trust Picasso if he was going to agree to Picasso's deal. However, he never trusted anyone in politics.

He needed a way to shield himself if the shit hit the fan and it turned out the vaccine was a scam. He needed a fall guy. He knew just the person. His lieutenant governor Kevin Bates. Vitti would have Bates agree to Picasso's deal, insulating Vitti from any blowback—if there was any. Vitti would deny approving the deal and blame it on Bates. If the vaccine succeeded, Vitti would claim the credit.

Vitti knew CYA was essential for success in politics. *Always blame failure on someone else.*

Chapter 32

A fortyish guy clad in jeans, a bolo tie, a black blazer, and a black porkpie hat tore across the parking lot in front of the bowling alley. Holding his porkpie hat pressed to his head so it wouldn't fall off, he ran from a mob of maniacs foaming at the mouth, who were catching up to him rapidly thanks to their superhuman speed.

His face sweaty with both fear and exertion, he spotted the bowling alley door and ran for it as three choppers hovered overhead.

Phoebe dashed to the front door.

"Let him in," she said.

"How do we know he's not one of them?" said Bud, standing at the door, Louisville Slugger in hand.

"Look, he's not foaming at the mouth," she said, pointing at the guy. "They'll kill him if you don't let him in. They're infected."

"Let him in," said Wally.

"How can we be sure he's not infected?" said Bud, unconvinced.

"They wouldn't be running after him if he was infected," said Phoebe. "They don't attack each other, just healthy people."

"I dunno."

"You can't delay. They're closing in on him."

"I don't want any of those infected maniacs or whatever they are inside my alley."

Their eyes popping out of their sweaty faces, their arms outstretched, their hands curled like claws, the maniacs muttered gibberish as they chased the guy in the bolo.

"Do something," said Crystal, jumping from her seat in the food court, worried at his plight. "I saw what they can do. They'll tear him apart."

Bolo reached the door and tried to open it. His face frantic, he pounded on the plate glass.

"Help," he cried.

The infected mob would reach him in seconds. They became more frenetic the closer they got to him.

"Open it," cried Phoebe, dreading to see him torn to pieces.

Grinding his teeth, Bud tried to decide what to do. He made up his mind, unlocked the door, and flung it open.

Bolo burst through the open door, gasping for breath, windmilling his arms, desperate to escape the bloodthirsty mob.

"Shut it," cried Phoebe, springing to the door to help Bud close it.

Bud didn't need any encouragement. He slammed the door shut as the leader of the mob crashed into it, trying to grab Bolo.

The leader of the mob was a stocky twentysomething woman wearing a postal uniform, a brass chain dangling from her belt. Foaming at the mouth and drooling, she managed to insert her arm through the doorway before Bud could get the door shut. He couldn't shut the door on account of her arm sandwiched between the door and the jamb.

She yelped in pain as the door smashed her arm.

Bud forced all of his weight against the door trying to keep the mob out.

"I can't keep them out much longer," he said, grimacing as he shoved his shoulder against the door trying to get it to close. "Somebody, get her arm out of there."

Drawing a jackknife out of his trouser pocket, Wally approached the door. He flicked open the blade. The postal woman's arm flailed around as she growled and tried to shove open the door. Wally stabbed her forearm, aiming for the radial artery. Blood jetted six feet into the air. She howled in pain and tried to jerk her arm away, but it was trapped between the door and the jamb.

Bud eased up a little on the door to let her pull her bleeding arm out. As she jerked her arm out, he slammed the door shut and locked it.

Two infected maniacs shoved the whimpering postal woman out of their way and pounded their fists on the door, growling and drooling.

"What is wrong with people?" said Bolo, gathering his breath. "I was walking outside, and that mob of psychos charged me."

"They're infected. I'm Phoebe."

"I'm Will Geiger. Thanks for saving my life. I'm convinced they would've killed me. Did you see how fast they can run? It's unreal."

"They're infected with a lethal virus."

Geiger rubbed his brow. "I thought I was a goner for sure. When I tried to open the door and found out it was locked, my heart stopped. I thought the bowling alley was closed."

"We have to protect ourselves from the infected," said Bud, stroking the barrel of his bat with his left hand while holding the handle with his right.

"He didn't want to let you in at first, Will," said Crystal.

"Never mind," said Phoebe. She turned to Geiger. "He thought you were one of the infected."

"I don't have any craving to eat people," said Geiger, shaken. "I saw them eat—" He caught his breath. "I don't want to talk about it."

"They're all messed up," said Herman.

Chapter 33

Geiger exhaled loudly. "I thought the killer mob was running amok on crack or speed. This confirms my view of life."

"You must have a low opinion of life, then," said Phoebe.

Geiger nodded yes. "I believe life itself is a virus. When we mate, we spread the virus."

"What are you?" said Bud. "Some kind of Satanist?"

"I'm a reverend."

"A reverend who hates life? I don't believe it. Religions cherish life. They don't hate it."

"A lot you know."

"More than you, I bet."

"I've lived in pain all my life. I feel like piranhas are chewing on my flesh every minute of the day."

"This has got to be a movie," said Herman. "A reverend who hates life has now joined our cast. This is one whacked-out horror flick." His eyes lit up. "I know, you're suffering a crisis of faith like Father Damien Karras in *The Exorcist*. Right?"

"That's my favorite horror movie," said Crystal.

"*Exorcist III* was good too."

"Movie?" Geiger eyed Phoebe. "What is he talking about?"

"He thinks we're all in a horror movie."

"Those psychopathic killers out there seem real to me." Geiger took a deep breath. "I saw them tackle a teenage girl and tear her limb from limb outside of a laundromat in the nearby strip mall," he said, disconcerted. "I'll never forget that sight as long as I live. When they saw me watching them, they tore after me like a pack of hyenas, howling and drooling."

"Special effects these days can work wonders," said Herman.

"You're lucky to be a live," Phoebe told Geiger.

"I'm not so sure," said Geiger. "My entire life has been a descent into the nether reaches of gloom and desolation."

"Are you the one the scriptwriter sent to save us?" said Herman. "The emotionally wounded hero suffering a crisis of faith who must prove himself?"

"Save you? I can't even save myself. I can barely tolerate all my pain."

Geiger's answer puzzled Herman.

"Then why were you sent here?" said Herman.

"Nobody sent me. I guess I was in the wrong place at the wrong time."

"You want us to feel sorry for you, Geiger?" said Bud. "Is that it? Nothing doing, buddy. If you want to wallow in self-pity, wallow alone."

"I don't feel self-pity. I feel anger, anger at the evil thing called life."

"Because you're a Satanist."

"I don't believe in Satan. Life is evil, but it's not because of a mythical being called Satan. Life is evil because it's a cancer. It grows unchecked and spreads all over the world."

"Growing unchecked doesn't make it evil."

"The only way you can free yourself from the disease called life is to see the evil for what it is and refuse to take part."

"Well, I don't want to free myself. I want to go on living. We should've left you out there to get murdered, since you hate being alive."

"I need to go on living in order to spread the word that life is an evil virus. The only way you can stop it is to refuse to breed."

"Don't worry in that department," said Crystal. "Nobody would want to breed with you. You're a coward. You don't know anything about pain. I was held as a sex slave by the Jalisco New Generation Cartel for most of my life, but I still want to live."

"Then you understand life is evil."

"I understand living in a cartel jail is evil, living as a sex slave is evil."

"You're preaching to the converted."

"But I don't think life is evil like you do."

"If he wasn't sent here to save us, how are we supposed to get out of this mess?" said Herman, addressing the group. "I don't understand this movie." He faced Geiger. "You're supposed to get your faith back and save us, like Karras in *The Exorcist*."

"We're in the middle of an epidemic," said Phoebe. "What I don't understand is why the government is shooting innocent people."

"How do we know they're shooting innocent people?" said Bud. "They're shooting the infected maniacs, the way I see it."

"Why don't they try to cure them?"

"You yourself said there's no cure. The only way to stop the spread of the epidemic is to kill the infected."

"But they're also killing people who aren't infected."

"We can't be sure of that."

"I saw them shoot my uninfected father," said Phoebe, raising her voice.

Two AR-15s protruding from the hovering choppers fired continuous bursts at the infected maniacs standing outside the bowling alley front door. Crying out in pain, the maniacs flailed their arms and fell to the ground as bullets plowed into their flesh, painting the tarmac red with blood.

Phoebe leered at the massacred victims lying in puddles of their own blood. It was the Strip all over again, she decided. The government started out killing the infected maniacs and ended up killing everyone in their vicinity.

Which meant Phoebe and her group didn't have much longer to live.

Chapter 34

Bud gazed out the plate-glass door at the choppers hovering overhead.

"I think those guys in the choppers are trying to help us," he said. "After all, they killed those maniacs. The infected, you call them."

"And they'll kill you if you go outside," said Phoebe.

"Why? I'm not infected."

"As near as I can figure, they must think everybody in the neighborhood of the infected must be infected."

"But that's not true," said Crystal. "We're not infected."

Herman scratched his head in thought. "Wait a minute. Maybe this is a plot twist in the movie. Maybe we really are infected and don't know it."

"I don't know about the rest of you, but *I'm* not infected," said Bud. "I don't have any desire to eat human flesh."

"Just thinking about it makes me sick to my stomach," said Crystal.

"The problem is you have to prove to the cops that you're not infected," said Phoebe.

"How do you do that?" said Bud.

"You can't."

"I don't believe this. You're saying the cops are gonna whack out all of us just because we're here?"

"That's what they did on the Strip."

"Well, nobody lives forever," said Wally. "I never thought I'd reach eighty, and here I am—still vertical. If it's over, it's over."

"Easy for you to say," said Crystal. "You're old. I'm young, and I don't want to die yet."

"Just because I'm old doesn't mean I want to die. I want to go on living as much as you do."

"Say what you want, but I don't believe the cops are gonna blow us away," said Bud. "My brother's a cop, and he's a stand-up guy. He doesn't go around blowing away people for no reason."

"Those chopper cops are *not* our friends," said Phoebe. "I've seen them in action. As soon as we set foot outside this bowling alley, they'll shoot us."

"Are you calling my brother a killer?" said Bud, taking umbrage, glowering at Phoebe.

"I'm talking about those cops flying above us," said Phoebe, looking up at the sky.

"Why should we believe you? You come in here with your bullshit stories about infected maniacs and killer cops. This is crazy stuff you're saying."

"I know how it sounds, but it's true."

"There's only one way to find out for sure," said Wally. "Someone has to go outside."

"No, don't," said Phoebe, striding to the front door and blocking anyone from reaching it. "I'm telling you they will kill you."

"I bet she's right," said Geiger. "Look at all those bullet-riddled corpses strewn on the parking lot."

"What do you care?" said Crystal. "You *want* to die."

"I said life is an evil virus. I never said I wanted to die."

"If I decide to go out there, nobody in this building is gonna stop me," said Bud, flourishing his Louisville Slugger. He stared at Phoebe. "Standing in front of that door isn't gonnna stop me."

"If you want to go on living, don't go outside," said Phoebe.

"I'm not taking orders from a batty woman."

"I figured it out," cried Herman.

The others stared at him.

"I figured out who's gonna die next in this horror movie."

Chapter 35

"Remember what the three rules of horror movies are?" Herman asked Crystal.

"Do you mean, who dies first?"

"Right."

"The ones who die first are the drinkers and dopers, the ones having sex, and anyone who says, 'I'll be right back.'"

"Which means . . . ," Herman trailed off.

"What are you yammering about?" said Bud.

"I was toking weed in the restroom when this started," said Herman, chewing his fingernails with worry. "I'm the one who's gonna die first."

"This isn't a horror movie," said Phoebe. "There really is an infectious virus outside, driving people insane, making them want to kill and eat people."

Herman's face drained of color. "I wonder how I'm gonna die."

"If it's a movie, you won't really die," said Crystal. "But it's not a movie."

"It has to be a movie. Nothing this crazy could happen in real life."

"I don't know who's crazier," said Bud. "You or Phoebe. Killer cops?" he said to Phoebe. "Come on."

"Let's look at the bright side," said Wally. "Nobody in this bowling alley has died."

"Yet," said Geiger.

"We can't stay here," said Phoebe.

"Why not?" said Wally. "Bud says the front door is bulletproof. Nobody can get in."

"Sooner or later the cops are gonna burn down this entire neighborhood like they did to the Strip."

"Why the hell would they do that?" said Bud.

"To stop the virus from spreading. We've gone over this a hundred times. Going over it again and again isn't gonna change anything."

"If this movie is part of the *Saw* franchise, the only way we can escape is to find the one way out," said Herman. "There's usually a key hidden somewhere. All we have to do is find it."

He surveyed the bowling alley, trying to figure out where to look for the key.

"What makes you think it's a *Saw* movie?" said Crystal. "Maybe it's *The Walking Dead*."

"Do the infected rise from the dead like zombies?"

"That's right," said Phoebe. "Unless they're burned or have their heads bashed in."

"Now I know you're crazy," said Bud. "You expect us to believe in zombies?"

"Some of the best horror movies have zombies," said Herman. "Take for example Lucio Fulci's *Zombi 2*."

"Why do they call it *Zombi 2*?" said Crystal. "Where's *Zombi 1*?"

"Fulci's movie was supposed to be a sequel to Romero's *Dawn of the Dead*."

Phoebe was looking out the front door when one of the bullet-peppered maniacs stood up.

Wearing yellow shorts she was in her thirties with bangs and shoulder-length, fine blonde hair. The hair was hanging farther down her back than usual thanks to the condition of her neck that had been almost severed from her torso by a swath of parabellum rounds fired by one of the AR-15s in the choppers. Her plump face was lying on her shoulder held there by a strip of flesh, which was the only part of her neck that remained intact and attached to her torso. Without that strip of flesh, her head would fall off. Blood splotched her salmon blouse.

"How in the hell can she be alive?" said Bud, following Phoebe's gaze. "She's as good as decapitated."

"The infected come back to life after they die."

"Impossible. She must still be alive somehow. There must be enough blood in her brain to keep her alive."

"The other corpses will start rising soon too," said Phoebe, picking up on movement among the cadavers sprawled in the parking lot.

Some of them were squirming. Others were sitting up.

"I guess all of them were only wounded," said Bud with surprise.

"The infected don't stay dead unless you cremate them."

As if on cue, Phoebe heard a whoosh outside. She gazed through the plate-glass door at the three choppers hovering over the parking lot. Flamethrowers were sticking out of the cockpits of two of the copters and unleashing streams of flame at the bloodbath in the parking lot.

The flamethrowers ignited the infected corpses strewn in front of the bowling alley.

"*Night of the Living Dead*," said Herman, watching the flames and nodding. "Nobody escaped the farmhouse in that movie. In the end the cops and vigilantes threw all of the corpses in the farmhouse into piles and lit bonfires."

"Your problem is you watch too many horror movies," said Bud. "Horror movies aren't reality. The flight crews are burning the stiffs to stop the spread of the virus, not to prevent them from returning to life. That makes sense."

"It's not gonna make sense when they start shooting us," said Phoebe.

"You expect us to take your word for that? Cops shooting innocent people? No way."

"We need to get out of here before they burn the neighborhood," said Phoebe.

"They're not gonna burn innocent, healthy people."

"There should be a tape recorder that says Play Me on it hidden around here," said Herman. "Jigsaw will tell us on the tape to confess our evil deeds and make amends or die a horrific death."

The air outside became thick with smoke from flaming corpses.

Bud ignored Herman. "Someone ought to go outside and thank the cops for killing those psychos who attacked Geiger."

"Don't go outside until the choppers leave," said Phoebe.

Bud strutted toward her. "I want to open my alley for business."

"I should tell the cops I was attacked," said Geiger.

"Me too," said Crystal.

"Count me in," said Wally, getting up from his seat in the food court.

"None of you know what you're doing," said Phoebe. "You can't go outside."

"Attention. Attention," said a chopper crewman into a bullhorn. "This is the California Highway Patrol. Attention. This is a health mandate. You are hereby ordered by the governor of California to shelter in place. Do not leave your buildings under any circumstances. Your lives are at grave risk on account of a new virus. Resistance will not be tolerated."

Chapter 36

"I guess we're stuck here for a while," Herman told Crystal as they headed for the food court to find a place to sit.

"I thought you were looking for the tape recorder with Jigsaw's message on it," said Crystal.

"I don't know where to look. Can you give me a clue where it is?"

"How would I know? I'm an actor, not a writer."

They sat down at a round white plastic table with bread crumbs scattered on it. Crystal wiped them off with her hand.

Herman smiled. "I can't believe I'm sitting with a movie star. If I'm gonna be trapped, I'm glad I'm trapped with you."

"Thanks."

"Let me make a confession," said Herman, fidgeting because he was about to confide in someone. "I don't have a life. I don't have friends or anything. That's why I watch a lot of horror movies. I have nothing else to do." He paused a beat. "I like horror movies because I can escape into a world that's even worse than my life. My life is so empty."

"Reality can be worse than a horror movie. I know from experience," said Crystal, her face glum.

"But you escaped the cartel and now you're a movie star. Pretty cool."

"It would be a lot cooler if the producers would ever pay me for the work I did for them. I've been working at Uber to make ends meet. My movie wasn't a humongous hit."

"That's odd. Horror movies usually make money."

"Oh, it made money, but it wasn't boffo, like they say. In any case, the producers haven't paid me."

"Maybe you could sue them."

"If I do, nobody will hire me again. It'll give me a bad rep as an actor. Someone who's difficult."

"I can't work at Uber. I can't afford a car."

"If we're trapped here for the rest of our lives, you don't need a car. None of us do."

"Can you tell me how to get a job in the movies?"

"Like I'm an expert?" said Crystal, amused at the idea.

"Well, you *did* act in a movie. It's almost impossible to get a speaking part in a movie."

"For me, it was a matter of knowing the right people and being in the right place at the right time. And being prepared, of course. When I was in the cartel jail, I used to act out scenes from movies I had seen, so when I got my chance to audition for *Green Hell Alive*, I was ready."

"I bet."

"I could do horror because I've had a lot of contact with murder and death. The cartel killed my younger brother Eduardo," said Crystal, her throat tightening with emotion.

"Sorry."

"The Jalisco New Generation Cartel attacked him with a narco-tank with a machine gun mounted on top of it," she said, grief welling up inside her.

"Narco-tank?"

"They also call them 'monsters' and 'rhinos.' They're SUVs or pickups outfitted with armor plating welded onto them. They look like something out of *Mad Max*."

Widening his eyes Herman gulped. "How did you ever survive?"

"I vowed they would never kill me and I would escape," she said, composing herself.

"And now you're a movie star. It's fabulous."

"It's not fabulous to be trapped in this bowling alley."

Bud banged his baseball bat against the floor in frustration.

"How long are we gonna be trapped here?" he yelled.

"Until they start burning the buildings in this neighborhood," said Phoebe.

"What do they expect us to do?"

"They expect us to die."

Bud did a double take.

"This joke or movie or whatever it is has gone on long enough," he said. "Time to return to normal, so I can open my business."

"You see," Herman told Crystal. "That's how I know this is a movie. The CHP would never burn down an entire neighborhood. That's not real. And this kind of excitement never happens in my dull life. It has to be a movie."

"I dunno," said Crystal. "I think Phoebe knows what she's talking about. I can tell from her face she's been through the wars. She's seen stuff. Cartel stuff."

"It's a vile, corrupt world we live in," said Geiger, approaching Crystal, adjusting his bolo. "How can anyone get through it without seeing stuff?"

"If you don't have a life, you don't see all of this stuff you two are talking about," said Herman.

"You must live in a hermetically sealed bubble."

"I wasn't held as a cartel sex slave."

"Weren't you ever bullied in school?"

"I don't want to talk about it," said Herman, embarrassed, his ears turning red.

"I thought so. You prefer to forget the bad things that happen to you. You're not alone in that."

"Two bullies ganged up on me in high school. Some fat guy and his buddy used to pelt my face with spitballs at lunch and laugh at me when I ate their spitballs on my peanut butter and jelly sandwich."

"Exactly. You can't escape the vile, corrupt world even when you're only eighteen."

"Things will get better when I'm older and can figure out what's going on."

Geiger snickered. "You think? I got news for you. It doesn't get any better when you're an adult. The bullies don't hit you with spitballs anymore. They order you around at work. They're called bosses."

"I'm not listening to you," said Herman, holding his hands over his red ears.

"You're not the only one who got bullied. I got bullied in high school. They used to call me Geiger Counter—like I was radioactive—so other students stayed away from me."

"That's mean," said Crystal.

"I don't want to talk about this," said Herman. "Where are the cameras hidden? That's what I want to know."

"There aren't any cameras," said Geiger. "Nobody cares about us. Why would they make a movie about people nobody cares about?"

"Why do you have to be so mean?" said Crystal.

"I'm not the one that's mean. The world is mean. Life is a virus. We're all infected. We're all fucked."

"Things will get better."

"What happens next, Phoebe?"

"The choppers napalm the bowling alley," said Phoebe, who was standing at the door watching the choppers hover overhead.

"Where is the miniature tape recorder that says Play Me?" said Herman.

Phoebe said nothing. She kept watching the choppers with a grim expression.

"You people don't understand horror movies," said Herman. "There has to be a way out. All we have to do is find it."

"Kids," said Geiger. "You believe in happy endings."

"Leave him alone," said Crystal. "You're the bully. Go pick on someone else."

"I'm trying to educate him about the ways of the vile, corrupt world. With your history you ought to know how evil the world is better than anyone."

Crystal said nothing.

A scream ripped across the parking lot, scything through the racket of the choppers.

Chapter 37

A gust of wind blew a white plastic trash bag across the parking lot. The bag billowed with wind as it bounced off car roofs and caromed off the side of a van in its frantic haste to escape. The downdraft from the hovering helos threw the bag off course, sending it somersaulting back and forth across the parking lot, trapped in brisk crosscurrents.

A fiftyish surgeon in green scrubs fled across the parking lot, his face a rictus of horror, the wind tossing his brown hair hugger-mugger.

Foaming at the mouth, grimacing, and slavering, a mob of a dozen enraged maniacs chased him. They opened their mouths wide, desperate to sink their teeth into his white flesh. They howled and jibber-jabbered in hot pursuit. Infected with the virus, the herd ached to tear him apart. The only reason they existed was to feed on living humans. The virus could not go on living without devouring fresh human flesh and blood.

The surgeon waved his hand at the choppers, supplicating them for help.

"They're gonna kill me," he cried up at them.

Phoebe watched the unfolding scene, feeling her nerves tighten, her blood pressure rising. She dreaded seeing another murder committed by a mob running amok.

She wanted to yell at the surgeon to run to the bowling alley, but she knew he would never make it to the door before the psychotic throng pounced on him and scarfed down his body.

A cropped teenage black guy riding a bicycle outstripped the mob, latched onto the surgeon's arm, and, growling, bit into the guy's shoulder. The infected teen shook his head back and forth like a shark, tearing the flesh out of the surgeon's shoulder. The surgeon screamed in pain. Blood started from his gaping wound.

"Why didn't the cops shoot those monsters before they reached him?" said Bud, standing beside Phoebe, furrowing his brow with concern.

"It doesn't matter," she said. "They're gonna kill everyone in the parking lot anyway."

"They're supposed to protect and serve. It's their job. Watching someone get murdered in cold blood and doing nothing about it is wrong."

"They don't want witnesses. Everything that happens here must be suppressed. That's how they operate. I've seen them in action."

"It's not right."

"The government must believe the only way they can stop this virus is by killing all of the infected and covering it up."

"That's not the kind of government I voted for. Government-sponsored wholesale slaughter? No way."

"I'm with you. They took my best friend and my father from me. I'll never forgive them for that."

The mob converged on the surgeon and fell to ripping off his limbs and gobbling down his flesh as he hollered for help. Blood jetted from the surgeon's body and rained down on the mob during their feeding frenzy. They bathed in it, relishing the downpour.

A tall thirtysomething blonde with an acne-scarred complexion snagged the surgeon's head with both of her hands, tore it off his blood-soaked torso, and, holding his head by the hair, bit off his nose.

Phoebe closed her eyes in horrified aversion at the bloodbath.

The barrels of AR-15s protruded from the hovering choppers and let loose bursts at the ecstatic mob invigorated by their consumption of the surgeon. Flailing bodies dropped in the parking lot as 9mm Parabellum slugs cut them down.

"Too little too late," muttered Bud, watching the massacre with an incredulous visage.

"Let's look at the bright side," said Wally.

"Bright side?" said Geiger. "What bright side?"

"Those infected maniacs can't kill us now that they're dead."

"They won't stay head," said Phoebe as if to herself, knowing the virus would resurrect their corpses.

The blood-drenched pile of corpses writhed on the asphalt. The AR-15s kept showering the bodies with bullets till the bodies remained motionless.

The muzzles of the flamethrowers emerged from the helo cockpits and trained golden arcs of fire on the corpses, lighting them up.

"Enough," said Bud, his gorge rising.

"It's the only way to keep the infected corpses from coming back to life," said Phoebe, imagining she was sitting in a sailboat on a lake instead of watching this bloodcurdling debacle.

Anywhere but here, she decided.

She could pretty much say that about her entire life. If only she could have a life full of happiness, love, and success instead of one filled with misery, betrayals, and bitter failures. But that wouldn't be *her* life. She would have turned into another person living such a life. To be that person would be fine with her.

She watched the fires consuming the corpses in the parking lot with a blank gaze. The sickening stench of burning human flesh crept under the plate-glass door and uncurled into her nostrils. She heard her stomach gurgle in revolt.

She had smelled the odor before on the Strip, but she couldn't get used to it. She would never get used to it. The same way she could never get used to the misery in her life even though it was almost constant.

She felt herself descending into a funk.

"We need to get out of here," she said, getting a grip on herself.

"If the wind spreads those fires over here, we're toast," said Bud.

"If the wind doesn't do it, the napalm from the choppers will."

"Can we have some good news right about now?"

Silence.

"If we can find Jigsaw's Play Me tape recorder, it will tell us the way out," Herman piped up.

"No stupid answers allowed," said Bud.

Chapter 38

Zandorf was examining Jason, who lay in bed in his hospital room attached to a wheezing life support system, when Steve Strus burst into the room, his face flushed.

Zandorf looked up at him.

"I just got a report from the police that there has been another outbreak in our city," said Strus.

"No," said Zandorf, dumbfounded.

"It's true. It's near the bowling alley. The cops are trying to contain it."

"Do they know how many have been infected?"

"Scores, at least. The CHP in choppers circling over the area reported rabid mobs racing around, killing people."

"Are you sure they're infected? I heard there are reports of angry townsfolk rioting at the blockades on the road out of town."

"The CHP says the rioters at the bowling alley are foaming at the mouth and are running at superhuman speeds."

"Damn. I was hoping we had contained the virus when the cops burned down the Strip." Zandorf thought about it. "One of the infected must have escaped the Strip and is spreading the virus."

"The people won't stand for it if we keep burning down the city."

"We can't let the virus spread beyond Costaguana. If it gets out of here, we can say good-bye to the United States."

"Our citizens are already rioting at the blockades. If they find out we're deliberately setting fire to the city, there's no telling what they will do."

"We have only one other chance to stop the spread of the virus," said Zandorf, removing his spectacles and wiping the lenses with his smock.

"Yes?"

"The lieutenant governor—I forget his name—phoned me and said he has found a vaccine for the virus."

"Kevin Bates?"

"Yeah, that's his name."

"How could he find a vaccine so fast? Is that possible?" said Strus, narrowing his eyes with skepticism.

"As he tells it, there was a similar outbreak of this same virus in Mexico. A pharmaceutical company called Cobygenex, I believe he said, told him they used the new mRNA technology and created a vaccine and are willing to sell it to us."

"How long will it take to get here?"

"They can get it here in a matter of hours, maybe less."

Strus gazed at Jason's expressionless face as Jason breathed with the help of the respirator.

"Can we use it on Jason?" said Strus.

"We need to use it on everyone. I don't know how many doses they're shipping to us. Seniors living near the outbreak areas should get the first doses."

Strus balled his fist. "I'm gonna do everything in my power to save Costaguana. Did you hear that, Jason? We're gonna save this town."

Jason's face remained expressionless.

"Can he hear me?" Strus asked Zandorf.

"It's possible," answered Zandorf, folding his arms on his chest. "There is evidence that patients in comas can hear voices without being able to react to them."

"I hope he can."

"Frankly, it's a miracle he's still alive what with the amount of fractured bones and damaged internal organs in his body. Has anyone figured out how he fell?"

"The police are investigating, but haven't reported back to me yet. It was no accident. That's all they know for sure."

"Then it's either a homicide or a suicide. Hmm."

"Why would he suicide? He's a successful mayor. He has everything to live for."

Zandorf rubbed his nose. "If he was in a lot of pain, I could see him killing himself."

"Why would he be in pain?"

"Infected victims suffer unbearable agony as the virus worms burrow through their brain and turn it into a warren."

"Are you saying he was infected?"

"We can't tell at this point. All we know is the virus, *if* it has infected him, is not active now because of his coma. Of course, there are types of pain other than that inflicted by a virus that he could have been suffering from."

"Like what?"

"He could've been suffering from psychological torment."

"It doesn't sound like the Jason I know. If anyone in this world has his shit together, Jason does. He's a solid citizen."

"If he *is* infected, we need to know how he got that way. We believe he could've got the virus from the hooker Val Lewton."

Strus shook his head no. "That's not Jason. He's a happily married man with a beautiful wife."

"Any news about the location of his wife yet?"

"No."

"That's unfortunate. She may be the key to stopping the outbreak."

"How can one person stop it?"

"We believe she could be a carrier who's immune to the virus. Or hopefully she's immune without being a carrier. We need to study her and find out if it's true and, if so, why she's immune. We have learned she was down at the Strip when the virus first broke out. She escaped the fire. How did she escape ground zero without becoming infected?"

"If she got infected, she could be dead by now."

"Possible," said Zandorf, twisting his mouth with displeasure. "Nobody has reported finding her body though."

"If it was cremated, nobody would recognize it."

"True."

"Why do we need to find her if we're getting the Cobygenex vaccines?"

"There's no guarantee they're gonna work." Zandorf shrugged. "I always think of the worst-case scenario. The virus here might have mutated since the outbreak in Matamoros, making the vaccine ineffective in our case. Viruses are constantly mutating."

Strus sighed. "I'm not gonna worry about it. What good does worrying do? All it does is cause ulcers."

Looking ill he rubbed his stomach.

"I'm paid to worry," said Zandorf.

"I'm paid to save this city, and I'm gonna do it."

"If all else fails, we burn the city to the ground."

Strus stared at him, aghast, as if Zanodorf had committed murder and was standing in front of him, his hands dripping with blood.

"I won't let that happen," said Strus. "Not under my watch."

Zandorf's expression remained grim. "The president's orders are clear, and the governor has agreed."

"This is madness."

"It's the final solution."

"Our mission is to save lives, not take them."

"We're talking about saving the country, not just one city."

"I can't believe Vitti would agree to the destruction of our city. I've got to change his mind. Is he going nuts? Only a madman would order the destruction of an entire city. The city is already in its death throes, locked down and ripped apart by riots."

Strus bolted out of the room.

Chapter 39

Clad in tan suede cowboy boots and faded blue jeans, sporting aviators, Rigo Alvarez stood behind his friend Tex's silver Ford F-150 pickup in a Home Depot parking lot and watched the fires from the riot burn in the distance under a smoke-hazed sky infested with hovering police helicopters. In his late thirties with a stocky build, he was five nine and weighed over two hundred pounds.

He ran an extermination business, which was losing money because he couldn't service customers who lived out of town.

A group of three men and one woman were standing beside him watching the riot-racked city, all wearing jeans, two of the men wearing Stetsons.

The one wearing a white Stetson was Tex. Pushing fifty he was chewing a wad of tobacco, his cheek bulging on his craggy, tanned, weather-beaten face. He worked for the city, collecting the change from parking meters.

"I don't like the looks of this," he said in a gravelly voice, squinting at the conflagration.

"Did you hear Joe Mack's show earlier today?" said Rigo. "He knows the true gen. He tells it like it is."

"I listen to him every day," said Tex, nodding, "but I missed him today."

"He said the president is getting ready to nuke Costaguana."

"What?" said Tex. He stopped chewing.

"Joe Mack knows what's what. I'm betting it's true."

Tex lifted his left boot onto the pickup's rear bumper and leaned his elbow on his raised knee, interlacing his knotty fingers, bronzed and sere from long hours toiling under the sun.

"What about us, the folks who live here?" he said.

"The president's more worried about the virus spreading, even though he hasn't publicly admitted the virus exists. He doesn't give a damn about us. That's what Joe Mack says. It's all part of this surveillance state we live in. The government is constantly surveilling everybody in the country, and they decided our city must go. We don't fit his concept of an ideal community. In other words, we didn't vote for him."

"It's a national security state if you ask me. And I could care less about his ideal community."

"There are different names for it. The bottom line is the people are screwed. The suits in power care only about themselves and staying in power."

"Next thing you know they're gonna take our guns from us so we can't resist."

"I thought you said you didn't hear Joe Mack today."

"I didn't. But he's the only I guy I trust on radio or TV these days."

"Well, he said on his show the exact same thing you did. He said they're coming for our guns next."

Tex spat out tobacco juice onto the blacktop. "We can't let them wreck our town."

"If they think we're gonna just stand here and do nothing while they nuke us, they got another think coming."

"Was Joe Mack talking about resisting on his show?"

"He was, but then the show went off the air."

"Huh?"

Rigo made a cutting motion with his forefinger across his throat.

"They cut him off the air," he said.

"Sons of bitches."

"Haven't you noticed nothing works anymore? Does your cell phone work? Mine doesn't."

Tex dug his cell out of his trouser pocket and tried to make a call. He shook his head no.

"They cut off all comms in our town," said Rigo. "They cut us off from the rest of the world. Even the radio and TV don't work. The landlines don't work. Nothing works."

"What about the Internet?"

"Forget it. We can't connect to it. E-mails and texts don't work either. I've tried everything."

"And we can't leave town thanks to their roadblocks," said Tex, glancing at the fiery riot unfolding under the hovering choppers.

"They're strangling our city."

"No wonder they cut off our comms. They don't want us to organize and resist them."

Rigo's face clouded. "They know what they're doing, all right."

"What about our mayor Jason? Isn't he sticking up for us? He's our mayor. We elected him."

"Haven't you heard?"

"What happened?"

"He fell out his office window, so they say, and he's in a coma."

"Fell out his window? They expect us to swallow that bullshit? How do you fall out of a window you can't open? I know that building. Come on."

"Joe Mack says somebody pushed him."

Tex spat more tobacco juice. "Yep. I guess our mayor didn't toe the party line. See where it got him. I'm telling you . . . they're coming for us next."

Rigo hitched up his jeans, tugging his sweat-stained leather belt.

"We need to fight back," he said. "We got plenty of ARs between us. I'm not letting them destroy our town without putting up a fight. Am I right?"

Tex lowered his boot from the bumper, stood straight, and spat.

"I'm all in," he said. "Life's not worth living if we can't live free. It ain't freedom when they take away our comms. They're taking away our First Amendment rights by taking away our comms."

"They don't care about freedom. All they care about is power. That's what Joe Mack says, and he knows what's what."

"Yep."

Rigo eyeballed the choppers through his shades.

"Them look like CHP helos," he said. "The state cops are controlling the city takeover."

"I wouldn't put anything past Vitti. I didn't vote for the guy and never will."

His gaze steady, Rigo faced Tex. "Joe Mack says helos napalmed the Strip."

Tex quirked an eyebrow. "The news said the Strip fire was an accident."

"It was no accident. The government told the media to say it was an accident. The media's bought and paid for. They're a mouthpiece for government propaganda."

"Can we believe Joe Mack?"

"That's why they shut him down. Because he tells the truth. You tell the truth, you get canceled."

"This is looking worse by the second."

Rigo tilted his head up and stroked his throat.

"I'm beginning to wonder if there really is a virus outbreak here," he said. "Maybe it's all a smokescreen so the government can wipe out our city."

"Why would they want to do that?"

"I dunno. Reprisals for not voting for the governor? This whole thing smells fishy. That's what I'm saying. How does cutting off our comms wipe out the virus? It makes no sense."

Tex nodded yes. "I see your drift."

"One thing's for sure, and it's the only thing that matters. Our. Lives. Are. In. Danger."

"Another thing's for sure. I'm not going down without a fight."

"We need a plan of attack," said Rigo, and gazed at the fleet of choppers circling over the smoking, riot-torn roadblock like bluebottles over dung.

"We can start by shooting down some of those choppers. If they napalmed the Strip like you say, they deserve to be shot down."

"I got a Browning M2 in my garage."

"We gotta use guerrilla tactics. Hit and run. Because they're gonna come after us with everything they got—and they got the advantage in firepower."

Chapter 40

Phoebe watched a black Ford Explorer drive into the bowling alley parking lot and park in a slot.

A guy in his late twenties clad in an aloha shirt and khaki board shorts clambered out of the driver's seat. In her midtwenties, dressed in silver spandex pants and a shocking pink T, his wife exited the passenger-side door. They opened the rear doors and withdrew bowling bags from the Explorer's backseat. The guy clutched a sapphire leather bowling bag while his wife clutched a pink one. They shut the rear doors.

Joking and smiling, carrying their bags, they made for the bowling alley front door.

"Customers," said Bud, beaming. "It's about time."

Watching them with concern, Phoebe ground her teeth. She glanced up at the three choppers hovering over the parking lot, poised for attack.

She sprang to the front door and frantically waved for the approaching couple to return to their SUV.

"What are you doing?" said Bud, appalled at her behavior.

He pulled her away from the door.

"The choppers will shoot them," she said, struggling to free herself from his grasp.

"Those two aren't infected. Why would the choppers shoot them? Look. They're not frothing at the mouth or yelling and screaming like maniacs. They're perfectly healthy. They're happy because they came here to relax and bowl a few games."

"We have to warn them."

"You need to pull yourself together, or I'm gonna have to throw you out."

"You can't throw her out," said Wally. "The infected will kill her."

"What infected? My two new customers aren't infected. Look at them." Bud turned away from the front door and surveyed everyone in the bowling alley. "You all need to calm down.

Everything is gonna be all right. The cops wasted all of the infected victims."

"Can't they cure them with meds instead of killing them?" said Crystal.

"I don't know about you, but I'm not gonna tell the cops what to do."

"Go back," Phoebe cried at the approaching couple. "Drive away. Your lives are in danger."

Phoebe didn't think they could hear her through the bulletproof glass, but she had to try to warn them.

Bud put his hand over her mouth, shutting her up.

"I'll gag you if I have to," he snarled.

She tried to pull his hand away from her mouth, but he was stronger than her.

The couple saw the commotion inside and paused in the parking lot in puzzlement on their way to the entrance.

Out of the corner of her eye Phoebe picked up on an old cop with his white hair in a crew cut sprinting toward the couple, glaring, holding his mouth open like he was getting an enema. The couple didn't see him because he was behind them. Oblivious to their danger, they resumed walking toward the bowling alley entrance.

Bud grinned politely and waved at the couple with his free hand, welcoming them.

Phoebe bit his hand.

"Ouch," he said, jerking it away from her mouth and shaking it.

"Why are you encouraging them? An infected cop is chasing them. Look."

"You bit me. How do I know you're not infected?"

"I'm not."

Bud didn't know what to make of the running cop.

"How could a cop get infected?" he said.

"Anyone can get infected."

"I thought the cops burned all the infected maniacs in the parking lot."

"Run," Phoebe cried at the couple. "Look behind you."

She pointed at the bloodthirsty cop closing in on them.

How could they hear anything with the din the copters were making overhead? she wondered with annoyance.

The couple looked at her in bafflement, confused by her overheated gesticulations.

Chapter 41

His face lathered with foam, breathing through his mouth, the psychotic cop caught up to the couple, grabbed Pink T by the shoulders, yanked her toward him, took a bite out of her cheek, and commenced gobbling the bloody flesh. Dropping her bowling bag Pink T shrieked in agony and shock. She held her hand to her mangled cheek, tears welling in her eyes.

Infuriated, Aloha Shirt raised his bowling bag with his fifteen-pound ball inside and slammed it against the cop's head in retaliation for the assault on his wife. Stunned by the stinging blow, the cop reeled backward, shaking his bleeding head, trying to clear it, looking like a punch-drunk boxer trying to get his bearings in the ring.

Bud flinched in shock at the brutal attack.

"We need to help them," he said, gripping his bat. "I can take that maniac cop."

He unlocked the front door, fixing to dash out to aid the assaulted couple.

As soon as the words left his lips, three infected maniacs stormed across the parking lot, stretching out their arms and yammering, their faces screwed up, flecks of spit flying from their open mouths. Running at superhuman speeds they would reach the couple well before Bud.

He hesitated at the door, weighing his chances against four infected maniacs.

"We can't help them now," said Phoebe, downcast.

"I dunno. I'm pretty good with this bat."

Of the three newcomers, the first maniac was a suit, the second a pregnant woman clad in a powder blue maternity dress, and the third a twentyish guy who slung hamburgers at the local Burger King. Burger King grabbed Aloha Shirt by the head, chewed the guy's ear, and tore it off. Blood spewed out of the side of Aloha Shirt's head as Burger King munched happily on the ear.

Screaming and wincing in pain, Aloha Shirt clapped his hand on his bleeding ear stub.

Pink T tried to make a run for it, blood pouring from her mauled face. The suit was on her in a flash. He snagged her arm, whipped her toward him, and sank his teeth into her nose. He ripped it off and chewed on it. More blood gushed out of Pink T's mutilated face.

The suit threw her to the asphalt, pinned her on her back, and straddled her stomach. She hammered him with a flurry of fists trying to repel him. Fighting her off, lowering his face to her throat, he tore out her carotid artery.

Phoebe knew it was over for the woman.

Her face drained of blood, Phoebe turned away from the heinous sight, feeling sick to her stomach.

At that moment, the AR-15s in the choppers opened fire on the assailants. A burst of slugs tore into the brawlers, indiscriminately taking out the infected and their victims. Fresh blood paved the asphalt like a sheet of grease in a sump pit.

Parabellum slugs ripped through the infected cop's chest, felling him. Bullets mowed down the hapless bowlers.

"Jesus," said Bud, recoiling in horror at the bloodbath, relocking the front door. "All they wanted to do was bowl. What the hell? You can't even go bowling anymore without getting blown away by AR-15s."

"The chopper cops take out everyone," said Phoebe.

"How do we get out of this?" said Wally.

"Someone needs to go outside and tell the cops we're not infected," said Crystal.

"They won't listen," said Phoebe in a jaded tone. "They'll kill you."

"We need to find the tape recorder that says Play Me," said Herman. "Jigsaw will give us the instructions on how to escape our torture chamber."

"Are you still harping on that?" said Bud.

"That's how you escape in the *Saw* movies."

"You have to understand this isn't a movie, Herman," said Crystal. "There are no cameras. There's no director. Look around you."

Herman stamped his foot on the floor in an outburst of frustration.

"I don't believe it," he said. "This is too awful. Cops don't massacre people in the real world. It has to be a movie."

"You're too young yet," said Wally. "You haven't seen enough of the world."

"What's *your* solution, gramps?"

"Somebody has to contact those chopper crews and tell them we're not infected," chimed in Bud.

"Our cell phones don't work," said Wally. "The landlines don't either. We can't contact anyone."

"We do it the old-fashioned way," said Herman. "One of us goes out there and yells at the choppers. We tell them we're not infected."

"Do that and you're dead," said Phoebe.

"What makes you an authority on this?"

"If you had been listening, you would know. My father found out the hard way that it's impossible to deal with those chopper crews. Their orders are to shoot to kill everyone in an infected zone."

"Listen to yourself," said Herman, incredulous. "Why would cops be given such cold-blooded orders?"

"Maybe we're better off waiting for the choppers to leave," said Wally.

"They're not gonna leave till we're all dead," said Phoebe.

"You sound like Dr. Death," said Herman. "All you ever talk about is everybody dying. According to you, we're dead no matter what we do."

"If you're going outside, Herman, what's taking you so long?" said Bud.

Herman ran his fingers through his hair. "Uh—they might not listen to me because of my age."

Phoebe heard a whoosh as flames leapt out of flamethrower barrels aimed out the chopper cockpits at the corpses of the two bowlers and of their attackers. The corpses strewn on the asphalt caught fire and burned. Their sizzling flesh melted and dripped from their bodies, revealing their bright white skulls, which would turn tea colored after being subjected to flames for a while.

"Attention, attention," boomed a chopper crewman with a bullhorn. "By order of the governor of California, do not leave your buildings under any circumstances. You must shelter in place. Failure to obey orders will result in your deaths. The virus must be stopped before it is safe for you to leave your premises. God bless all of you."

"That last part sounds like it's our funeral," said Wally in the bowling lounge. "I wonder if he was crossing himself when he said it."

"We need to get out of here before they start napalming every building in this cursed neighborhood," said Phoebe. She fetched a long sigh. "Let's hope they don't plan on burning down the whole city."

"The whole city?" said Bud in disbelief. "Why in the name of all that's holy would they do that?"

Overwhelmed, nobody said anything, trying to get their heads around the enormity of what was happening.

Herman cleared his throat. "I'm the one who's supposed to die first because I smoked pot. I guess it's time for me to go outside and have a word with the chopper pilots."

"This isn't a movie," said Crystal. "If they shoot you, you'll die. Blood squibs aren't gonna explode in your shirt. Your heart will explode when a real bullet pierces it."

"It's time for me to play my role," said Herman, approaching the front door.

"Wait. You're not the one that's supposed to die first."

Chapter 42

Herman stared at Crystal with astonishment. "I know what I'm talking about. I've seen the *Saw* movies."

"So have I," said Crystal. "The one who dies first is the one who takes life for granted. The one who doesn't enjoy life and treats people like dirt. If you don't make the most of your life, you should be killed, according to Jigsaw."

"I agree. But that doesn't follow the rules of horror movies about who dies first."

"It doesn't matter. You said this is a *Saw* movie. *Saw* movies have their own rules."

"Then who's supposed to die first, according to you?"

"Geiger," said Crystal, cutting her eyes toward him.

"Do you do drugs?" Herman asked Geiger.

"I have a drink of pinot grigio now and then," answered Geiger.

Herman shook his head no. "That doesn't qualify for drinking and taking drugs. Not according to the three rules of horror movies about who dies. Do you have a lot of sex?"

"I divorced my wife five years ago after her overspending drove me into bankruptcy. I've abstained from sex ever since."

"He's disqualified from dying in a horror movie," Herman told Crystal. "No sex and no drinking or doping. He has no chance of dying."

"But he hates life," said Crystal. "Remember? He said life is a disease. It's corrupt and vile. That's not someone who's grateful to be alive. He's the type of person Jigsaw targets for torture and murder."

Herman thought about it. "Then maybe this isn't a Jigsaw horror movie. It could be another franchise. *Halloween* maybe. Michael Myers."

"Why are you humoring him?" Phoebe asked Crystal. "This isn't a horror movie."

"I'm trying to talk him out of going outside," answered Crystal.

"I'm the doper," said Herman. "I'm the one who has to die first. There's nothing any of us can do about it. I'll go outside and tell the chopper cops we're all healthy inside the bowling alley. Somebody has to do it, or we'll never get out of here."

"I agree with him," said Bud. "Somebody has to tell the chopper cops that we're here and we're not infected. Then they'll go away, and I can reopen for business."

"That makes three of us," said Wally. "Let Herman do his thing."

"What are you saying?" said Phoebe, surveying the others. "You're condemning him to death."

"I know I'm older than dirt and don't have many days left. I suppose I should volunteer to go. But, damn, I really like living. Not like Geiger there."

"I said the world is corrupt and vile because life is a disease," said Geiger. "That doesn't mean I don't like living."

Wally harrumphed. "It doesn't sound like a ringing endorsement of being alive."

"I spent a lot of my life punching a timeclock at a job I didn't like. I felt like a robot following orders ten hours a day, shoving pieces of paper into metal slots. I didn't feel like I was accomplishing anything. It gave me a sour disposition. I asked myself, why am I spending most of my life doing something I don't want to do? Is that any way to live?"

"For money. Like everybody else."

"I needed job satisfaction. Money isn't enough if you have to throw away your life chasing it."

"What would you rather be doing?"

"I'd rather be a rich artist."

"Of course. Nobody wants to be a starving artist, which is the reality of that job."

"Ain't it the truth?"

"What was this job you used to have?" said Herman.

"Postman."

"You were going postal," said Wally with a hint of a smile.

"I didn't start shooting people if that's what you mean."

"Of course not," said Wally, becoming serious.

"I say *you* should volunteer to go outside because your life is almost over," said Geiger. "You're old. You're gonna die any day now. It might as well be now."

"That's not nice to say," said Crystal.

"I want to live forever," said Wally. "What can I say? I never said I was a hero of some cheapjack horror movie."

"This isn't about volunteering," said Herman. "This is a horror movie. We don't have a choice. I'm the doper. The rules say I'm supposed to die first. I'll go outside and talk to the chopper crews."

"And they'll shoot you," said Phoebe.

"I'm playing my part. I don't have a choice." Herman shrugged. "I guess, if I had it to do all over again, I never would've smoked any weed. I had no idea it would lead to this."

"Nobody's forcing you to go outside and get killed."

"Horror movie rules are written in stone," said Herman, resigned to his fate.

"You're my man," said Bud, approaching Herman and laying his hand on Herman's shoulder. "I'm all for you. Tell those flyboys they can fly away because everybody's A-OK in my bowling alley." Bud glanced outside at the parking lot littered with burning corpses. "Can you get them to cart away those stiffs too? They're bad for business."

"No problem."

"Attaboy," said Bud, patting him on the back. "You're a good kid, and we're never gonna forget this. I tell you what. I'll let you bowl five games for free when this mess is over with."

"Don't listen to him," said Crystal. "You only get one life. If you don't stand up for yourself, nobody else will."

"Don't let it be said Herman violated a horror movie rule," said Herman. "I would never live that insult down."

"Sure, you're a little bonkers," said Bud, "but that's OK with me. You're doing the right thing."

Bud and Herman walked to the front door.

"I'm not doing this for you," said Herman. "I'm doing it because it's my role."

"No call to get pissed. We appreciate what you're doing."
Smiling, Bud patted Herman on the chest. "I'm proud of you, kid.
Let me get the door for you."

"If you insist on going, act calm," said Phoebe, giving up on
convincing Herman to stay inside. "Don't act excited like you're
infected. Don't drool or spray flecks of spit when you talk."

"I'm gonna have to yell to be heard above that racket the helos
are making," said Herman, eying the hovering choppers.

"And walk. Don't run. Take my advice, you're better off not
going outside."

"Is this where I say my fatal last words, 'I'll be right back'?"
said Herman, cracking a smile.

Nobody laughed.

"You don't have to go," said Phoebe. "It's your choice."

"I'm a diehard horror movie fan. I can't bring myself to
violate their rules. What am I saying? They can't be broken
anyway. They're ironclad. *I'm* the character who's gonna die first. I
might as well do it now."

"You're a brave kid," said Bud.

"I have no choice."

"Remember to tell them nobody in here is infected."

Herman surveyed the parking lot that looked like a
battleground as smoke drifted from the smoldering corpses and
burning cars scattered on the asphalt.

"It's just a movie," he said, trying to convince himself. "I'll be
right back."

Gulping, he opened the door and walked outside.

Chapter 43

Phoebe ran to the door as Bud closed it behind Herman and locked it.

"We need to stop him," she said, trying to open the door.

Bud prevented her from grabbing the handle. "No way. It's his decision."

She watched Herman advance tentatively toward the hovering aircraft. He held up his hands in surrender.

"They're not gonna blow him away," said Bud. "Look how calm he's acting. He's not slobbering and growling like those infected maniacs that bushwhacked you."

She remembered her father acting calm and getting butchered by chopper cops when he approached them to ask what was going on.

She pounded on the plate-glass door with her fists and waved feverishly at Herman, motioning for him to come back.

Herman kept making for the three choppers.

"Hello," he cried up at them. "I'm not infected. The people inside the bowling alley aren't infected." He glanced back at the bowling alley.

With alarm Phoebe picked up on an AR-15 muzzle extending from the nearest chopper's cockpit.

"Oh no," she said.

"Not looking good for the kid," said Wally, who was now standing behind Phoebe and peering out the plate-glass door at Herman and the choppers.

"I'm not infected," cried Herman, eying the AR-15 muzzle with trepidation. "You must believe me. None of us are infected. Listen to me."

The shooter in the cockpit opened fire on Herman, cutting him down with a burst of Parabellum slugs that etched a jagged line across Herman's throat and chest. Herman crumpled on the asphalt.

"Fuck," said Wally, watching with wide eyes. "Why'd they waste the poor kid?"

"I thought he had it made," said Bud. "What the hell happened?"

"They're gonna kill everybody in this neighborhood," said Phoebe, stricken. "Now do you believe me?"

"I believe those cops are nuts," said Wally. "That's what I believe. What's their problem?"

"This is their answer to the spread of the virus."

"Then what's the difference between them and the virus? The way I see it, we got two options. Get killed by the virus or get killed by the cops."

"Look," said Bud in disbelief. "The kid's standing up."

"He must be right," said Wally, feeling relieved. "This really is a movie, and he was playing dead."

"Not good," said Phoebe, taken aback.

"What do you mean? He's still alive."

"How could he be alive unless there are some of those blood squibs he was talking about on his chest and throat?" said Bud.

"It means he must have been infected," said Phoebe.

"How do you figure that bullshit?" said Bud, screwing up his face.

"After the infected die, they return to life as ghouls."

"That can't be true. Look at him. He's walking. He was playing dead for the movie. His scene's over, so he's heading back here," said Bud, smiling.

His shirt soaked with blood, Herman shambled toward the bowling alley entrance.

"The kid's OK," said Wally. "Let's go outside and congratulate him for a great performance."

"No," said Phoebe. "It's not over till he's really dead."

"Whaddaya mean? Look at him. He's fine."

"He's one of the undead now."

"I'm thinking you're the one who's crazy, lady," said Bud. "The kid was way ahead of us. He knew all along that we're in the middle of a movie shoot."

"Look at his eyes."

Bud checked out Herman's milky eyes that stared ahead without seeing.

"Man, what's going on?" said Bud. "What happened to his eyes?"

"I used to have a little pet green turtle when I was a kid," said Wally. "I fed it pieces of ground round. The turtle was slimy as hell. Anyway, when it died, its eyes looked milky like that."

"There's one way to find out what the hell's happening. Let's ask him when he gets back here."

"Whatever you do, don't let him in," said Phoebe. "He'll infect the rest of us."

"You're batshit crazy, lady," said Bud.

Phoebe chewed it over and surveyed the others. "Since he's infected, maybe more of us are too."

"I feel fine," said Bud.

"He was standing next to us, breathing the same air. I don't know how the virus spreads. How did he get infected in the first place?"

"Ah, phooey," said Bud, dismissing her. "You're nothing but a flake."

Phoebe watched the flamethrower barrel protrude from the cockpit and take aim at Herman.

Chapter 44

A flame leapt from the muzzle and set Herman on fire. His hair flared into a crown of jagged gold then frizzled. His white eyes turned black. Consumed by flames, he flailed his arms and writhed in agony. He coughed clouds of grey smoke like empty dialog bubbles in a comic strip.

He collapsed on the asphalt next to a blue Toyota RAV4. He rolled over and over, trying to put out the flames without success. His smoking body came to a halt. His flesh continued to burn as he lay motionless in a charred heap.

Bud watched in awe. "Jesus. I thought his scene was over after he got shot."

"Why isn't he getting up?" said Wally. "How long is he supposed to lie there?"

"I'm confused. Is it or isn't it a movie?"

"It's not like the movie I was in," said Crystal from the food court. "If the scene's over, he should be getting to his feet. I can't see him from here. I can't bear to look. Is he standing up?"

"He's flat on the pavement like a crispy critter," said Bud.

"It's no movie," said Phoebe. "It's the site of an infectious, hundred percent lethal virus."

"This is terrible," said Crystal. "He was a nice guy. Why'd they have to kill him?"

"How could they tell he was infected?" said Wally.

"They couldn't," said Phoebe. "They're ordered to shoot everybody in this area."

"Who's giving those orders?" said Bud.

*Not my husband*, thought Phoebe.

"Someone at the top of the food chain," she said.

"How do you know they're not rogue cops up there?" said Bud, nodding toward the chopper-cluttered sky.

"There are too many of them. They did the same thing at the Strip."

"How do you know so much about this? That's what I want to know."

"I was at the Strip when they napalmed it. How many times do I have to tell you?"

"How do we know you're not a spy for them?" said Bud, jutting his jaw at her.

"Why would you even think that?"

"Because you know so much about them."

"I got news for you. They want me dead."

She wasn't going to tell them there was an arrest warrant out for her. They might figure out she was the mayor's wife. She didn't think revealing her last name would help her under such circumstances. She doubted the mayor was popular these days.

"None of this matters," said Wally. "I learned long ago that the only thing that matters is getting through the day. We're all just passing through, and none of us will leave a trace when we're gone."

"I can't get through the day unless I have income from my business to pay for food and rent," said Bud. "I don't want to live in a pasteboard box on the sidewalk. Those choppers are preventing me from making a living."

"You got that right," said Geiger. "Whoever's in those choppers wants us dead in this vile and corrupt world where nobody gives a damn about any of us."

"We can always bowl while we wait to die," said Wally, checking out the bowling lanes.

"At least we can thank the kid for proving this ain't a movie," said Bud. "We know we got a life-or-death problem on our hands."

"It's still about getting through the day. That's all."

"You sound like a defeatist."

"I disagree. If we can get through the day, we've succeeded at staying alive. How is that defeatism?"

Bud tapped the crown of his bat against the linoleum floor twice.

"I believe we're gonna have to fight our way out of this mess," he said. "Sitting around doing nothing won't save us."

"How are we supposed to fight the whole police force who are armed with AR-15s and flamethrowers and are spying on our every move in choppers?"

"We have to convince them we're not infected before they let us go," said Phoebe.

"Which is impossible, according to you," said Bud.

"I didn't say it would be easy."

"I wish this was a horror movie like Herman said," said Crystal. "Then we would know Geiger is gonna die next because he doesn't appreciate being alive. Just the kind of person Jigsaw wants to torture and kill."

"Will you stop harping on that?" said Geiger. "I haven't had an easy life."

"You think I have?"

Wally coughed. "Let's not get into a fight over whose life sucks the most. It won't help anyone."

"My husband betrayed me," said Phoebe as if to herself, staring at the floor. "I haven't got anything to cheer about. He's a professional scammer, and I fell for it."

"Men have betrayed me all my life," said Crystal.

"Great," said Bud. "We're all a bunch of losers. Wake up, people. This isn't a group therapy session. Now how do we get out of this clusterfuck without getting killed? I for one am not gonna let my enemies destroy me."

"Throw your bat at the choppers," said Wally, chuckling. "Maybe that'll scare them away."

"Watch your mouth, Geritol Man," said Bud, tapping the barrel of the bat against his open hand. "I could knock your grey head off with one swing."

"What good would that do? The cops are still gonna take you out."

"It would do me a lot of good. I wouldn't have to listen to your geezer wisecracks."

Wally scowled at Bud.

"Why can't they let us die with dignity?" said Geiger. "Why do they have to pick us off in the parking lot like they're hunting rabbits and then toast us like marshmallows?"

"I can see why you're worried, since you're the next one who's gonna die, according to the kid," said Wally. "Horror movie rules and all that."

"Let's drop the movie BS. Herman isn't playing dead for a movie shoot. He's dead and cremated. End of story."

"Don't forget our new problem," said Phoebe.

"What's that?" said Bud.

"Herman was infected. Which means one or more of us could be infected, because we were in the same room with him."

"You're saying one of us will turn into a homicidal maniac foaming at the mouth and will attack the others?"

"We can't rule it out."

They looked at each other suspiciously.

"Who's the infected?" said Wally. "Now's the time to reveal yourself."

Nobody said anything.

"Does anybody see foam on someone's mouth?" said Wally, narrowing his eyes and inspecting mouths.

"Let it die," said Bud. "We're acting like a bunch of paranoid psychos."

"Is that foam I see on your mouth?"

"Codger, you're gonna be seeing stars after I get through swinging this bat at your face," said Bud, raising his bat.

"The name's Wally. Is that so hard to remember?"

"The symptoms may show later," said Phoebe. "This doesn't prove anything. We don't know enough about the virus to be sure. One or more of us could be infected."

"That's what I'm talking about," said Wally, continuing to inspect everybody's face. "We need to keep our eyes on each other. If anybody sees a foaming mouth, holler."

"I hope it's your mouth, so I can belt your head with Babette," said Bud.

"Is that foam I see on the corner of your mouth?" said Wally, craning his neck closer to Bud's face.

Bud raised his bat, preparing to swing at Wally. "I'm warning you. Get your stinking breath off my face."

"Killing each other isn't gonna help matters," said Phoebe.

"I just want to kill Geezer Breath."
Wally laughed in Bud's face.
"Get the fuck away from me," said Bud.
"I was looking for foam."

Chapter 45

To find Phoebe, Hardy used his Pegasus spyware created by the Israeli cyber-intelligence firm known as the NSO Group. For a hefty price, Pegasus had the ability to use remote zero-click surveillance of smartphones. Knowing the government was jamming comms in the city, Hardy used his satphone to avoid the jamming. He hacked into Phoebe's phone via Pegasus and located her at the bowling alley.

As he drove to the bowling alley, he picked up on the three helos hovering over its parking lot, which was hazy with wafting smoke. He slowed down. He saw car wrecks burning out of control. Sooty human cadavers lay around the wreckage.

Hardy had seen this movie before. He had been at the Strip when the chopper cops napalmed it. He wasn't going to enter the bowling alley parking lot and get perforated with Parabellum slugs.

The question was, how was he going to get Phoebe? His Pegasus spyware had indicated she was in the bowling alley. If he tried to enter the alley, the chopper cops would cut him down with a hail of bullets and burn his ass. He knew the drill.

He had to get Phoebe out of the building alive and well. Jackson wanted her in one piece so he could grill her. Hardy parked on the side of the street out of sight of the choppers.

He knew if he wanted to enter the bowling alley, he couldn't use the front door while the choppers guarded it. The building must have a back entrance. He would drive around to the other side of the building and find it.

He extended his satphone's antenna outside his car window and called real-estate tycoon Jackson Albright's direct number, bypassing the reception desk.

"I've located her," said Hardy.

"Excellent," said Albright. "Bring her here on the double."

"There's a bit of a snag."

"What do you mean?" said Jackson, sounding testy.

"She's in the middle of a new outbreak zone."

"What? I thought the outbreak was contained after the Strip burned down."

"Apparently not," said Hardy, having difficulty hearing Jackson courtesy of the clamor ginned up by the hovering choppers in the background.

"I need to speak to her."

"I have to figure out a way to exfil her from the bowling alley she's sheltering in."

"Just do it."

"The cops aren't gonna let me inside."

"I don't want excuses."

"No excuses. It's gonna take a little time, is all."

"I don't have time," Jackson snapped.

He terminated the call.

Another rich bastard for a client, decided Hardy with loathing. Of course, they were the only ones who could afford his unique, much-in-demand services. He wished someone would hire him to whack Albright. It would be a pleasure.

He telescoped his satphone's antenna. He tossed the satphone onto the shotgun seat.

Even if he managed to get inside the bowling alley, he would still have to find a way to spirit Phoebe out without getting shot by the chopper sharpshooters. This mission was losing its luster.

However, Jason owed him two million bucks and was in no shape to pay him. The guy would probably croak and never pay him, decided Hardy. Which meant Hardy needed money. Which meant he needed to do this job for Big Daddy Albright. Hardy made a living doing difficult and frequently illegal assignments for rich clients. It had never been easy, and it was the reason he got the big bucks. Why should today be any different?

Chapter 46

Zandorf had received the vaccine doses from Manuel Picasso and was administering them at the local high-school gymnasium with the help of masked nurses.

Even without comms, word of mouth had spread about the vaccines, and Zandorf had no problem recruiting volunteers for the shots.

Five hundred volunteers, sixty-five or older, were standing in a long line that snaked around the gym, waiting their turns on the gleaming parquet floor. On the gym's perimeter, basketball backboards and their nets hung above the crowd like bearded spectators.

Zandorf stood at the front of the gym in his white smock, watching the volunteers. If it was this easy to get hundreds of volunteers, it should be no problem getting thousands more once he organized a concerted effort to spread the news of the availability of the vaccine around town, he decided.

He hoped he could trust Picasso's test results of the vaccine in Matamoros. They were all Zandorf had to go on as to the vaccine's efficacy. He had never heard of Cobygenex Pharmaceuticals, but Big Pharma was loaded with start-ups he had never heard of. Just because Cobygenex was new didn't mean it wasn't any good.

Besides, Lieutenant Governor Kevin Bates had vouched for the company.

Zandorf had inspected the Matamoros vaccine data Bates had sent him, and it had checked out.

Zandorf watched nurses inject the vaccines. He saw no ill effects so far in any of the recipients. If he spotted any, he would cease the injections on the spot.

"Remember not to give them embolisms," he said, trying to alleviate the tension in the air with a joke.

A middle-aged nurse with her grizzled hair in a bun laughed as she inoculated the next person in line, a seventyish man with his neck permanently tilted to the right, who looked horrified after hearing Zandorf's joke.

"You're such a flirt," she said, withdrawing the hypo from the patient's arm.

Vaccines were the way to go, decided Zandorf. They were a much better option than killing every citizen in Costaguana and razing the town to ashes. The virus must not be allowed to spread beyond this city. If it did, the consequences would be a monumental debacle on an unheard-of scale.

"We're gonna kick this sucker in the teeth," he said, clasping his hands behind the small of his back and rocking on his heels as he oversaw the inoculations.

Dressed in a navy blue suit and a crimson necktie, Deputy Mayor Steve Strus entered the gym and cast around it until he clapped eyes on Zandorf. Strus approached him.

"How is everything proceeding?" said Strus.

"Fine," said Zandorf.

"I'm sure I don't need to tell you this vaccine must succeed. I want to open up the city ASAP. People are rioting in the streets and setting fires to vent their anger at the lockdown."

"Nobody wants this vaccine to succeed more than me."

"We have another outbreak at the bowling alley. We need to start injecting everybody in the city, not just these volunteers, so I can open up the city."

"I'm doing everything I can to speed along this process."

"It doesn't seem like it."

"We must take precautions," said Zandorf, his face stern. "This is a new vaccine. It has only been used in Matamoros—"

"I know but—"

"Let me finish. We need to see if there are any side effects from the vaccine and how severe they are before we issue mass inoculations."

"They're not gonna do us much good if the rioters tear down the city before we can vaccinate everyone," said Strus, flustered, his face sweaty. "Arsonists tried to torch the town hall. Our police force is stretched to the max. They don't have enough manpower if these riots continue."

"We must proceed in an orderly fashion. So far we haven't had any severe reactions to the vaccines."

"How long do we have to wait for you to OK the vaccine?"

"At least a day."

Strus yanked his necktie. "That's too long. The rioters' ranks are swelling and sweeping across the city, trashing buildings, and setting fires."

"I'm not gonna authorize a vaccine that could have disastrous side effects. I want to wait at least a day before approving it."

"We might not have a day. The city could turn into a war zone tonight."

Zandorf folded his arms across his chest, resolve setting his jaw.

"I'm not shirking my responsibilities as a medical officer of the CDC," he said. "We're testing the vaccine on five hundred people before we approve it."

"This is ridiculous. Manuel Picasso and his company guaranteed the effectiveness of the vaccines. Why do you even need to test it? I ought to halt the testing right now and order every citizen inoculated."

"Over my dead body. You have no authority to overrule me. The only one who can overrule my decisions is the president himself."

"My city is being torn apart by civil war."

"If the virus spreads, everyone in this city will die."

"What am I supposed to tell the rioters?"

"That you'll lift the lockdown after the virus is contained."

"How can I tell them anything when all comms are down?"

"You can't blame that on me. I have no control over the city's communications."

Strus shook his head in frustration, turned on his heel, and stalked out of the gym.

Chapter 47

Phoebe couldn't believe what she was hearing.

"I vote we put Phoebe in charge, since she seems to know what's going on with those helicopters outside," said Crystal, buying a can of diet Coke at one of the vending machines in the bowling alley food court.

Why would they want her to lead them? wondered Phoebe. Her life was filled with bad decisions that had made her miserable. She had been inches away from filing for Chapter 7 bankruptcy thanks to a bad investment. And she had picked a philandering husband.

"She sure knows more than the rest of us about this virus that's infecting people," said Wally. "She said the cops would shoot the kid, and they did."

"I'm not taking orders from her or anybody else," said Bud. "This is my business. When I'm here, I'm running the show."

"All I'm saying is we need to listen to her to get out of this mess," said Crystal. "I'm not saying she's in charge of your business."

Crystal took a pull on her Coke.

"We should listen to Phoebe before we decide what to do next when we're dealing with the virus," said Wally.

They had no idea what they were saying, decided Phoebe. They didn't know how bad her track record was at making decisions.

"I'm not telling anyone what to do," said Phoebe. "If I can help us get out of here, I will."

"So what's your plan?" said Bud.

"We can't go outside without getting shot as long as those choppers are out there."

"That's not a plan."

"It sounds like a good plan to me," said Wally. "In other words, stay put for now."

"But we can't stay here forever," said Phoebe. "Eventually the choppers are gonna napalm this building and the rest of the neighborhood."

"How long do we have?"

"I wish I knew. I don't think we have long."

"We could make a run for it," said Geiger, peering out the plate-glass door at the parking lot, which was hazy with billowing smoke generated from the smoldering corpses lying scattered on the blacktop.

"We'd never make it."

"What other options do we have?" said Geiger, turning around to face Phoebe.

"What do you care if we die here?" said Crystal. "You said you don't like living."

"Why do you keep saying I said that? I said life is a vile disease. It even spreads like a disease."

"There you go. You proved my point."

"There's no talking to you. You distort everything I say. You've watched too many of those brain-dead *Saw* movies."

"*You* have to take responsibility for your actions. If you don't like living, change your life. You make your life what it is."

Not always the case, decided Phoebe. *Sometimes crap happens to you no matter what you do, no matter what kind of a life you lead, whether you're good or bad. Still, you can't let it get you down.* Jason had betrayed her with a streetwalker, but she wasn't going to let it interfere with her life. She wasn't going to fill her heart with hatred for him. Nor was she going to kick herself for the rest of her life for making the wrong decision of choosing him for her husband.

She would live her life without dwelling on past indiscretions. Dwelling on the past was a waste of time. In the future she would try to make fewer mistakes. Jason's betrayal had been a gut punch to her, but she wasn't going to give up and crawl into a cave to die.

She wasn't going to give in to the outbreak cops either, or whatever they called themselves. She called them murderers.

In any case, things were not looking up.

She had escaped the fire at the Strip only because of the hit man Hardy's help. He wasn't in the bowling alley to help this time. *Help*, she thought derisively. A more accurate word for it would be *kidnap*. He kidnaped her in order to ransom her off to her husband. At least, those were his plans, which she managed to knock into a cocked hat by escaping him.

She was going to have to escape this time on her own.

"I vote we get rid of Phoebe," said Bud.

Chapter 48

"What are you talking about?" said Crystal. "Without her, we wouldn't know what's going on with those choppers killing everyone."

"Everything was fine until she showed up," said Bud. "She's the one who brought trouble here. She brought those killer choppers. If we hand her over to them, they'll leave."

"I don't believe it," said Wally. "She saved my life outside."

Bud tapped the crown of his bat against the floor twice.

"How can you be sure?" he said. "Maybe they wouldn't't've attacked you if she hadn't been with you."

"Ah, you're talking through your hat."

"Maybe he's right," said Geiger. "The point is, we really don't know what's going on."

"The cops in the choppers are gonna shoot us if we go outside," said Crystal.

"How can you be sure?"

"Because they said they wouldn't allow anyone to leave these buildings. And you saw what they did to Herman."

"I bet they'd leave us alone if we gave them Phoebe," said Bud.

"They're gonna come after all of us, not just me," said Phoebe. "They know the virus is here, so they can't let any of us live. They believe we'll spread it if we keep living."

She approached the front door.

"Why don't you give yourself up and save the rest of us?" said Bud, watching her.

"The only way we can save ourselves is by getting out of here before they burn down the neighborhood."

Bud retreated behind the front desk and retrieved a package of black plastic zip ties.

"Put your arms behind your back," he said, making his way to Phoebe.

"Leave her alone," said Wally.

"What are you gonna do about it, old man?"

"You have no right to throw her out of here."

"I have every right in the world. This is my bowling alley. I can eighty-six anyone I want. Possession is nine-tenths of the law."

"Throwing me out won't save your life from the choppers," said Phoebe, eying the zip ties in Bud's hand with apprehension, her pulse accelerating.

She knew he was bigger than her and could overpower her with ease.

"She's right," said Wally. "She's not the enemy."

"We have no chance against them," said Crystal. "If the government wants us dead, we're dead. We might as well kill ourselves and save them the trouble," she added, her voice trailing off.

"It's not as bad as you think," said Wally.

"No, it's worse. Does anyone have a gun with one bullet?" said Crystal, looking around.

"That's crazy talk."

"You can't fight the government. They always win. The only way we can escape is by killing ourselves."

"You make this sound like Jonestown. Pass around the Kool-Aid."

"As long as we're breathing, we have a chance," said Phoebe.

She picked up on a crowd gathering outside. Approaching the choppers, they looked angry. Middle fingers flashed at the choppers. Many of the crowd members were clutching rocks or bottles. The members gesticulated angrily at the choppers.

But they weren't infected, decided Phoebe. None of the mob were foaming at the mouth or moving rapidly.

"Something's happening outside," she said with concern.

"More maniac killers?" said Wally.

"I don't think they're infected. They're not attacking anyone on the ground. They're mad at the choppers."

Bud came up to her and peered outside. "They're pissed at the choppers, all right. Maybe they saw the choppers massacre people in the parking lot."

"Maybe they came here to help us," said Wally, perking up.

"I don't see how they could know we're here."

"This isn't about us," said Phoebe. "They're on their own mission."

"I don't like their chances," said Bud. "Rocks and bottles against AR-15s? No way."

Chapter 49

A furious, dark-haired, mullet-cut man clad in an olive drab wife beater stood in the throng gesturing wildly with his left hand. At least a head taller than the others, he yelled an obscenity, cocked his heavily tattooed right arm, and flung a rock at the low-flying chopper nearest him. The rock slammed into the Plexiglas cockpit, bounced off, and fell to the pavement.

The enraged mob broke into a chant.

"End the lockdowns," they hollered. "End the lockdowns."

They brandished their fists at the choppers.

Becoming angrier they flung rocks and bottles at the choppers, which ascended into the sky to avoid damage to their rotor blades.

"They're protesting the lockdowns," said Phoebe.

"It looks more like a riot than a protest," said Bud.

Three AR-15s protruded from the choppers and opened fire on the boisterous mob.

"Oh no," said Phoebe, raising her hand to her mouth.

Several in the mob screamed as Parabellum slugs shredded their bodies. Blood fountained from wounded necks and splattered the throng. Wounded in his shoulder, grimacing with both pain and vengeful fury, Mullet Cut slung another rock at the choppers. An AR-15 nine mil cracked open his head and catapulted his blood-streaked parietal bone across the parking lot.

Wally stood behind Phoebe and Bud. "Why the hell are they shooting them? The protesters aren't even armed, except with bottles."

"They don't look infected," said Bud. "It makes no sense."

"They did the same thing on the Strip," said Phoebe. "The chopper crews killed everybody in the immediate area—the infected and the healthy."

"Why the healthy?" said Wally.

"The chopper crews must figure everybody in the area will become infected sooner or later."

"We're dead meat. Those rioters just got here, and they're killing them. We've been here for a while. For sure, they're gonna waste us."

"We have no chance," said Crystal from the food court. "Why do we have to keep pretending things will work out? Where does a girl get a gun around here? It's not like I'm asking for a million bucks. Just one bullet."

Silence.

"Or does somebody want to do me a favor and strangle me?" she said.

"We'll figure something out," said Phoebe, unsure of herself. "I got away from the Strip in one piece. Why not from here?"

"How did you get away?" said Wally.

"I had help."

"We could use some of that."

Phoebe turned to Bud. "Do you have any weapons we can use, besides your bat?"

Bud thought about it. "Let's see."

He strode to the main desk, stooped behind it, and pulled out a fluorescent lime battery-powered eighteen-inch chain saw.

"How about this?" he said, holding it up.

"Why in the world do you have a chain saw in a bowling alley?" said Wally.

"I prune the trees in the parking lot with it."

"We can use a chain saw," said Phoebe. "Do you have anything else?"

"Why? Are we planning a jailbreak?"

"We can't stay here. They're gonna burn this building till it's nothing but ashes."

"They better not," said Bud with the determined visage of a pit bull clamping a large bone between his teeth. "This is my livelihood. I can't exist without it. They might as well shoot me in the head as burn me out."

"The only way to stop them is to chase them away."

"And we're gonna do that with a baseball bat and a chain saw?"

"I'm open to suggestions."

Phoebe heard the choppers descending. She peered out the plate-glass door and saw them closing in on the rioters they had butchered. Flamethrowers protruded from the helos and unleashed streams of fire that ignited the bullet-riddled corpses sprawled in the parking lot.

"Why are they torching the corpses if they're not infected?" asked Wally.

"To cover up their murders," answered Phoebe. "No one can prove the rioters weren't infected with the evidence destroyed."

"Bastards," said Bud.

"Why doesn't the new mayor stop them?" said Wally.

"He must not know what's going on," said Phoebe.

"Or worse," said Bud. "He *does* know and thinks he's saving the city by killing the protesters."

Chapter 50

Strus and Zandorf were standing in Jason's hospital room at St. Luke's studying Jason, who remained in a coma, when Chief of Police Coffin flung open the door and burst inside.

At well over two hundred pounds, five ten with broad shoulders and a beefy face with a complexion as ruddy as fresh raw ground round, dressed in his uniform, forty-two-year-old Coffin trained a fixed blue-eyed glare on Strus.

"The rioters attacked one of my helos," he said, his snow-white flattop glowing under the overhead track lights and dominating his face.

"Crap," said Strus. "Why aren't you implementing crowd-control measures?"

"We are. There are too many rioters. The citizens are revolting against the lockdowns. We don't have enough men to control them."

"What did your men do to retaliate and control the attackers?"

"They shot them."

"What?" said Strus, dumbfounded. "They shot uninfected citizens?"

"We can't be sure they were uninfected."

Strus heaved a sigh. "What exactly happened?"

"What we know for sure is the citizens were rioting and assaulting my men with rocks and bottles. My men fired on them to protect themselves."

"Did any of your men get hurt?"

"One officer got hit in the head with a brick. Others required medical attention."

"Let me think." Strus paused two beats. "Were there any eyewitnesses to the attack?"

"How could there be? My men killed all of the attackers—and—uh—incinerated them in case they were infected."

"Were they infected or not?"

"They were acting crazy. You said that's a symptom of the virus."

Strus stared at Jason. "As long as nobody saw the attack, we should be able to survive this."

Jason's face showed no reaction.

"My men are up in arms," said Coffin. "They don't want to kill any more fellow citizens."

"Tell them if they don't kill the infected, they will become infected too and die a horrifying death."

Coffin nodded, but didn't look convinced his men would buy it.

"Tell absolutely nobody what your men did to the attackers," said Strus.

"Nobody's gonna talk. Don't worry about it. Your job is safe."

"I'm worried about our citizens, not my job," retorted Strus.

"Uh-huh."

"You can't let this leak out. Do you understand? We got enough problems with the lockdown. Rioters are tearing apart the city. It's a damn insurrection."

"Why would I tell anyone? Do I look like I want to shoot myself in the foot? I'm the guy that's gonna get blamed for this fiasco if anyone hears of it."

"Promise me, no leaks."

"The leaks are gonna come from your office before they come from mine."

Strus shot Coffin a baleful glance.

"Your office is always leaking to your media pals, and you know it," said Coffin.

"Watch your mouth, Chief. Your job is on shaky ground, especially with riots everywhere."

"We're not causing the riots. *You* are with your lockdown. That's why the people are rioting."

"Just because I'm subbing for the mayor doesn't mean I don't have the power to fire you," said Strus, his face livid. "Do you want me to take your badge and send you home without a job?"

"I'll be without a job, anyway, if the city falls apart, the way things are going. And so will you. We're heading straight for anarchy."

"Is that a threat?" said Strus, bridling.

"If the vaccines work, you'll be able to open up the city on a dime," said Zandorf, trying to defuse the animosity in the room.

"Why are we even testing them?" demanded Strus. "Cobygenex's CEO promised the lieutenant governor they work."

"These vaccines have not passed USDA inspection. Therefore, the CDC does not consider them safe without testing them first. We're dealing with a virus we've never encountered before."

"Your pussyfooting caution is costing lives. The sooner we administer the vaccines, the sooner we eradicate the virus."

"You need to show some patience. We'll be getting test results soon."

"The Mexicans wouldn't dare send us a bunch of shit."

"Of course not."

"Then let's start injecting more people, so I can open the city and calm everybody down," said Strus, champing at the bit. "We can't handle many more of these riots. We're already stretched to the limit."

"That's for sure," said Coffin.

"I know it and you know it."

"Let me tell you," said Coffin, wagging his thick forefinger. "If people find out we're shooting the infected to stop the spread of the virus, there will be hell to pay. Mark my words."

"And you'll the first to be shitcanned. Are we on the same page, Chief?"

Coffin blew out his pink cheeks, flabbergasted.

Smiling, Strus patted him on the shoulder. "I thought so."

"Get your hands off me."

The smile disappeared from Strus's face. "As long as you know who's boss."

Amira, a thirtysomething black nurse wearing horn-rimmed glasses with lenses shaped like butterfly wings, burst through the door and interrupted them.

"Dr. Zandorf, hurry," she said, her face animated.

"Hurry where?" said Zandorf.

"Come with me. We're getting scores of patients entering the ER and dying."

"Do they have the virus?" said Strus, furrowing his brow.

"We don't think so," said Amira.

"Why do you need me if it's not the virus?" said Zandorf.

"*It's the vaccines*. The people entering the hospital were all vaccinated for the virus today."

"Good God," said Zandorf, shock registering on his face.

He bolted out of the room, Amira in tow.

Chapter 51

Phoebe didn't like their chances. She wasn't ready to give up, however.

"What good's a chain saw against helicopters?" said Wally, watching Bud approach, his chain saw in hand.

"What do you expect?" said Bud. "A bazooka behind my desk?"

"Herman said this was a horror movie," said Crystal. "No horror movie worth its salt is complete without a chain saw."

"If only those choppers would leave," said Phoebe, "we could make a run for it. A chain saw will work against the infected maniacs if you cut off their heads. They can't return to life without heads."

"The question is, how long do we got?" said Bud.

"Before they burn us out, you mean?"

Bud nodded yes.

"Not long, I bet," said Phoebe. "The situation is going sideways fast what with rioters and infected maniacs running amok."

"Does that chain saw have fuel in it?" Geiger asked Bud.

"It's battery-powered," answered Bud. He glanced at the chain saw dial. "It's got a full charge."

"Is it heavy?"

"Nah. About two pounds," said Bud, lifting the chain saw up and down.

"Good. Then all you gotta do is turn it on and throw it at a chopper."

"Are you trying to be funny?"

"You gotta have a sense of humor in a world as rotten as this one."

"Like I'm gonna knock a helo out of the sky by throwing a chain saw at it," said Bud. "Ha."

"I dunno," said Wally. "It would damage a rotor blade if it hit one."

"Meanwhile, what are the other choppers gonna be doing? Filling me full of lead is what."

"I'm telling you we have to get out of here before they torch us," said Phoebe.

"I thought you said they're gonna shoot us if we go outside," said Geiger.

"They will."

"Then why do you expect us to go outside?"

"It's either that or burn to death."

"What's our third option?"

"There is no third option."

Bud cleared his throat. "The third option is we hand her over to the cops, and they'll leave the rest of us alone."

"What makes you think that?" said Wally.

"Because all my problems started when she entered my bowling alley and said they're gonna kill us."

"All I know is one of those infected maniacs tried to kill me and she helped me get away from them."

"How do you explain her knowing so damn much?"

"Why does that make it her fault we're in this pickle?"

"Maybe she was sent here to lure us out so they could blow all of us away," said Geiger. "Maybe we're safe inside."

"Yeah," said Bud. "That makes more sense than anything else I've heard."

"I'm thinking she's right about their burning us," said Wally. "Remember how the chopper cops burned all their victims with flamethrowers after they shot them?"

"That doesn't necessarily mean they'll burn us out," said Bud. "Remember what they said? They told us to stay inside and we'd be OK."

"Why should we believe anything they tell us? They're cold-blooded murderers, for Chrissake."

"The thing is, they told us to stay inside on the Strip and then they napalmed the entire neighborhood," said Phoebe.

"I heard about that fire on the Strip," said Wally. "The news said it was an accident."

"Yeah, that's right," said Bud. "I saw the news on TV."

"The news media didn't see what I saw," said Phoebe. "I was there when the fire started. I saw everything."

"Why should we believe you?"

"People are skeptical in horror movies," said Crystal. "They don't believe the horror is real. They end up dying because they don't believe their lives are in danger."

"Will you shut up with the horror movies," said Bud. "You're starting to sound like Herman."

"Even if this isn't a horror movie, it sure feels like one."

"What's the news saying about our situation here?" said Wally.

Bud glanced at the flat-panel TV set mounted on the wall behind the main desk.

"There is no news," he said. "There's nothing on TV. The TV's as dead as our cell phones. All comms are dead as roadkill."

"They're jamming everything," said Phoebe. "They jammed our cell phones before they napalmed the Strip."

"Who's they?"

"Whoever's telling the chopper cops what to do."

Chapter 52

"Let me get this straight," said Bud. "You want us to believe our own government is trying to kill us? The cops work for the government."

"I know it sounds crazy, but it's true," said Phoebe.

"Why would they do such a thing?"

"They're trying to stop the spread of the virus. That's all I can figure."

"Haven't they heard of doctors? Their job is to cure diseases. Nobody cures diseases by killing the infected victims."

Phoebe shook her head in bafflement. "I can't get my head around it either."

Frowning in thought Bud took two steps across the floor and wheeled around.

"Or maybe you're making this shit up out of whole cloth," he said.

"Why would I?"

Phoebe felt like he would attack her any second. Her pulse raced. The guy had a chain saw in his hand. She had nothing.

"Hold on a second," said Wally. "We all saw what the chopper crew did to the innocent people outside. They mowed them down with bullets like they were nothing."

"Those 'innocent' people threw rocks and bottles at the choppers," said Bud.

"So that gives the cops the right to shoot them in cold blood?"

"It was self-defense."

"The cops could've flown away without hurting anybody. They overreacted big time."

"I'm not gonna argue about it. I still say she"—Bud pointed at Phoebe—"has brought us nothing but trouble. She's bad news."

Bud strutted toward her.

Wally inserted himself between Bud and Phoebe.

"That doesn't mean she's causing it," said Wally.

Bud glared at him.

"What difference does it make who's causing it?" said Crystal. "What matters is we gotta deal with it."

"It makes a lot of difference if the choppers are waiting for Phoebe to come out," said Bud. "They'll go away and leave the rest of us alone if they get her."

"We don't know that's the case," said Wally.

Phoebe knew the cops would arrest her or kill her if they saw her. However, she wasn't going to tell the others. Even if she surrendered, the choppers would still napalm the bowling alley because it was the site of another outbreak of the killer virus. They were going to kill everybody here no matter what she did.

She might be able to save herself if she surrendered. On the other hand, she figured the cops were just as likely to kill her as to kill the others. She wasn't sure why they had issued a warrant for her arrest. Either because she was a witness to the murders they had committed at the Strip or because they thought she was infected since she was at the Strip, and therefore they wanted to quarantine her. Or cure her. In other words, kill her.

She wasn't going to entrust her life to the chopper cops. She had seen them in action.

Sneering at Wally, Bud raised his chain saw. "Want me to turn this baby on?"

"Killing all of us won't get the choppers to leave," said Wally.

"Ah, you don't know nothing," said Bud, lowering the chain saw, a grimace-grin on his face.

"I want to put in my two cents," said Geiger. "I'm a truck driver."

"I thought you said you were a reverend."

"I thought you said you were a postman," said Phoebe.

"I used to be a postman," said Geiger. "I've had a lot of jobs, because I never liked any of them. Being a reverend doesn't pay the bills, so I do some long-hauling."

"Maybe what you really are is a lying bum," said Bud. "I sure wouldn't go to your church—with all your preaching that life is a virus. Who wants to hear that?"

"As I was saying before you interrupted me, I just finished a long haul across country in a semi, and I came here to bowl a few games to unwind. It's no fun being cooped up in a big rig all by yourself twenty-four hours a day."

"What's your point?"

"My point is maybe we're better off on our own. I'm an independent trucker. Why do we all have to act together?"

"You just got through saying you don't like being alone all the time."

"Not all the time, but it's how I make a living—nowadays. Maybe if we go our separate ways, the choppers will leave us alone. There are five of us and only three choppers. We each leave one at a time. They can't chase all of us if we split up."

"They'll just pick us off one at a time as we leave the alley," said Phoebe. "I don't see how that makes us better off."

"Any other bright ideas?" said Bud, his face smug, eyeballing Geiger.

"I don't hear you coming up with anything," said Geiger.

"The choppers are gonna napalm this area no matter what," said Phoebe.

"Maybe they'll do it after we leave," said Geiger.

"They're not gonna let us leave. They believe we're infected and have to be killed to stop the spread of the virus."

"We have to take your word for that."

"Why should we take her word for anything?" said Bud. "That's what I'm talking about."

"Look where acting alone got Herman," said Crystal.

"The kid was messed up," said Geiger. "He was so stoned on weed he thought he was in a horror movie. He was out of it."

"Being that you hate living, Geiger, why don't you go outside by yourself and see what happens?" said Bud.

"How many times do I have to tell you I don't hate living? I said life is a disease. It spreads like a virus."

"Now you're changing your tune. You want to live as much as the next guy."

"If I wanted to kill myself, I would do it," said Geiger, adjusting his bolo. "Well, I'm still here, aren't I?"

"You're a bullshitter. That's what you are."

"And you're good at volunteering other people to go outside. Why don't *you* go outside?"

"This is *my* bowling alley. I don't want to go outside. I want people to come *inside* and have a good time and bowl."

"That's not gonna happen with those killer copters in the sky."

"My life keeps getting worse," said Crystal, standing up from her table in the food court and cutting across the room toward the others. "I escaped the cartel and now we're gonna get napalmed. I'm sick of this shit."

"I'm telling you life is a terminal disease," said Geiger.

"Don't talk to me about terminal diseases," said Bud. "My mother died from pancreatic cancer. *That's* a terminal disease. She was miserable for the last days of her life."

"Sorry for your loss," said Crystal.

Bud rubbed his face like it was a slab of meat. "I don't want to think about it."

"Holy shit," said Wally, standing near the front door and peering through its plate glass.

Chapter 53

"What is it?" said Phoebe, running over to Wally.

"That pickup over there just pulled into the parking lot," said Wally, pointing at a silver Ford F-150.

"What about it?"

"A guy in the flatbed's got a .50-caliber Browning M2 machine gun in his hands."

Phoebe gazed through the glass at the pickup.

"That's what we need," said Bud, approaching Phoebe from behind. "A fucking Ma Deuce. I used to be a marine. Gimme a Ma Deuce any day."

The pickup came to a halt beside the smoldering remains of the cremated mob beneath the nearest hovering chopper. The muscular, tattooed guy holding the heavy M2 trained the barrel on the chopper and fired a burst, which ripped into the chopper cockpit before a crewman could return fire with an AR-15.

Making a humming racket, its tail rotor broken by a bullet, the copter yawed to the right, unable to keep its balance. It descended and crashed in the parking lot, where it burst into flames. Black smoke commenced unfurling from it.

The two other choppers ascended at speed and flew away from the pickup.

Rigo trained the M2 on the nearest one and fired. The chopper gained speed and was flying out of range as a host of .50-caliber slugs tore past it.

"Yeah," cried Bud, unleashing a wide grin and pumping his fist.

"The only way to deal with killer cops," muttered Wally with a glum expression.

"Who is that guy?" said Phoebe.

"One of the rioters getting revenge for the murder of his comrades."

"I dunno," said Geiger, coming up behind Phoebe. "Killing a cop is bad news. Cops pull me over all the time on the road, but I would never whack one of them. The cops are gonna go after that guy in the pickup like you wouldn't believe."

"They're maniac cops," said Crystal, joining the group. "You saw what they did to the people in the parking lot. Snuffed 'em and torched 'em."

Bud got a hold of himself. "I like and respect cops. I'm pro-cop all the way. I give to the Police Benevolent Association every Christmas. They got a hard job holding the line. They earn my respect every day. But those cops in the choppers, man, that's not right what they're doing, wasting innocent folks. I know they were defending themselves against the protesters who attacked them, but—"

"But nothing. They deserved to get shot. Maniac cops, I'm telling you."

"And they're hovering up there, waiting to whack us," said Wally.

"You're right," said Bud, thinking about it. "We got the right to defend ourselves against these psycho cops. If we don't fight back, they're gonna waste every last one of us. Wasting people because they're infected with a virus—that ain't right. I don't want to catch this virus any more than the next guy, but why can't doctors treat the infected? Who's giving these cops such brain-dead orders?"

"Damn straight," said Crystal.

"Still . . . ," said Bud tenuously.

"Still what?"

Bud hung his head. "Sill, I shouldn't have cheered for cops dying."

"Why not? They're gonna kill us. If they're gonna off us, we got the right to off them."

"This city is turning into an armed camp with us against them," said Wally. "And *them* is the cops."

"And us against the infected," said Phoebe. "Don't forget the infected are the real maniacs. They go stark raving mad when they catch the virus, and they kill every healthy human in sight."

"Is it time to make a run for it?" said Crystal.

Wally peered at the choppers hovering in the distance.

"Those choppers haven't left," he said. "They're hovering out of range of the Browning, is all."

"What am I cheering for?" said Bud. "I don't want cops to get killed. Cops come here to bowl all the time. They're some of my best customers. What's happening to this city?"

"It's their bosses that need killing," said Wally.

"The cops don't want to kill us, but that's not stopping them from doing it," said Phoebe. "We don't want to kill them, but if we don't do them, they'll do us."

"Should we make a run for it now?" said Crystal.

"We can't stay here. They're gonna burn this building to the ground."

"Not while I'm alive," said Bud.

"If you leave with us, you can find another job," said Wally.

"I don't want another job. I have no marketable skills. This is all I'm good at. I love bowling and I love watching people bowl. It's all I'm interested in. I invested all of my money in this building. I'm ruined if I let it burn."

"Don't you have insurance?"

"I couldn't afford insurance."

"You can open up another bowling alley."

"How can I afford to? I'm staying."

"Then they'll burn you with your alley," said Phoebe.

"Only if we believe everything you're telling us," said Bud.

"I believe her, and I don't want to die," said Wally. "I'm gonna do everything in my power to stay alive one more day. If she says we gotta beat it, let's vamoose."

"I'm staying."

"Is there a rear entrance?" asked Phoebe, scoping out the back of the bowling alley.

"There used to be. I had it welded shut to keep punks from robbing me. The front door's the only way out."

"Not good."

"Let's go," Wally told Phoebe.

"Where are we going?" she said. "The road that leads out of town is blocked."

"Then we'll stay in the city."

"I don't know how long the rest of the city will be safe," she said with a pensive expression.

"Well, they can't burn down the entire city. That would be suicidal madness."

Phoebe wasn't convinced it couldn't happen. If the government was willing to burn down the Strip to stop the spread of the virus, why not burn down the rest of the city, since the virus was continuing to spread?

Chapter 54

When Zandorf arrived at the ER, to his dismay he saw dead bodies everywhere. Strus followed close on his heels.

"What are they dying from?" Zandorf asked a blonde, thirtyish roly-poly intern wearing red plastic glasses with a silver lanyard hanging from them, her hair in a perm. "Are they infected with the virus?"

"We believe they're dying from overdoses of fentanyl," she answered.

Two EMTs wheeled a new DOA body in on a gurney.

"Fentanyl?" said Zandorf. "Are you sure these people were all vaccinated today?"

"Positive."

"How could they be dying from fentanyl?" said Strus.

"Are you sure *all* of them died from fentanyl?" Zandorf asked the intern.

She nodded yes. "According to our preliminary tests on the first victims."

"How can that be possible?" said Strus, incredulous.

Zandorf considered it. "That fucking Cobygenex vaccine must be laced with fentanyl."

"Why would they do such a thing?"

"The drug cartels lace everything with fentanyl. The governor must've bought this vaccine from a drug lord."

"That idiot Vitti."

"We need to make sure," said Zandorf, turning toward the intern. "Stop administering the vaccines and have one tested for the presence of fentanyl."

"On it," she said, and burst out of the ER's swinging doors.

"Can this really be happening?" said Strus, holding his sweaty forehead in shock.

"I'm afraid so," said Zandorf with an ashen complexion, surveying the corpses laid out around him.

Strus grabbed Zandorf's arm. "No one must find out about this. If the news spreads, it will incite more riots. They'll come after me with pitchforks."

"What are we gonna tell relatives of the deceased?"

"I dunno. Think of something."

"If all of the vaccinated die, people are gonna figure something's wrong."

"Put a lid on it. Don't let anyone outside the hospital know what happened."

"The relatives will find out."

Strus dug out a handkerchief from his jacket pocket and wiped his brow.

"Nobody must find out," he said.

"You're lucky all comms are out."

"It's not luck. Vitti had comms shut down in the city. You must keep your lips sealed about these vaccine deaths."

"Let me remind you, I don't work for you," said Zandorf, bristling. "I work for the CDC and the president. You have no jurisdiction over me."

"I'm trying to get you to understand the gravity of the situation. If this news leaks out, the people will become enraged. They'll blame us, because we offered them the vaccines. Our very lives may be in jeopardy, including yours, because you were in charge of administering the vaccines."

"Your lieutenant governor gave them to me. What's his name?"

"Uh—Bates," said Strus, snapping his fingers. "Kevin Bates."

"He's the one who gave me the information that the vaccines are safe and effective."

"I'm not blaming you, but the people *will* if they find out about the deaths the vaccines caused."

"Somebody needs to tell Vitti he bought poison from the cartels and tell him or Bates or whoever not to buy any more."

"I'll talk to him."

"It's more important than ever that we find Phoebe Albright," said Zandorf, fidgeting.

"Why is she so important?"

"She could be immune to the virus."

"What makes you think so?"

"She escaped the Strip without becoming infected. If she's not infected, we have to find out why."

"How do you know she's still not infected? Maybe it's taking longer to infect her."

"Possible," conceded Zandorf reluctantly. "That doesn't change our priorities. It is imperative we find her so I can examine her."

"She could have died from the virus by now."

"She's our only possible lead. If the cops killed her and burned her, we're doomed," said Zandorf, frowning.

Strus clasped Zandorf's arm and lowered his voice.

"You need to promise me you won't say a word about these vaccines to anyone," he said. "It would trigger more riots."

Zandorf stared at Strus. "Your vaccines murdered five hundred innocent people."

"*My* vaccines? Vitti ordered them. I didn't. Don't put this on me."

"We can't let murders of this magnitude go unreported. It would violate the Hippocratic Oath to ignore five hundred murders."

"It was an accident," said Strus, gesticulating wildly. "We didn't do it on purpose. Cobygenex scammed us."

Zandorf bowed his head, crestfallen. "Innocent people died because of us."

"The townspeople will put our heads on stakes when they hear about this," said Strus, anguished. "They're gonna blame us, and you know it."

Zandorf heaved a despondent sigh. "We're not without blame."

"At least keep mum about this until we've got the city under control. Can you do that? This is vital to the health of the city."

His conscience weighing on him, Zandorf hemmed and hawed.

"I'll take it under advisement," he said at last.

"I'll talk to the CEO of the hospital to get him onboard and put a lid on this tragedy. There's no way he would want news of this horrific accident to spread. His hospital's reputation would be tarnished forever."

Strus bustled to the C-suite corner office on the top floor.

Chapter 55

When Strus emerged from the hospital entrance onto the sidewalk after his discussion with the hospital CEO, a freshly washed black late-model Audi with tinted windows pulled up to the curb and halted beside him.

The passenger-side door swung open, and a five-nine guy in a black suit stepped out. Pushing thirty-five he unbuttoned his jacket, letting his turquoise silk moiré necktie flap free, and strode around the front of the car to Strus.

The musclebound driver, who was wearing a black suit and Oakley wraparound shades, kept the motor idling. Above the driver's razor-creased white shirt collar, Strus could make out the tail section of a tattoo of a scorpion etched on the guy's bull neck.

Strus didn't recognize the guy approaching him.

Rawboned, smooth-complected, he had a slight scar grooved over his right eye. A pencil-thin mustache rode his upper lip.

"Hello, Mr. Mayor," he said, grinning. "I'm Enrique."

"I have work to do," said Strus, in no mood to talk to strangers.

"It's not gonna be that easy."

"What are you talking about?"

"To get rid of me. I have an important message for you from the Cobygenex group."

Strus's eyes flared. His blood boiled. They were the double-crossing crooks that had sent him toxic vaccines.

"I want nothing to do with you," he said, ducked his head, and tried to brush Enrique aside.

Enrique didn't budge. "You're not gonna dis me. Look at me when I talk to you."

Strus raised his head and looked daggers at him. "Do you know who I am?"

"I do, indeed. Do you know who _I_ am?"

"If you work for Cobygenex, you're a crook."

"With all due respect, those are strong words for a partner."

185

"I'm not your partner."

"We saved your bacon with our vaccines. I'd watch your mouth if I was you."

"Your vaccines are poison," hissed Strus, apoplectic with rage.

Enrique stiffened. "You're looking at a lawsuit with accusations like that. We have an ironclad contract with the governor. He's not gonna be happy if you fuck us."

"You're looking at a prison sentence for the first-degree murders of five hundred people."

"With all due respect, Mr. Mayor, we will sue you if you don't keep up your end of the deal."

"You can sue us from your jail cells when you're doing time."

"It's called breach of contract."

"Nobody made a deal to buy fentanyl from your cartel," spluttered Strus.

"Your governor made a deal with us to buy another thousand vaccine doses from us for thirty million USD."

Strus blew out his cheeks. "He made a deal to buy *vaccines* from you, not *fentanyl*."

"A deal's a deal. You can't welsh on it without breach of contract. Tell that to your governor," said Enrique, jabbing his index finger at Strus. "Do you think you're dealing with hicks?"

"Thirty million dollars for another load of poison? You can't be serious. People are dying from your vaccines."

"We're not responsible for the administration of the vaccines. You're inoculating your patients incorrectly."

"Bullshit. The hospital tested the vaccines after patients started dying. We found toxic doses of fentanyl. End of story. Now get out of my way."

Enrique didn't move. "Tell the governor to wire thirty million USD into our Cobygenex bank account in the Cayman Islands with our ABA routing number ASAP."

"You're out of your mind. He's not gonna pay thirty million bucks for toxic doses of fentanyl."

"Remind him we have a deal. Tell him his career's on the line if he stiffs us. The boss never forgets a welsher."

"Is that a threat?"

"It's a business promise. And unlike you, we keep our promises."

Steamed, Enrique returned to the open passenger-side door of the Audi and clambered into the shotgun seat, slamming the door.

The Audi peeled away from the curb, burning rubber, the tires shrieking.

Chapter 56

Furious, Strus strode a block away from the hospital, withdrew his satphone from his inside jacket pocket, and extended its antenna. He glanced into the sky to make sure there wasn't any cloud cover which could block transmission. A few wispy white clouds floated overhead.

He punched out Vitti's direct number.

"This better be important," said Vitti.

"This is Mayor Strus. You got a major problem."

"Me? You're the one with the problem in Costaguana."

"Listen closely. You're the one that's gonna take the fall."

"Do you know who you're talking to? I'm the fucking governor of California, the most powerful man in this state."

"The vaccines. Do I have your attention?"

"What about the vaccines?"

"The vaccines you sent us are killing all of the recipients."

"What?" exploded Vitti.

"The vaccines are laced with fentanyl. Cobygenex is a cartel. You signed a contract to buy the vaccines from a goddamn cartel."

"Your information is wrong."

"I am not wrong. St. Luke's Hospital tested the vaccines after patients started dying from the inoculations. The interns found toxic amounts of fentanyl in the doses we received from Cobygenex. Enough to kill the recipients."

Silence on the line.

"I didn't sign anything with any cartel," said Vitti.

"Enrique was just here demanding that you send him another thirty million bucks for additional doses of the vaccine."

"I don't know any Enrique."

"He said he works for Cobygenex."

"I don't care if he works for El Chapo. I didn't sign any contract with them."

Strus digested Vitti's words with confusion. "Then who did?"

Was the bastard going to try to blame him for signing the contract? wondered Strus. There was no way Vitti could prove such a bald-faced lie.

"Kevin Bates cut the deal with Cobygenex. He's the one who signed the contracts. I always suspected there was something hinky about that outfit. They're from Matamoros. That's cartel country. Everybody knows that."

Strus realized what Vitti was doing. He was hanging the lieutenant governor out to dry and saving his own skin in the process. There was no one better at CYA than Vitti. It was the reason he had advanced so far in politics. Strus wouldn't want to be in Bates's shoes. Once word got out about the toxic vaccines, Bates would have to fall on his sword and leave Vitti squeaky clean. Vitti would no doubt take credit for not signing a contract with a drug cartel.

"What's plan B?" said Strus.

"Be clear."

"The vaccines aren't gonna work. How do we handle the virus?"

"You need to continue the lockdown. You must not allow the virus to spread outside of your city."

"We're getting more outbreaks. The virus is not under control."

"*You must not let it spread outside of your city*. Do you understand?"

Strus fetched a long sigh. "We'll have to continue our current methods, I'm afraid, since the vaccines are useless."

"The virus must be stopped at all costs."

Strus wished Jason was conscious. Maybe he would know how to handle this debacle. Strus doubted Jason would ever regain consciousness. Lucky him.

"The lockdowns are inciting riots," said Strus.

"Under no circumstances are you to lift the lockdown," said Vitti.

"But the city is dying—"

"No *ifs*, *ands*, and *buts*."

"I'm not gonna stand by and let my city die."

Strus knew if the city died, he would die with it, as would every other citizen in Costaguana.

"Let me remind you. I have absolute authority over your city, because your city is an existential threat to the state of California," said Vitti, and hung up.

Strus heard police sirens in the distance. Racing to quell another riot, he supposed. Or an outbreak of the virus. The city was in its death throes. Racing to Armageddon.

Satphone in hand, he stared into the infinite, glorious blue sky and wondered if there was a god in heaven. He doubted it. If there was one, he must be the crown price of sadism. How were they going to stop the virus without a vaccine that worked? The vaccine had given them hope. Now there was none.

Chapter 57

"How are we supposed to survive when our government is corrupt and wants us dead?" said Wally, watching the distant choppers through the bowling alley plate-glass door.

"I'm telling you, life itself is corrupt," said Geiger from the food court, where he was trying to buy a bag of Fritos from a vending machine. "It's a vile disease—"

"Will you shut up?" said Crystal, sitting at a table the better part of six feet from him. "I'm sick of listening to your bullshit."

"Not only do we have to fight the infected, we have to fight the cops," said Phoebe, standing beside Wally.

"Moping about it won't do any good," said Bud, a few feet from her.

"You're right. Let's get out of here while we have a chance." Phoebe scoped out the parking lot. "I don't see any of the infected maniacs."

"Life is evil," said Geiger, struggling with the vending machine, unable to get it to dispense his Fritos. "It's a highly contagious virus that can't be stopped from spreading."

Crystal bolted to her feet. "I can't stand listening to him anymore. Let's make a run for it and leave him behind."

"You're not getting rid of me that easy. I'm not staying here alone."

Geiger kicked the metal vending machine in frustration.

"Don't damage the equipment," growled Bud, wheeling around at the clanking sound of Geiger's kick.

"A junky vending machine for junk food," said Geiger, throwing up his hands.

"No one's forcing you to use it."

"It stole my money," said Geiger, and pounded the machine with the bottom of his fist.

"Watch out. You break it, you pay for it."

"It's already broken."

"We need to go while that guy in the pickup is holding the choppers at bay," said Phoebe, gazing at the hovering choppers keeping their distance because of the M2 manned by Rigo in the pickup flatbed.

"Where are we going?" said Bud.

"We can't stay here. This building is bound to get napalmed because it's close to where the infected maniacs attacked."

"What's to stop the choppers from shooting us?" said Crystal.

"They're out of range now and keeping their distance."

"They don't want to lose another aircraft to the M2," said Wally.

"They probably radioed for reinforcements," said Phoebe, narrowing her eyes at the choppers. "That's why we should bug out now."

Distraught, Bud surveyed the interior of his bowling alley and its deserted pinewood lanes gleaming with mineral oil.

"Is there some way I can get them to spare my business?" he said.

"How do you keep your lanes so shiny?" said Wally, impressed.

"I oil them at least once a day. If the place is busy, I oil them more often to keep them spick and span."

"They're gonna fry this neighborhood with napalm," said Phoebe. "This building will be ashes."

"If you're not going with us, can you give me your chain saw?" said Wally.

"It's not gonna do you any good against bullets," said Bud.

"It'll work on the infected maniacs."

"Are there more of those things outside?"

"We have to figure there are," said Phoebe. "Where there's one, there are others."

"Can I at least have your bat?" Wally asked Bud.

"I guess," said Bud, handing his Louisville Slugger to Wally.

"Thanks."

"What about the rest of us?" said Crystal. "Where are our weapons?"

"This ain't no armory," said Bud.

Crystal scanned the alley. She headed to a lane, walked down it, careful not to slip on the slick wood, and retrieved a tenpin at the end of it.

"I can use this," she said, holding the tenpin upside down and brandishing it. "Anyone else want one?"

"Yeah," said Phoebe.

"Me too," said Geiger.

Crystal carried three tenpins with her as she returned to the group. She handed a tenpin to Phoebe, but hesitated when it came to Geiger.

"Come on," he said. "I need a weapon too."

Crystal looked at him with suspicion. "How can we be sure you won't use it on us?"

"Why would I do that?"

"You keep saying life is a virus. You might try to kill us because we're alive."

"That's ridiculous," said Geiger, reaching for the tenpin.

Crystal pulled it away from him. "I'm not so sure."

"You make me sound like a homicidal maniac. I'm not gonna hit anyone unless they attack me first."

Tenpin in hand, Phoebe flung open the door and pelted outside.

Chapter 58

She looked around and didn't see any pedestrians in the parking lot. She dashed away from the choppers.

Crystal and Geiger followed her. Slower than the others thanks to his age and to hip surgery, Wally pulled up the rear.

Phoebe paused and looked behind her. "Where's Bud?"

"Guarding his bowling alley, I guess," said Crystal.

Just then, Bud burst out of the bowling alley front door, chainsaw in hand. He turned around, closed the door behind him, and locked it.

"What are you waiting for?" he barked over his shoulder.

Phoebe smiled with half her mouth and looked forward—and saw a twentysomething woman with long chestnut hair walking toward them. She wore olive green stretch pants, a powder blue sweatshirt, and pink sneakers.

"Why did you lock your door?" Wally asked Bud, who ran up to them.

"I don't want vandals to enter and loot my alley," answered Bud.

"Phoebe says they're gonna burn your alley to the ground, so you don't need to lock it up."

"The verdict's still out on what Phoebe told us, as far as I'm concerned."

When the woman with chestnut hair saw Phoebe and her crew, she stopped in her tracks. A look of sheer terror swept over her face.

Phoebe didn't see any foam on the woman's mouth. The woman wasn't grimacing in agony either. She just looked scared to death.

Phoebe didn't think the woman was infected. Phoebe couldn't understand why the woman was so scared of them.

"Hello," said Phoebe, smiling.

Her eyes starting from their sockets, the woman fled down the sidewalk that bordered the parking lot.

"What the hell's wrong with her?" said Crystal.

Phoebe and the others gave chase.

"Wait a second," Phoebe cried after the woman. "Wait for us."

The woman screamed when she saw Phoebe and her group chasing her.

"What's her problem?" said Bud.

"She's scared out of her mind," said Wally, trying to keep up with the others.

"She's running pretty fast. Do you think she's infected?"

"If she was, she wouldn't be running away from us," said Phoebe. "She'd be attacking us and trying to tear out our throats. The infected aren't afraid of anything."

"She's acting nuts if you ask me," said Bud.

"Maybe she thinks you're Patrick Bateman with that chain saw in your hand," said Wally.

"You should talk. You got a baseball bat in yours."

Seeing them chase her the woman screamed for help.

"They're infected," she cried. "They're gonna kill me."

"We're not infected," said Phoebe. "We're the good guys."

"What's wrong with everyone?" said Crystal. "Everybody's acting crazy."

"Nobody wants the virus," said Geiger.

They chased the woman for a block and reached a strip mall, where all hell was breaking loose.

Chapter 59

Phoebe gasped at the nightmarish sight.

People were running amok, screaming and yelling. Dozens of infected were chasing people in the parking lot, grabbing them, and chewing hunks of flesh from their bodies.

A blonde pushing thirty wearing a charcoal grey pencil dress was kneeling over a teenage man who lay on his back on the asphalt. Phoebe couldn't believe her eyes as she watched the blonde tearing a coil of his blood-soaked intestines out of a gaping, ragged hole in his stomach and stuffing them into her mouth.

A twentysomething guy in lime board shorts and a cropped grey T was jumping up and down in rage on the hood of a scarlet Dodge Charger, howling like a beast consumed with bloodlust, while another guy about the same age frothed at the mouth, gnashed his teeth, and tried to drag the resisting driver out of the driver's-side open window.

The fortyish driver wearing a blue chambray shirt grabbed the steering wheel to prevent his attacker from dragging him out of his car. But his young infected attacker had superhuman strength thanks to the virus-triggered adrenaline surging through his system and managed to break the driver's grip on the steering wheel and haul his torso through the window. Kicking and screaming, the driver tried to wedge his feet in the steering wheel to prevent the infected maniac from dragging him completely out of the Charger.

Undeterred, the maniac kept tearing the driver out of the car as the guy on the hood kept hooting like a savage, pumping his fists, and jumping up and down on the hood, stamping large dents in the metal.

The driver's passenger, a thirtyish woman with brilliant red hair, was shrieking in terror, her face flushed. She snagged one of the driver's feet and tried to prevent him from being dragged out of the car, but her grip wasn't strong enough to resist the strength of the infected. She ended up holding the driver's empty shoe in her hand as the bloodthirsty maniac wrenched the driver's entire body out of the Charger, threw him on the pavement, and fell to chewing the guy's face.

"Where are the choppers when you need them?" said Phoebe, aghast.

"Be careful what you wish for," said Crystal. "They'd probably just massacre all of us if they were here."

Phoebe nodded, her face grim. She knew Crystal was right.

The infected maniac chewed the driver's right eye out of its socket and scarfed it down with relish.

Phoebe thought she was going to be sick.

The better part of twenty feet away, an infected heavyset female bus driver with a crew cut was hunched forward, throttling a dress-clad, white-haired woman in her fifties, forcing her down on her back, and shoving her head under the water in a fountain in the middle of the strip mall as water splashed around them. Foaming at the mouth the bus driver yanked her victim's head up out of the water, chewed the victim's cheek, and twisting her head back and forth, tore a slab of flesh out of the victim's face.

Crying, the white-haired woman screamed in agony, blood gushing out of her face and tinting the fountain water crimson. The blood-soaked water shimmered under the bright sunlight at the base of a statue of an upright bronze dolphin mottled with green patina. The dolphin stood in the middle of the fountain spewing bloody water from its open mouth, spraying red rain and tears on the pool surrounding it.

Not six feet away from them, a whey-faced, bespectacled doctor in his forties with a stethoscope hanging around his neck snatched a fortysomething woman's hair, jerked her head back, bit her throat, and tore it out. Arterial blood jetted out far enough to reach the water fountain and splatter the back of the bus driver's head.

His lips dripping with blood, the doctor howled with frenzied glee. He tore his victim's head off from her mutilated throat and tossed it into the water fountain, dousing himself with the blood pouring from her severed throat. Drooling, he commenced tucking into her shoulder as he propped her body up in front of him to keep her from falling.

The sneering bus driver lifted her victim's head out of the water and chewed off the woman's remaining cheek. The white-haired woman screamed. Irritated by the woman's screaming, the bus driver continued to throttle her and thrust her bleeding face underwater to muffle her screams and drown her.

His face covered with lather, an infected, uniformed rent-a-cop with a shaved head stretched his hands in front of him and lunged at Bud. Bud whipped his chain saw toward the maniac and pulled the trigger. The chain saw roared into action and severed the rent-a-cop's arms off as Bud swiped the blade in a rapid arc. The rent-a-cop grimaced in pain. Growling, he kept on coming toward Bud.

Bud swung the chain saw blade through the maniac's throat and decapitated him. The torn carotid artery spurted a powerful stream of glistening blood skyward, drenching Bud's face.

A suit with neatly coiffed, grizzled hair attacked Phoebe, who swung her tenpin at the guy's head and connected with his temple. The impact from the blow sent the suit reeling.

Phoebe chased him and smashed his blood-streaked temple again with the tenpin with all her might, thrusting her entire body into the blow. The suit staggered and fell on his face on the pavement, knocking out two of his front teeth, which clicked like dice as they hit the ground. She smashed the back of his skull with the tenpin to make sure he was either out cold or dead.

She preferred him unconscious. The problem with his being dead was that he would come back to life as a flesh-eating ghoul. She didn't want to have to kill him all over again. On the other hand, if she had damaged his brain, maybe he wouldn't reanimate. She believed the infected maniacs couldn't come back to life with their brains destroyed.

"Good one," said Wally, flashing her a thumbs up.

"We can't stay here," she said, surveying the mayhem around her.

Wally swung his bat to bean a rangy guy with a receding hairline who was launching himself at Phoebe. Phoebe heard the guy's skull crack like a tree branch snapping and watched him drop face down to the pavement in a senseless heap.

Crystal bopped a bare-chested dwarf on the top of his brainpan with her tenpin when he growled and lunged at her. He stumbled and fell to his knees, dazed. Charged with adrenaline, Crystal rapped his head again and again till he fell forward on his face and barked it on the pavement.

Phoebe spotted the chestnut-haired woman she had chased into the strip mall. An infected teenager wearing earphones was dragging her into a deserted laundromat and trying to bite her face. Screaming, she was fighting him off, but losing the battle. He swung her body into an open drier and, collaring her throat with two hands, shoved her head into it. He proceeded to strangle her.

Feeling helpless as she watched the woman's plight, Phoebe knew she couldn't reach the laundromat in time to help her.

Out of the corner of her eye Phoebe caught sight of a sewer worker growling in dirty coveralls and darting toward her, his hands outstretched. Her heart jackhammering, she smelled raw sewage as he neared her. She spun out of his way, whipped her tenpin at him, and delivered a glancing blow to his head. Blood poured down the side of his head. He didn't go down. He shook his head, got his bearings, and charged her again.

At that moment, Bud swung his chain saw and sliced through the sewer worker's throat.

The guy's head blew off his severed throat, propelled by a fierce stream of arterial blood that pumped out of his gaping wound.

Phoebe nodded in gratitude at him. She cut her eyes toward the chestnut-haired woman in the laundromat, who was lying backward, motionless, her torso stuffed in the drier as Headphones grimaced and chewed one of her ears off. The woman's face was chewed beyond recognition.

Phoebe looked away in horror. Nobody could help the woman now.

Phoebe looked up at the sky and screamed in frustration and fear.

"We can't stay here," said Wally, holding his blood-and-brain-smeared bat at his side, his clothes splattered with blood, watching infected maniacs wandering around the parking lot, growling and slobbering on themselves.

Chapter 60

Sitting behind his desk in the governor's office in Sacramento, Vitti was reading the riot act to his lieutenant governor Kevin Bates.

All of forty-seven, Bates was a graduate of Berkeley Law School. He had played basketball at Cal as a point guard when he was an undergraduate. Freshly barbered with skintight cropped hair, he was black and stood over six feet tall. He was wearing a bespoke black suit.

"You really blew it," said Vitti.

"What are you talking about?" said Bates, puzzled.

"The vaccines you authorized for Costaguana. They're defective."

"With all due respect, Governor, you're the one who told me about the vaccines in the first place."

"I was always suspicious of them," said Vitti, shuffling papers on his desktop. He cleared his throat. "I naturally thought you would check them out before authorizing the payment for them."

"I never would've known about the vaccines if it wasn't for you."

"Be that as it may, you blew it big time. What I'm gonna tell you doesn't get out of this office, or they're gonna be asking for your head on a plate."

Bates shook his head in confusion. "I want to know what's going on."

"Listen up. Those Cobygenex vaccines you authorized are toxic. They're laced with overdoses of fentanyl. Everybody who got vaccinated died."

"Jesus Christ," said Bates, stricken. "This is horrible."

"It is, indeed. You should have known better than to deal with a Mexican pharmaceutical company based in Matamoros. That's cartel country."

"You're the one who told me about Cobygenex."

"That's not gonna wash. You're the one who signed the documents that authorized the deal and the payment of thirty million bucks."

Nonplussed, not believing his ears, Bates stared at Vitti.

"Look," said Vitti. "We need to keep this under wraps for now. Nobody knows about this but you and me and a select few in Costaguana."

"I'm not gonna tell anyone."

"I knew I could count on you," said Vitti, smiling.

"But when this comes out—and it will—I'm not gonna fall on the sword for you. You're the governor. Ultimately, you are responsible for everything that happens under your administration."

Vitti shrugged. "I wouldn't want to be in your shoes, Bates. When it hits the fan, everybody is gonna see your name on the Cobygenex documents. No matter what you tell anyone, you can't erase your name from the documents."

"I was doing what you told me to do. I was carrying out your orders."

Vitti snorted derisively. "I never ordered you to sign anything."

"Liar," cried Bates, fuming.

"I'm the good guy here. I'm the guy who saves the day after you bungled everything in Costaguana. Unfortunately for you, the heinousness of your act will no doubt get you impeached, I'm sorry to tell you."

"How can you live with yourself after all the lies you tell? How can you sleep at night?"

"I sleep like a baby," said Vitti, smiling.

"This is unconscionable. How can you do this? Do you care about nobody but yourself?"

"You're not gonna be able to blame me for this clusterfuck with your signature on the incriminating documents." Vitti shook his head, grim-faced. "I heard at least five hundred people died from your inoculations."

"*My* inoculations," said Bates, outraged. "I don't work for Cobygenex."

Vitti eyed Bates with commiseration. "I feel sorry for you, Bates. My heart goes out to you."

"You think I'm gonna believe that? In a pig's eye. You set me up."

"The best I can offer you is to keep a lid on this tragedy for as long as possible. But sooner or later it's gonna get out. In the end, you and I both know everything leaks out no matter what anyone does to stop it. That's why I believe Lee Harvey Oswald acted alone when he whacked JFK. If he had help, the identities of his coconspirators would have been leaked by now. Nothing can stay hidden forever—and that assassination was over sixty years ago."

"By the same token, you can't hide your involvement with Cobygenex."

"Arguing about this won't change the facts. I don't see how you avoid impeachment after the facts come to light," said Vitti blandly.

"You're crazy if you think you're gonna get out of this shitstorm unscathed."

Vitti took umbrage. "You ought to be thanking me for telling you what happened with the vaccines. Without me, you never would've known about this terrible tragedy and your impending impeachment."

"There's no way I'm gonna thank you for making me the fall guy."

"If you want to make it in politics, you gotta have a pair of these," said Vitti, opening his desk drawer, removing a pair of cue balls, and slamming them on the desktop. "It's a blood sport. If you don't have a pair, you shouldn't get into it."

"You're the one without balls because you won't man up and take responsibility for your actions. *You* hired Cobygenex. I didn't."

"There you go again, weaseling out," said Vitti, shaking his head with disdain. "You're a wimp. You haven't got what it takes to make it in politics."

"If you think I'm a pushover, you're nuts. I'm gonna fight you every inch of the way."

Vitti picked up a pencil and, staring at it, tapped its eraser on his desktop, deep in thought.

"Remember Nixon?" he said.

"What's Nixon got to do with anything?"

"You could learn from him."

"Learn what?" said Bates irritably.

"He made the only move open to him when confronted with impeachment." Vitti stopped tapping his pencil. "He resigned."

"How dare you assume I'm gonna get impeached," said Bates, stiffening with resentment. "You have no control whatsoever over impeachments."

"If you don't want to get impeached, follow Nixon's example."

"I'm not doing anything Nixon did. The guy was a crook."

"A word to the wise is sufficient. Good-bye," said Vitti, waving at Bates without looking up at him.

"You're not gonna get rid of me that easy. I can sue you."

"Sue me for what?"

"Uh—uh—simple," said Bates, snapping his fingers. "Defamation."

"*Your* signature is on the Cobygenex documents. There's no way you can put that on me. And there's no way you can prove I defamed you when the facts implicate you. You as a lawyer should know that." Vitti flung his pencil across the room and bolted to his feet. "Now get your sorry ass outa here. I have work to do. I have to stop that virus in Costaguana before it wipes out our whole state."

"You haven't seen the last of me," said Bates, smoldering.

He wheeled around and stalked out of the office, slamming the door behind him.

"The next time I see you they'll be impeaching you in the House," muttered Vitti.

Chapter 61

Standing on his pickup flatbed, gripping his M2, Rigo heard the commotion of the riot behind him. He turned around to check out the yells and screams, but saw nothing. The brouhaha was several blocks away.

He turned back and faced the choppers, who were keeping their distance thanks to his M2.

Sitting in the driver's seat minus his Stetson, Tex stuck his head out the window and looked back at Rigo.

"Want to check out that yelling?" said Tex.

Rigo squinted and scoped out the empty blue sky over the commotion.

"There aren't any choppers over there," he said. "I don't know why they're rioting."

"The people have had it with these lockdowns. They're taking to the streets. I don't blame 'em."

"They sound like they're trashing the strip mall."

"There could be cops at the mall in squad cars. Not all the cops are in choppers."

"The cops are doing more harm than good these days, because they spend all their time enforcing the lockdowns."

Tex spat tobacco juice out the window. "If we go over there, the choppers are gonna come back here."

"I'm thinking they'll follow us and try to take us out."

"They're gonna get reinforcements any time now. Maybe it's time for us to beat it."

"I dunno. They're stretched pretty thin these days what with the whole city rioting. Where are they gonna get reinforcements?"

Tex hawked. "I gotta tell you. I don't like killing cops. A couple of my cousins are cops. They're good folks. I respect the men in blue."

"I do too. But these cops in choppers are wasting innocent people. Look at that car wreck smoking in the parking lot. There are burnt human stiffs next to it. And there are other burnt stiffs next to the bowling alley entrance."

Tex chewed his tobacco wad. "Yep."

"We heard shooting and drove over here. Those chopper cops were blowing away people in the parking lot. There's no denying it."

"And the victims weren't even armed."

"Here's the thing. There are good cops and bad cops. These cops are rotten," said Rigo, glancing at the nearest chopper hovering in the distance.

"I hear ya."

"We can't let 'em get away with murder."

"What's happening to this city? Killer cops? What next?" said Tex, bewildered, and stopped chewing his tobacco.

"We're gonna have to stick up for ourselves. The cops aren't gonna help us. They're the enemy."

"It goes against the grain for me to kill cops. But we have to defend ourselves. I never thought I'd see the day when we'd have to kill cops to stay alive."

"Neither did I."

"Our founding fathers saw the day coming. That's why they wrote the Second Amendment, so we'd have guns to defend ourselves."

"We could blame the city's upheaval on the virus, but blaming it on the virus won't change anything. We have to become self-reliant. We have to fill in for the corrupt cops and do their job for them."

"Which is?"

"To protect and serve the citizens."

"Count me in."

Rigo paused in thought. "I'm thinking we should mount an attack against city hall. The mayor's the one giving the cops their orders."

"I dunno. I hear tell it's the governor calling the shots. I seen CHP cops at the roadblocks."

Rigo nodded yes. "I heard there's feds in town too, helping the cops."

"The feds don't take orders from the mayor."

"Still, if we hit city hall, it would send a message to the powers that be."

"What are you talking about when you say 'hit'?" said Tex, raising an eyebrow, his neck hurting from craning around so long to look back at Rigo in the flatbed.

"I got an RPG-7 in my garage. A couple of missiles fired at city hall would put the mayor on notice."

"Something to chew over."

"We gotta let them know we're not gonna let ourselves be slaughtered in the streets like lambs. We gotta put up a fight. Hell, we elected these politicians. And now they're trying to whack us out."

"Double-dealing politicians. Fuck 'em," said Tex, and spat tobacco juice onto the parking lot pavement. "When push comes to shove, they don't represent us. All they care about is lining their pockets. They're narcissist sociopaths."

"A couple of missiles tearing holes in city hall will make them think twice about massacring us."

Chapter 62

Wally swung his baseball bat and bashed in the brains of an infected young mechanic in a grease-stained grey uniform who was trying to take a bite out of his face.

Wally sighed with exhaustion. "I'm getting too old for this."

He saw the mechanic squirming on the strip-mall parking lot pavement and took two more swings at the youth, which, when they landed, turned the guy's head into mush. Blood splattered the leg of Wally's trousers.

"Phew," said Wally, and leaned on his bat like it was a putter and he was waiting his turn on the green. "I'm beat."

An infected maniac snuck up behind him and bit Wally's neck.

Wally screamed in agony and grabbed the back of his neck. He felt a jaw clamping his neck, hot blood spurting between his fingers.

Phoebe wheeled around at the sound of Wally's scream and saw him trying to fight off an infected pudgy twentysomething pie-faced woman clad in a loose yellow maternity dress who was tearing out strips of his neck and gobbling them down, her lips smeared with blood.

Phoebe scurried around Wally and slammed Pie Face in the back of the head with her tenpin. Pie Face jerked her head away from Wally's neck and gawped at Phoebe, who delivered a second blow, bashing her on the top of the head. Pie Face squeezed her eyes into slits under the impact of the blow, but refused to go down.

Pie Face must have had a hard head, decided Phoebe with frustration. Screaming in attack mode, she jumped into the air and, coming down, cracked Pie Face on the crown of her head with a savage blow from her tenpin. Phoebe felt queasy as she heard the distinct crack of the parietal bone. Pie Face dropped on rubber knees and sprawled motionless on the pavement, her riven skull spilling brains and blood.

Wally collapsed on the pavement, bleeding profusely.

"No," cried Phoebe, and rushed over to him, her eyes tearing. She knelt beside him.

"I'm not feeling so good," he said, lying on his back. "You didn't save me this time," he said, cracking a smile as he groaned.

"I tried."

"I'm not blaming you. It's my fault I don't have eyes in the back of my head."

Phoebe laughed in spite of herself, tears streaking her face.

She dreaded the thought that she would have to split his skull to prevent him from turning.

"I'm seen enough of the world," he said. "Don't waste any tears over me. I wasn't gonna last much longer anyway."

Bud came up, blood-soaked chain saw in hand.

"Jesus," he said, his face wan, staring down at Wally.

"No way," said Wally. "I'm not even a saint."

"You're a good fighter, old man."

"Nah. I prefer saving people to killing . . . ," said Wally, his voice trailing off.

Phoebe realized he wasn't going to live much longer.

"I'm gonna miss your wisecracks," said Bud.

"Like missing boils on your ass," scoffed Wally, and snorted a laugh.

"I know we had our differences—"

Before Bud could finish his sentence he saw Wally's eyes roll up in his head.

Weeping, Phoebe rose to her feet.

"Cut his brain in half," she said.

"What?" said Bud, dumbfounded.

"You have to do it or he'll reanimate," said Phoebe, her face gaunt.

Wally's eyes snapped open. "Are you gonna give me a lobotomy?"

He stared into space and hung his mouth open.

Her eyes popping out, Phoebe held her chest. "He scared me to death."

Bud blew out his cheeks. "Are you sure he's dead?"

Phoebe leaned over and felt for a pulse in Wally's wrist. Nothing.

"He is now," she said.

"Is this really necessary?" said Bud.

She nodded yes.

Chapter 63

Bud triggered his chain saw and, wincing, brought the churning blade down through Wally's forehead, a half inch above the eyes.

Phoebe turned away from the grisly sight. She could hear the chain saw cleaving Wally's skull, sounding like slicing a watermelon. She wished she was dead.

"I don't see any more of those maniacs around here," said Crystal with a blood-streaked tenpin in her hand as she walked up to Phoebe. "What's wrong?"

At that moment, Crystal picked up on the chain saw slicing through Wally's face.

"What the hell are you doing?" she said, retching.

"She told me to," said Bud, blood spurting from the chain saw cutting through Wally's skull and spattering the front of his shirt as he leaned close to Wally.

Crystal brought her hand down her face.

"Not Wally," she muttered.

"He got bit," said Phoebe, downcast. "The virus infected him. We don't want him to reanimate."

Geiger approached. "They got Wally, I see. Maybe he's the lucky one."

"How can you call him lucky?" said Crystal.

"He's out of this hellhole. He can't spread the virus called life."

"*You're* the one who should've died."

"How do you figure?" said Geiger, nettled.

"According to Herman, the guy who hates life is one of the first to die in a *Saw* movie."

"Are you still harping on that stupid movie?"

"He was right about you. Jigsaw would've tortured you to death."

211

"The kid was out of it. This ain't a movie. And I don't hate life. I'm just telling it like it is. It's a virus that spreads all over and can't be stopped."

"You don't sound like someone who likes living."

"What difference does it make? Whether you like living or not, you're still gonna die. A horror screenwriter isn't deciding your fate."

Crystal eyeballed Geiger's tenpin. "Why isn't your tenpin bloody? Didn't you kill any maniacs?"

"Are we keeping score?"

"Maybe you're chicken."

Bud killed the chain saw after carving Wally's brain.

"I'm hungry," said Geiger. "Let's get something to eat."

"We need to get out of here before the choppers come," said Phoebe. "They'll torch every stiff."

"I didn't see you kill a single maniac," Crystal told Geiger.

"You guys took care of them without me," he said. "What do you want me to do? Kill them twice?"

"That's a good idea," said Phoebe. "They're gonna turn if their brains weren't destroyed."

"Go smash heads, Geiger," said Crystal.

"We don't have time," said Phoebe.

"Can we at least grab a pizza at that pizzeria next to the laundromat," said Crystal, pointing.

"My stomach's growling," said Bud. "Let's do it. I need food in my belly. Slicing and dicing homicidal maniacs burns a lot of energy."

Phoebe looked up at the sky. She didn't see any choppers heading this way yet.

"We need energy," said Geiger. "We gotta eat."

"All right," said Phoebe. "But we have to hurry."

They ran to the pizzeria tucked between the laundromat and a Super Cuts.

When they burst into the restaurant, the middle-aged owner with a receding hairline, who was standing behind the counter wearing an apron, took one look at them and fled. Screaming, his two teenage coworkers clad in jeans and white button-down shirts hightailed it after him.

"What's their problem?" said Bud, his blood-soaked, brain-smeared chain saw in hand.

"I don't blame them," said Geiger. "Look at you guys. You look like you just stepped out of a slaughterhouse."

"We look better than you," said Crystal. "You look like a chicken."

"How are we supposed to order pizzas?" said Bud, and knocked on the counter with his fist three times in frustration. "Can we have some service here? We're hungry as hell."

Chapter 64

"Do you smell smoke?" said Bud, sniffing the air.

He exited the pizzeria and peered at the sky.

Phoebe followed him. She could see smoke drifting toward the strip mall from the direction of the bowling alley. Two choppers were hovering over the building, which had a column of smoke issuing from it.

"No," said Bud, taking in the devastating scene, heartbroken.

"At least you're not inside," said Phoebe, knowing it was cold comfort, but it was the best she could do.

"My life is over," he said, dropping his chain saw. "I put my entire life savings into that alley. It's all I got. I'm ruined. The bastards."

Phoebe knew that when the choppers finished burning the bowling alley and the immediate neighborhood, they would head to the strip mall and torch it to eradicate the infected residents, since it was clear from the scores of mutilated corpses sprawled on the parking lot that the virus had spread in this direction.

"You can open a new alley somewhere else," she said.

"With what? I don't have any money. All my money was tied up in the alley. Nothing's gonna be left but ash."

"You're still alive," said Crystal, emerging from the pizzeria. "Be thankful for that."

"I'm still alive, but my life is destroyed without my business to keep me going. Those cops are so evil, they deserve to die." Bud shook his fist at the choppers, not knowing if they could see him. "I'm gonna kill them."

"You don't want to draw their attention," said Phoebe. "The last thing we want is for them to come here."

"I don't care if they come here. I got nothing to live for. Without my business, I got nothing."

"As long as they're preoccupied elsewhere, we can make our escape. Come on."

His face determined, Bud picked up his chain saw and headed toward his burning bowling alley.

"I'm gonna go to my alley and fight those evil bastards," he said.

Phoebe grabbed his arm and stopped him. "You haven't got a chance. They got napalm. They'll burn you alive."

"I gotta defend myself. When they burn my property, they burn me at the same time. I'm not letting them get away with it."

"How can we fight them without guns? You can't fight choppers with a chain saw."

Bud shook his arm free and stood gaping at the conflagration, watching his livelihood go up in smoke.

"They're taking the food out of my mouth," he said. "I can't make a living."

"When this is over, the whole city will be a shambles," said Geiger, taking in the choppers as they sprayed napalm on the bowling alley and its neighborhood."

"They're killing me," cried Bud, his anger welling inside him and choking him.

"We can't do anything now," said Phoebe. "We'll get them another time."

"When my alley's nothing but ashes?" said Bud, standing and staring into space like he'd just been clobbered on the back of his head with a sledgehammer.

"She's right, dude," said Crystal. "You got no chance if you go back there now. Those cops are blowing away everybody—infected and noninfected."

"You have no idea what it's like to lose your livelihood. It took all of my life to make my business a growing concern. And they're taking it away in the blink of an eye."

"You have no idea what it's like to be a cartel sex slave for five years. What livelihood? I didn't even have a life, let alone a livelihood. I was a slab of meat filthy animals passed around."

Bud looked at her, feeling her pain. "What kept you going?"

"I made believe I was somewhere else. And I swore I'd get back at them some day."

"But not now," said Phoebe. "We're outgunned. We got no chance against killer copters."

Bud clutched his forehead in anguish. "What am I gonna do?"

"You think you got it bad?" said Geiger. "I was locked in my pint-sized crib for two years because of Covid and because I couldn't get a job. I'm uniquely untalented at anything."

"What brought you out?" said Crystal.

"It got worse. I was lonely being locked up by myself for so long, so I went onto one of those dating websites and met a girl named Celeste. She was a tall blonde with blue eyes. She said she used to be a model. She came over to my place regularly and kept borrowing money. I had barely enough for myself, but I kept dipping into my savings account to help her."

"Why?"

"I know it sounds stupid, but I felt sorry for her. She said she lost her job because of Covid and was being evicted from her apartment. She didn't even have a bank account. She promised she would pay me back because she was inheriting a lot of money from her rich uncle. I had to sell my car so I could lend her more money to pay for her probate lawyers. I maxed out my credit cards. The bottom line is I went bankrupt. I filed for Chapter 7.

"I locked her out of my apartment and stopped talking to her. I found out she had given me a fake name and a fake address. It turned out she was working for a ring of professional crooks that included her sister who I paid most of the money to with Venmo. Her sister had a bank account because she was using her real name. Not like Celeste. The 'sister' might not even have been her sister. Who knows with all her lies—?"

"Does this story ever end?" cut in Bud.

"The bankruptcy trustee wanted to sue Celeste for all the money she borrowed from me, but the trustee lawyer couldn't locate her and her sister. He couldn't serve them with a suit. And I'm left with nothing. I can't even move to a cheaper apartment, because landlords won't rent to anyone who declares bankruptcy."

"If you're trying to cheer me up, it's not working," said Bud. "I still feel like shit."

"I'm also paranoid. I feel like people are out to get me and take what little money I have left. Celeste might send a hit man after me to force me to drop the lawsuit, even though I'm not the one suing her and I have no control over it."

"Your pep talk is falling flat on its face."

"Talk about revenge, I want revenge. If she really inherited all that money—over two million bucks—she could be anywhere in the world. I have no way of finding her to sue her for fraud, since she gave me a phony name."

"I thought you said you were a trucker and a reverend," said Bud.

"I've done just about everything that doesn't take any talent or skill."

"Either that or you're a bullshit artist."

"Talk about bullshit. At least I don't wax bowling balls for a living," retorted Geiger.

Sneering at Geiger, Bud triggered his chain saw. "I got nothing to lose by carving you up like a turkey."

"Killing each other isn't gonna help matters," said Phoebe, trying to get them to cool off.

"He started it," said Geiger.

"You're killing the chain saw battery, Bud."

Bud pulled a face and turned off the chain saw.

"We can't wallow in the past," said Phoebe. "First, we need someplace to hide. We can't stay here. They'll torch the strip mall when they see all the bodies strewn on the parking lot."

"Is there any place free of the infected?" said Crystal.

Bud let out a strangled groan, realizing he was powerless to do anything to defend his flame-engulfed property.

"What happened to those guys with the machine gun who were holding off the choppers?" said Geiger.

"They must've left," said Phoebe.

"Too bad they didn't take out those two choppers before leaving."

"Yeah," said Crystal.

"The choppers were staying out of their range," said Phoebe.

"How do we know?" said Crystal. "Maybe the choppers killed them. They're killing everybody else."

"We can't stand around here and wait for the machine gunners in the pickup to help us. Either they left or the choppers killed them. We have to figure we're on our own."

Chapter 65

Dressed in surgeon's green scrubs, his visage eager, Dr. Raspail found Zandorf in one of the hospital corridors.

"Come with me," said Raspail. "Quickly."

"What's this about?" said Zandorf.

"The mayor, Jason Albright."

"What about him?"

"He's conscious."

Zandorf widened his eyes with excitement. "I need to talk to him. He could shed light on the outbreak of this virus."

They hurried down the hallway to Jason's hospital room and flung open the door.

Jason was lying on his back in his bed, groaning, his eyes open, the respirator tube gone from his mouth.

"The worms," he said, screwing up his face. "Make them stop. They're chewing through my brain."

"Didn't you do a CAT scan of his brain?" Zandorf asked Raspail.

"I did."

"You didn't say anything about worms."

"The CAT scan didn't show any worms. I don't know what he's talking about."

"The worms are eating my brain," cried Jason, rolling his eyes. "I can't take it anymore. You can't believe the pain I'm in."

"Look at me," said Zandorf. "We did a CT scan of your brain. There are no worms in your brain."

Jason trembled in pain. "They're burrowing deeper into my brain. It's unbearable."

"When did you do the CT scan?" Zandorf asked Raspail.

"Only this morning," Raspail answered.

"How could worms appear in his brain in the short time since then?"

"They couldn't."

Zandorf turned to Jason. "You must be imagining them. There are no worms in your brain."

"If he *does* have worms, he must be infected with the virus," said Raspail.

"If he had worms, our equipment would detect them. Maybe hallucinating is part of his coma. When the brain has no input for a long time, it hallucinates."

"I'm infected," moaned Jason.

"Why do you think you're infected?" said Zandorf.

"Because the worms are in my brain. I was with Val on the Strip. She must have infected me."

"Do you know who this Val is?" Raspail asked Zandorf.

"She was an infected hooker. Do another CAT scan of his brain. We have to be sure he isn't infected."

"There's no way the worms could show up in just a few hours. He's been here in bed for the entire day. How could he have become infected lying in bed by himself in his room?"

"I think he's hallucinating about the worms. But let's double-check just to make sure."

"If he's infected, shouldn't we quarantine him?"

"I don't believe there are parasitic worms generated by the virus in his brain. If your CAT scan picks up the worms, then we quarantine him."

"I'll do it now."

"I can hear them nibbling on my brain tissue," said Jason in horror. He pulled on Zandorf's sleeve. "Can't you give me painkillers?"

"Give him some Vicotin after you do the CAT scan," Zandorf told Raspail.

"Can you hear them?" said Jason, terrified, hanging his mouth open. "They're making so much noise. It's deafening."

"I can't hear anything," said Zandorf. "What do they sound like?"

"They—they sound like—hmm—beavers gnawing wood."

Jason contorted his face with agony.

"You're coming out of a coma," said Zandorf. "You're hallucinating. That's all."

Screaming, Jason jerked his head back and forth.

"If you can't make them stop, give me cyanide," he said.

Raspail exchanged looks with Zandorf.

"Out of the question," said Zandorf.

"You have no idea how much pain I'm in," said Jason. "I want to die."

"No, you don't," said Zandorf. "That's your hallucination talking."

Jason writhed in bed, his face sweaty, his eyes glassy.

Raspail summoned two orderlies with a gurney to transport Jason out of the hospital room toward the CAT scan room. They lifted him out of bed onto the gurney.

"It's cruel and unusual punishment to make me go on living in so much pain," said Jason. "The worms. The worms are burrowing into my brain." He pointed at his eye. "They're gonna crawl out my eyes."

"Pull yourself together," said Zandorf. "There aren't any worms. It's all in your mind."

"They *are* in my mind. They are. That's the problem. Give me a knife so I can cut them out."

Zandorf shook his head. "You're burning up with fever and raving."

When the orderlies tried to wheel Jason out of the room, he grabbed the doorjamb and stopped the gurney.

Zandorf pried Jason's hand off the doorjamb. "After we're done, we'll show you the CAT scan results to prove to you there are no worms in your brain. Satisfied?"

"It won't do any good. I know they're there. I feel nothing but pain," said Jason, his eyes bulging in fear.

The orderlies wheeled Jason into the busy corridor.

"I can't believe he came out of his coma," said Raspail.

"Maybe it would have been better for him if he never had," said Zandorf.

Chapter 66

Strus and Chief Coffin bustled into Jason's hospital room, startling Zandorf and Raspail.

"I've been looking for you," said Strus. He glanced at Jason's empty bed. "Where's the mayor? Don't tell me he . . ."

"He regained consciousness," said Zandorf.

"Can he resume his duties?" said Strus, agog.

"I don't think that would be a good idea at this time," said Raspail.

"Where is he?"

"Getting a CAT scan."

"What do you want to see us about?" said Zandorf.

"We've had several more outbreaks of the virus," said Strus.

"Let's cut to the chase," said Coffin. "We're losing control of the city. Not only do we have new outbreaks, riots are racking the city."

"Who's rioting?" said Zandorf.

"People opposed to the lockdown. We don't have anywhere near enough manpower to handle the crisis." Coffin's normally pink face reddened in anger. "Rioters are shooting down our choppers. We need help."

"The president hasn't empowered me to authorize enforcement help," said Zandorf. "I'm only authorized to handle the virus outbreak."

"We're stretched too thin to deal with the virus. The infected are rampaging through the streets and attacking everybody."

"Is there no respite from this endless drumbeat of bad news?" said Strus in frustration.

"I can't change the facts," said Coffin. "The city's in its death throes if things continue the way they are now. I need more officers."

"I thought we wiped out the virus when the Strip burned down."

"I had hoped so," said Zandorf. "Some of the infected on the Strip must've escaped the fire and are spreading the virus throughout the city. Has anyone found Phoebe Albright yet?"

"No," said Strus.

"We have a BOLO out for her, but no sign of her yet," said Coffin.

"I must talk to her," said Zandorf. "She might have answers to the virus."

"Is she a doctor?"

"No. I want to understand why she hasn't been infected even though she was on the Strip at the time of the outbreak."

"Maybe we can't find her because she's dead."

"Possible. But I hope you're wrong."

"I'm not exaggerating," said Coffin. "I need help to manage these riots."

"I thought the governor was gonna send us the National Guard," said Strus.

"Where are they?"

"I'll have to call him to find out."

The orderlies wheeled Jason's gurney back into the hospital room and lifted him onto his bed. The taller of the two, who was skinny and wore wire-rim glasses straddling his prominent nose, handed a manila folder to Zandorf.

Zandorf inspected the X-rays.

"Now do you believe me?" Jason asked Zandorf from his bed.

"The CAT scan says there are no worms in your brain," said Zandorf, continuing to study the X-rays.

"What are you talking about?" said Jason, stunned. "They're eating me alive. I can feel them right now chewing on my brain tissue."

Zandorf looked at Jason. "There's nothing there. Now I need to ask you questions."

"First, give me something to stop the worms from digging through my brain," said Jason, his nerves frayed.

"There are no worms. You're imagining them."

"I'm not imagining them," said Jason, writhing in bed in agony.

"Where did you first meet Val Lewton?"

"Who?"

"The hooker Val Lewton. You said earlier that you met her on the Strip and you thought she infected you with the virus."

"I never heard of anyone named Val Lewton, especially not a hooker."

"The mayor doesn't know any hookers," said Strus. "He's a happily married man."

"Then why did you say earlier that you met her at the Strip?" said Zandorf.

"I don't recall saying any such thing," said Jason. "I must've been delirious."

"This is important," said Zandorf, raising his voice. "I need to know when you first met her. We have reason to believe she is patient zero for the virus."

"I never met her."

"Why did she keep saying your name when we were examining her?"

"I dunno. I'm a famous person. When you're famous, you get a lot of attention. Maybe she saw me on TV. Women fantasize about me all the time. They want to go to bed with me."

Zandorf shook his head. "You're not leveling with us."

"You're not leveling with me. You keep saying there aren't any worms in my brain, but I can feel them tearing my brain apart," said Jason, and screamed, his face contorted with pain.

"Can't you give him some painkillers?" said Coffin.

"There's nothing wrong with his brain," said Zandorf. "There are no worms in it."

"Then why's he screaming?"

"He's hallucinating. His mind is unstable from being out of use for so long in his coma. Now it's overreacting to stimuli."

"The worms are eating holes in my brain," said Jason, wincing.

"Do you think he's well enough to return to his position as mayor?" said Strus.

"No," said Zandorf. "He keeps slipping in and out of delirium."

"What's all this talk about worms? Is he infected?"

Zandorf rechecked Jason's CAT scan X-rays. "There's no sign of infection in his brain. But in his condition, I don't believe he can make rational decisions. I'm afraid you're stuck with his miserable job for the time being."

"Is there any way the president can send us more FBI agents?" said Coffin. "The rioters are gonna take over the city if we aren't careful. We need bodies. We also need more choppers."

"I could ask him, but he might well reach a different conclusion."

"Like what?"

Zandorf paused for effect. "He might decide to abandon the city."

"Abandon us?" said Strus, not sure he had heard Zandorf correctly.

"In the interests of the safety of the country."

"He's gonna leave our city to anarchy?"

"We must stop the virus dead in its tracks here. Nothing else is acceptable."

"What if we can't?"

"There is no alternative. We must stop the virus here."

Chapter 67

Hardy watched Phoebe and her gang escape from the bowling alley and followed them, ducking behind parked cars so none of the gang would spot him.

Clad in jeans and a black AC/DC T, a twentysomething guy with a high fade and three days' growth lay on his back with part of his shoulder bitten off, blood pouring from the wound.

"Help me," he said, reaching toward Hardy with his good arm.

Hardy withdrew his Beretta 92 Compact from his jacket pocket, screwed a sound suppressor from another pocket onto the muzzle, and shot the guy in the head.

He had seen infected maniacs in action at the Strip and wasn't taking any chances. He wasn't going to let anyone get in the way of his capturing Phoebe and taking her to his client Jackson Albright.

Hardy took cover behind a yellow Mustang when he picked up on Phoebe looking in his direction. He didn't want her to see him. She would recognize him and book. After all, this wasn't his first attempt at kidnaping her. This time would be different. This time she wouldn't get away.

He scoped out her friends, or whoever those guys were with her. The guy with the chain saw might be trouble. Though a chain saw versus a Beretta was a blowout for him as long as he got the drop on the guy from a distance, Hardy decided.

Hardy couldn't stay here in the blood-drenched corpse-strewn parking lot. None of them could, including Phoebe. It was only a matter of time before the choppers moved in and shot and torched everyone in the strip mall. Phoebe knew this as well as he did.

Hardy wanted to catch her by surprise, allowing her no time to flee. He would rather whack her than kidnap her after she had almost killed him in a car accident, but Jackson was paying good money for him to bring her in alive. Maybe the guy would let him waste her after he had finished talking to her and had no further use for her.

The city was in such a mess it was interfering with Hardy's plans. It wasn't just the killer choppers and the infected maniacs. It was also the rioters protesting the lockdowns. You had to be on your guard 24/7 in apocalypse city.

It used to be a nice place to live. Not anymore. But people couldn't move out thanks to the lockdowns. The politicians were wrecking the city, but they refused let anyone move. It was like they had a death wish for every resident.

After he delivered Phoebe to Jackson, Hardy decided he was going to put down stakes elsewhere.

Chapter 68

"Time to make the stinking politicians pay for their lies," said Rigo, cradling the M2 in his arms as he stood on the F-150 flatbed.

"I can't hear you," cried Tex out the open window as he drove the pickup. "There's too much wind rushing by my ear."

Rigo checked the sky to make sure none of the choppers had followed the pickup. The choppers were busy napalming the bowling alley and other buildings in the area. Rigo could see the grey smoke pluming from the alley.

"They're burning the bowling alley," he said. "They're not gonna follow us."

"They don't want to mess with Ma Deuce," said Tex, grinning.

"Let's go to my house."

Tex nodded, his hands on the wheel. "I thought we were going to city hall."

"First, my house."

They arrived at Rigo's place ten minutes later. It was a Spanish-style bungalow with red roof tiles and cream-colored stucco walls with black grilled windows. Agaves surrounded by redwood chips lined the front of the bungalow under the picture window.

Tex parked in the pebble drive and killed the pickup engine.

Rigo gazed into the skies, checking for signs of choppers. Seeing none he set down the M2 on the flatbed and hopped onto the white pebbles. He circled to the driver's-side window.

"Where's the RPG?" said Tex, sticking his elbow out the window.

"Be right back."

Rigo strode to the garage and lifted open the accordion door. He entered the garage and sidled past the pickup parked in it. When he returned to the entrance he carried an RPG-7 and two rockets in his hands. Together the three were a lot lighter than the M2.

"All *right*," said Tex, smiling as he saw the weapon.

"Time to pay a visit to city hall and the stinking, lying politicians that are wrecking our city."

"Let's send them a message they won't forget."

Rigo loaded the RPG-7 and its rockets into the flatbed then climbed in after them. He pounded the roof of the cab with his fist twice to signal Tex to go.

Tex fired the engine, backed out the drive, and made for city hall.

"We need to let them know we're not happy with their lousy rule," said Rigo, feeling the wind blowing through his hair.

"They're a bunch of congenital liars," said Tex through his open window. "They could care less about our city. All they care about is holding onto their power."

"They're liars and crooks. It's time for someone to tell them we've had enough," said Rigo, eying the RPG-7 that lay on the flatbed.

"The biggest liars get the most power and the most rewards. If I'm lying, I'm dying."

"I got customers for my extermination business who live out of town. How am I supposed to fumigate their houses if the cops are blocking the only road out? My clients are gonna hire someone else to do the job. I got a wife and three kids to support. Are the cops gonna pay my bills?"

"That'll be the day."

"In the end, we gotta stand up for ourselves. We can't count on the government's help."

"The only thing the government's good at is taxing us to death. We need to fight back."

"We're gonna have the element of surprise on our side when we launch our attack."

"They'd never expect us to take the battle to them. And the cops are spread so thin they won't have anybody guarding city hall. They're too busy blocking roads and shooting folks out of choppers."

"Do they really think they can kill us without our putting up a fight?" Rigo screamed into the wind rushing by his face in the back of the pickup. "They're crazy."

He heard a metallic noise and looked down at his feet. He saw empty Coors beer cans rolling around the flatbed.

"Where's my Coors?" he said.

"All out," said Tex, holding up an empty hand in a conciliatory gesture. "I'll treat us to a couple of sixpacks when we're done with city hall."

"With the roads blocked we're gonna run out of beer."

"Another reason to blame our rotten politicians."

Chapter 69

At city hall, sitting behind his desk in the mayor's office, Strus was using a satphone to contact Governor Vitti. The satphone lay on the edge of the desk two-odd feet from the window broken by Jason before his fall. The extended antenna reached outside the building and transmitted to the satellite overhead.

"Our city is being racked by riots in opposition to the lockdown," said Strus on speakerphone.

"That's why you have a police force," said Vitti.

"The police chief tells me his men are stretched too thin."

Coffin was standing in front of the desk, his attention riveted on Strus.

"Why are you telling me?" said Vitti. "My office is besieged with requests from the rest of the state 24/7."

"Our police need help."

"I already sent you all of the CHP officers I can spare."

Coffin mouthed the words *National Guard* at Strus.

"Can you send us the National Guard?" said Strus.

"What is the problem?"

"Not only do we have riots, we have more outbreaks of the virus. It's turning people into berserk cannibals."

"I thought you had the virus under control."

"Those vaccines you sent us didn't help," said Strus, smoldering.

"I'm not responsible for those."

"Every single patient who received that vaccine died from fentanyl poisoning."

Silence on the line.

"Bates signed off on that deal with Cobygenex," said Vitti at last. "Don't blame that fiasco on me."

"The point is, we need more police to keep the peace. Otherwise, we're gonna have anarchy and chaos."

"Calling out the National Guard is gonna draw national media attention. There's no way I can hide it from the media. They *will* find out. You need to take care of your problems without the guard."

"How are we supposed to keep the peace without enough personnel?" blurted Coffin.

"Who is that?" said Vitti.

"Our police chief," said Strus.

"Chief, if you don't know how to do your job, you'll be out of a job."

"Then the city will collapse in chaos," said Coffin.

Strus shushed Coffin, who was hopping mad.

"Don't you have any sympathy for your fellow Californians in distress, Governor?" said Strus, trying to strike a more agreeable tone, despite his anger at Vitti seething inside him.

"You're not the only city in this great state."

"If townsfolk escape the roadblocks here, the virus could spread to the rest of the state."

Vitti held his peace for a few moments.

"Your job is to make sure your city is locked down to prevent the spread of the virus," he said. "Can't you handle your job?"

"Not without help for our police. Riots and virus outbreaks are tearing the city apart."

"Deputize your citizens."

"Are you talking vigilantes?"

"*Volunteers*. You heard me."

"Nobody's gonna volunteer," said Coffin. "They're all against the lockdown. Even my own men are. We're shooting fellow citizens at the roadblocks, and they're firing back at us. They shot one of our choppers out of the sky, killing everybody on board."

"We can't let news of your situation spread," said Vitti. "You must contain the virus. Otherwise, panic will spread throughout the state. California will become a basket case, disrupted by violence and riots."

"If you want us to contain it, send us the National Guard," said Strus.

"Haven't you heard a word I've said?" said Vitti, raising his voice with irritation and impatience, his voice shrieking like a buzz saw in Strus's ears. "I'm not gonna repeat myself."

"My city needs help. You're the only one I can ask for it."

"Why are you still talking?"

"At least send us more CHP officers," said Coffin.

"Impossible."

Strus drank from a Styrofoam coffee cup on his desk.

"The city is a basket case, Governor," he said.

The building rocked with an explosion.

Strus grabbed his desk for support as the floor rolled.

"Quake?" he said, apprehensive.

"I heard an explosion," said Coffin, wide-eyed. "We're under attack. Get under your desk."

"What is it?" said Vitti. "What's happening?"

"We're being attacked," said Strus, crawling under his desk, his pulse racing.

"What?" cried Vitti.

Another explosion rent the air. The building shook again, spilling Strus's cup of coffee.

Coffin bolted out of the mayor's office to check out the source of the noise.

Chapter 70

Coffin barged into the hallway and looked for signs of damage. He didn't see any.

Thirty feet down the hall he picked up on a suit and a middle-aged woman in a pale green dress running out of an office on the opposite side of the hallway, their eyes bulging. Wincing, the woman was holding her arm.

"What happened?" said Coffin, pelting toward them.

"We were sitting in our office when out of nowhere the wall explodes," said the suit, shaken.

He brushed plaster dust off his jacket sleeve.

Coffin entered the office and set eyes on a gaping hole in the wall in the front of the building, with masonry, broken furniture, and other debris strewn on the floor. Twisted rebar stuck out of the front of the building at floor level. The hole was almost as big as the wall, and through it Coffin could see the street that skirted the building's frontage.

He picked his way through the debris on the floor and reached the hole. Outside he saw a pickup parked alongside the curb with a man standing in the flatbed with a weapon in his hand. On closer inspection Coffin realized the weapon was an RPG-7. The shooter was wearing a baseball cap low on his forehead. He was staring at the damage to the building. Coffin couldn't make out his face because of the cap's bill.

The pickup peeled away from the curb, almost knocking the shooter off his feet, and sped away from city hall.

A thirtyish uniformed cop darted into the office from the hallway.

"What happened, sir?"

"The shooter launched an RPG-7 at us," said Coffin, wheeling around to answer the officer. "He's in a late-model silver Ford pickup bearing south on Main Street. He's wearing jeans and a blue baseball cap."

"Got it," said the uniform.

"Is anyone hurt?" Coffin asked, looking around the damaged office.

The office worker in the green dress appeared at the door.

"A piece of debris hit my arm in the blast," she said, grimacing. "I think it's broken."

"Call EMTs," said Coffin.

"Yes, sir," said the uniform, activating the radio on his shoulder.

"And put out a BOLO for that silver pickup with a shooter in the flatbed. Treat him as armed and dangerous."

"On it, sir. But all of our men are dealing with riots and infected and enforcing the lockdown."

"Damn it. We can't let that shooter escape. This is an active investigation."

"Yes, sir."

"Did both grenades hit here?" Coffin asked the woman.

"What?" she said. "My ears are ringing. I'm having trouble hearing."

"There were two explosions," said Coffin, raising his voice. "Did both grenades hit your office?"

"The wall blew up only once," she said, nursing her injured arm.

"We got hit twice," Coffin told the uniform. "Where did the other grenade hit?"

The uniform ducked out of the office and cast around the corridor for signs of damage as he radioed Coffin's instructions to capture the shooter.

Coffin followed him. His ears were ringing too, he realized.

He would be willing to bet the second blast had been in this area as well.

"Down the hall," he said, pointing. "There's smoke coming from that office."

Smoke seeped under the office door in question and filled the corridor.

The uniform sprinted to the door and flung it open, releasing additional smoke that billowed into the corridor, propelled by the wind gusting through a massive hole in the office wall. Two motionless, bloody female office workers sprawled on the floor among bomb debris.

Coffin appeared in the doorway and scoped out the blast area, which looked similar to the previous bomb-damaged office, except there was a fire burning here. He strode to the bodies, knelt down, and checked them for signs of life. One of the women had a pulse, though faint. The other wasn't so lucky.

"We need those EMTs," he said, pulling the injured woman from the debris that covered her. "And the fire department."

The uniform radioed the fire department.

Coffin heard the floor creaking. He wondered how stable it was after the damage inflicted by the blast.

"Help me with her," he said.

The uniform complied.

Coughing on the smoke, the two of them lifted the injured, unconscious woman to her feet and hauled her into the corridor.

"Why would anyone blow up city hall?" asked the uniform. "Were they terrorists?"

"Must be."

"Which group?"

"Maybe they'll announce it on social media. They're always eager to lay claim to their terrorist acts."

"Bastards."

"It might not be terrorists. The mood of the people is ugly. They're incensed by the lockdown. They're venting their wrath on the government and us."

"We're just doing our jobs."

"They're gonna continue to retaliate, the way I see it, unless we open the city."

"There are fires burning out of control too. My brother's a firefighter. He says the fire department is like us. They don't have enough manpower to put out the flames."

"I'd bet dollars to doughnuts rioters are setting some of those fires."

Through the haze of the smoke, propping up the unconscious woman with the aid of the uniform, Coffin picked up on two EMTs pushing an empty gurney down the hallway toward him, their expressions earnest.

"Over here," he yelled, beckoning to them, his eyes smarting from the smoke.

His lungs were scorching. He needed fresh air.

Chapter 71

Phoebe and the rest of her group cut across the strip-mall parking lot and saw a donut shop facing them.

"Let's get donuts," said Crystal. "I'm starving."

"I'm hungry too," said Phoebe, "but we don't have time to take a break and eat donuts. When the choppers are done burning the bowling alley, they're gonna come after us. They saw us run here. We don't want to get trapped in the donut shop."

"We gotta eat. I got a headache because I haven't eaten anything in so long. If we don't eat, we'll become sick."

"I don't see anybody in there," said Bud, gazing through the shop's picture window.

"Good," said Geiger. "They won't run away from us when we enter their shop."

"The owners might've been killed by the infected maniacs," said Phoebe.

"Then they won't mind if we eat their donuts," said Bud, angling for the donut shop.

Phoebe followed him. She knew Crystal was right when she said they needed to eat to maintain their energy.

"We have to get a move on it," said Phoebe. "The chopper cops will fly here after they finish incinerating the bowling alley, and they will shoot us like they shot everybody else."

Bud swung open the door to the donut shop. He triggered his chain saw to scare away anybody who might be in a backroom. A white-haired middle-aged woman sprang out of the door behind the counter. Frothing at the mouth, growling, she charged him. He swiped his chain saw at her, slicing her head in half. Blood splattered the top of the glass counter as half her skull and brain thudded against the glass. Her body collapsed on the linoleum floor and painted the yellow tiles red.

Bud approached the doorway behind the counter and entered the backroom to make sure it was empty. He saw no one and returned to the counter, avoiding tripping on the body with half a head that sprawled at his feet.

He snagged a chocolate donut that lay on a glass shelf beneath the blood-smeared counter and devoured it in seconds. He smacked his lips.

Crystal and Geiger rushed inside after him.

"Who's she?" said Crystal, sickened by the body on the floor.

"The owner, I guess," said Bud, glancing at her. He munched a glazed donut. "Look at her mouth. She was infected."

Crystal scoped out the woman's foam-covered mouth.

She switched her attention to the varieties of donuts in the shop. She grabbed one with chocolate sprinkles on it and scarfed it down.

Tenpin in hand, bringing up the rear, Phoebe made sure no infected maniacs were following them before she entered the donut shop. She savored the aroma of sweet donuts that suffused the air in the bakery. She grabbed a cinnamon cruller and demolished half of it with one gulp. It tasted delicious. She snagged a donut with pink frosting and bolted it.

Preoccupied with her selection of donuts, she didn't keep watch of the rest of the strip mall.

Gripping his Beretta, hunching down, Hardy belted across the parking lot toward the donut shop and took cover behind a white EV SUV that had a Greenpeace bumper sticker on it.

"Like kids in a candy shop," said Geiger, inspecting a tray of jelly donuts.

"Anything's better than the gloom and doom that's outside," said Bud, glancing through the window at the corpse-strewn parking lot. "It's bad for your health to be bummed out all the time. A decent meal can do wonders for your well-being."

"It's the little things in life that I live for," said Crystal, holding up a chocolate éclair and taking a bite of it.

By this time, Hardy had made his way to the bakery's front door and flung it open, gun in hand.

"Who are you?" said Bud. "The owner? We'll pay. Don't worry about it."

"Then why'd you kill the woman lying on the floor?" said Hardy.

"She was infected with the virus. You can put that piece down."

"How do I know you won't saw my head in half too?"

"You don't look infected."

"Then drop the chain saw."

"No," said Bud, his back stiffening.

Phoebe recognized the fixer Hardy and stood petrified. She wondered if his presence had anything to do with her. She figured it did. She wondered how he had found her. Nobody knew where she was. She needed to be more careful about leaving a trail. If Hardy could find her, so could the cops.

"Have a donut," Crystal told Hardy. "We're not stingy."

Hardy sniggered. "You're not stingy with other people's goods. How generous of you."

"Then don't have a donut. I could care less."

"Yeah, leave us alone," said Bud. "Good-bye."

Hardy double-tapped Bud in the head.

Bud crumpled, a half-eaten donut in his mouth.

Chapter 72

"What'd you do that for, you bastard?" said Crystal, taken aback. "We're not infected."

"How do I know you're not lying?" said Hardy.

"Look, mister, we're sorry we broke into your store," said Geiger. "We didn't know you were the owner. We won't eat any more of your donuts."

"We'll pay for them," said Crystal. "What's the big deal? How much could they possibly cost? Are they worth killing someone for?"

"I didn't like that chain saw in his hand," said Hardy. "He should've dropped it when I said so."

"You're the one who's infected if you ask me."

"Hi, Phoebe," said Hardy, training his Beretta on Phoebe.

"You know this guy, Phoebe?" said Crystal.

"We've met," said Phoebe.

"That's a polite way of describing it," said Hardy.

"Huh?" said Crystal, not understanding.

"She tried to kill me in my car."

Phoebe shook herself out of her funk. "You were trying to kidnap me."

"Well, nothing's changed."

Phoebe didn't like the sound of that. She tried to calm her rapid heartbeat by taking a deep breath.

"I'm not going with you if that's what you mean," she said.

"It *is* what I mean."

"Are you planning on getting the reward for my arrest?"

"What reward?" said Crystal, pricking up her ears, holding a half-eaten glazed donut in front of her mouth.

"There's a reward for my capture."

"You been holding back on us?"

"It has nothing to do with you."

"What do they want you for?" said Geiger.

"I was at the outbreak of the virus on the Strip. I think it has something to do with that."

"So you didn't kill someone or commit a crime?"

"No."

"You attempted to kill me," said Hardy.

"You were kidnaping me," said Phoebe.

"Let's go," he said, motioning to her with his Beretta.

"She doesn't want to go with you," said Crystal. "Can't you tell?"

"I don't care what she wants. She's going with me."

"Don't you understand what's going on here, buddy?" said Geiger. "There's some kind of virus that's turning people into deranged cannibals. Did you see those stiffs all over the parking lot?"

"You don't say?"

"This is serious."

"So's this piece in my hand."

"What's your problem?"

"Don't you know the law? All looters will be shot. I'm exercising my right as a law-abiding citizen to execute you."

"Hold on, man. We're not looting anything," said Geiger, dropping the jelly donut in his hand.

"Those donuts aren't yours."

"I'll go with you," said Phoebe, attempting to defuse the tension in the shop.

"There was never any question of that," said Hardy.

"Let us go with you too," said Crystal.

"She's going with me as my prisoner."

"You can't trust him," Phoebe told Crystal. "Look what he did to Bud."

Crystal cut her eyes anxiously to Bud's corpse.

"Put your hands behind your back," Hardy told Phoebe.

Phoebe scoped out the piece in Hardy's hand and obliged.

He fished out a black plastic zip tie from his trouser pocket, stood behind her, wedged his Beretta in his waistband, and fastened the zip tie around her wrists. The Beretta was back in his hand in seconds.

"You're not gonna crash me into a tree this time," he said.

He peered out the plate-glass door at the parking lot and saw no movement. He checked the sky and saw the choppers hovering over the burning bowling alley.

"Let's get going," he said, jerking on the zip tie securing Phoebe's wrists. "The helos will be here any minute."

"What are *we* supposed to do?" said Crystal.

"I suggest you beat it—unless you want to end up barbecued."

"We'll follow you."

"I'm going where you can't go."

"What's that supposed to mean?" said Geiger.

"It means I'll whack you if you follow me," said Hardy, training his Beretta on Geiger.

"Why would we even want to follow you?" said Crystal, disgusted.

"It was your idea."

"That was before I figured out you're an asshole."

Hardy burst into laughter. "I need to save ammo for the infected maniacs or you'd be dead by now, stretched out next to that chain saw and that hotshot with two bullets in his head. Thank your lucky stars." He turned to Phoebe. "Get going."

"I can't open the door with my hands behind my back," she said.

"Complain, complain."

He pushed open the bakery plate-glass door for her, and she walked out onto the sidewalk.

She heard the choppers hovering in the near distance as smoke from the burning bowling alley wafted below them.

"I parked on the side of the street," said Hardy, glancing at the choppers. "Walk faster—unless you want to get napalmed. Not a pretty way to die. Your frying skin will turn into blistering jelly. The Viet Cong found out about that the hard way from our flyboys in Nam."

Chapter 73

"Now what are we supposed to do?" said Geiger, watching Hardy and Phoebe cut across the parking lot replete with blood-smutched corpses strewn every which way.

"We need to split," said Crystal. "We can't stay here."

"Why not? At least we won't starve," said Geiger, munching on a raspberry jelly donut.

"You heard Phoebe. The choppers are gonna burn down this strip mall after they finish with the bowling alley."

"She was right about the bowling alley, wasn't she?"

"I don't know how she got mixed up with that scumbag," said Crystal, leering at Hardy as he headed into the distance with his odd bandy-legged gait.

"Where are we gonna go?" said Geiger.

"Straight out of this godforsaken town—"

"Did you forget? The road out of town is blocked."

"We're gonna have to run the roadblocks."

"First we need a car. Do you have one?"

"No."

"My car's in the bowling alley parking lot, burned to a crisp no doubt."

Crystal surveyed the cars in the strip-mall parking lot.

"Then we'll have to get another one," she said.

"Jack one?"

"Who's gonna mind? The infected maniacs could care less if we jack their wheels. They're dead meat."

Geiger nodded, his face haggard. "Their victims won't mind either."

"We don't need dickhead's help to beat it."

"What about poor Phoebe? Do you think he'll kill her?"

"If he was gonna waste her, he would've done it by now. He's taking her to somebody."

"*Then* he'll kill her."

Crystal and Geiger exchanged looks.

"Are any of us gonna get out of this alive?" said Geiger.

"I don't know about you, but I'm not gonna sit here and wait to get killed."

"The more I see of life, the more evil and rotten it looks."

Crystal dropped the tenpin she clutched. She approached Bud's chain saw that lay on the floor near his corpse and picked it up.

"There could be more of those maniacs outside," she said, and made for the door, chain saw in hand.

"Is it really this bad?"

"Yeah, it is."

"I keep hoping I'm exaggerating how awful life is. I keep finding out I'm not. It's a never-ending bummer. Life's a virus, and we're all infected."

She looked at him with a weary visage. "Not another one of your pep talks."

"I call 'em like I see 'em."

"I can see why you don't have any friends."

"Who told you that?"

"It's obvious, once you start talking."

"I became a recluse after my ex-girlfriend borrowed my life savings and never paid me back. She took me to the cleaner's. I went out on a limb for her, borrowing money to help her pay all her bills while she lopped it off. I hope I never meet anyone as greedy and as evil as her again."

"You must not know many cartel members. Consider yourself lucky."

Geiger laughed despite himself. "I may be many things, but lucky isn't one of them."

"Herman was right about you. You should've been the first to die in this horror movie, because you don't appreciate being alive."

"Correction. I don't appreciate being fucked over all the time."

"Nobody does. We all take our lumps. You gotta learn to roll with the punches. You want everything handed to you on a silver platter?"

"I just don't want to get it in the neck every minute of my life. Is that too much to ask?"

"I admit it's bad now—"

"Bad? We'd be better off getting crucified."

"It's not *that* bad. Oh, I forgot, you think you're a reverend."

"It's worse than any horror movie. It's really happening."

Geiger paused. "Maybe Herman was right about one thing."

"What's that?"

"Maybe we *are* all gonna die before this is over."

They shared the eerie silence between them for a moment.

"We need to make ourselves scarce," said Crystal.

Chapter 74

Crystal bolted out the bakery door with the chain saw. She scanned the parking lot. She didn't pick up on any of the infected maniacs. She noticed the two choppers hovering in the sky over the smoking bowling alley.

If the choppers would just stay away a little longer, she could boost a car and be gone, she decided.

She felt Geiger running up behind her.

"Check the cars to see if any of them have keys," she said, and commenced peering into the cars parked near her.

Out of the corner of her eye she saw movement the better part of thirty feet to her right. A brunette's head bobbed into view from behind a yellow Mustang. Wearing stressed jeans and a torn glossy tangerine blouse with a black halter underneath, she looked about thirty-five. She saw Crystal the same time Crystal saw her. The brunette pulled a face and drooled.

Crystal gripped the chain saw tighter in her hand.

Foaming at the mouth, the brunette bolted around the Mustang and stormed toward Crystal. Fueled by the virus that gave her superhuman speed, the brunette reached Crystal in a few minutes and growled at her.

Crystal could make out a name tag in a transparent plastic sheath pinned to the brunette's blouse that said Cindy Lou.

Crystal swiped the chain saw at her and amputated one of her hands.

Blood jetting from her arm stub, Cindy Lou hissed at Crystal.

Geiger worked his way behind Cindy Lou in order to coldcock her with his tenpin. She was too quick for him. She darted away and took a bite out of Crystal's shoulder. Crystal couldn't swipe the chain saw fast enough to defend herself. She screamed as Cindy Lou tore a hamburger-sized chunk of flesh out of her shoulder, shaking the bloody clump back and forth and growling, splattering blood everywhere.

"Run," Crystal cried at Geiger, her face knotted with pain.

"Come with me," said Geiger.

"She infected me."

Cindy Lou lunged at Crystal again. This time Crystal swiped the chain saw at Cindy Lou and decapitated her. Cindy Lou's body dropped to the asphalt, blood gushing from her severed throat. The air became heavy with the odor of blood.

"I'm gonna turn," said Crystal.

"Maybe you won't. You can't be sure. Just because Phoebe said you would doesn't necessarily mean you will. She doesn't know everything."

"I saw others turn after they got infected. You need to get out of here before the choppers come."

"Let's go to a hospital. They'll fix you up."

"The virus is in my blood. How can they fix me?"

"They're doctors. That's what they do."

Crystal moaned in pain. "There's no cure for this virus."

"You can't be sure of that. Maybe now there *is* a cure."

"There is no cure. That's why the choppers are shooting the infected. The infected have to be destroyed. You saw what the choppers did to them at the bowling alley. You know what you have to do."

"What are you talking about?"

"I don't want to turn into one of those things. You have to kill me. I don't have much time left," said Crystal, groaning.

She felt like she was at death's door. She spotted another infected maniac weaving around the cars in the parking lot, searching for prey.

"I don't want to kill you," said Geiger.

"You said life's evil, so put me out of my misery," said Crystal, gnashing her teeth in torment.

"No," said Geiger, uncertain what to do.

Crystal held out the chain saw for him. "Here. Use this. Cut off my head. It's the only way to make sure I don't come back."

"If you don't want the chain saw, I'll take it."

Geiger accepted the chain saw.

"Now use it," said Crystal, motioning with her forefinger to slash her throat.

"That would be murder," said Geiger, his face sweaty.

"Don't you understand? I don't want to turn into one of those things."

"I'm not gonna murder you."

"Then give me back the chain saw. I'll do it myself," said Crystal, reaching for the chain saw.

Geiger pulled it away from her.

"I don't want to play games with you," said Crystal. "Do it and get it over with. I feel sick. I feel worms eating into my brain," she said, her eyes popping out.

"Worms?"

"They're burrowing into my brain. It hurts so bad. Are my ears bleeding?" she said, squirming in agony.

"I don't think so."

"If you're worried about them charging you with murder, don't. Tell them the truth. I told you to kill me. I'm the murderer. They can't put me in jail without a head."

"I'm the one they'll put in jail."

"Then don't tell them anything. How will they ever know you did it? Ow. The worms. Make them stop," said Crystal, a thin stream of blood oozing out of her ear canals.

She scratched her ears, trying to make the pain stop.

"I don't know what to do," said Geiger, brushing sweat from his brow with the back of his hand.

"Put me out of my misery, you fucking phony priest," she said, trying to rouse him into action.

Enraged, Geiger triggered the chain saw. He moved the churning blade toward her neck, sweating profusely.

"Hurry," said Crystal, her eyes starting to turn white. "A maniac's coming."

Closing his eyes, wincing, Geiger cut off her head. The chainsaw blade sliced easily through her throat. Her body crumpled, blood pouring from her mutilated throat. Her head thudded on the blacktop, rolled to a stop the better part of three feet from her body, and faced him. He couldn't tell from her blank expression whether she was accusing him or thanking him.

He wheeled around to defend himself against an attacking flesh-eating maniac.

He thought it ironic he should be the last one left alive— except for Phoebe who had been captured. Like Herman and Crystal had said, he was the one who least wanted to be alive after all the misery life had handed him. Yet he wanted to live, despite the suffering he had endured. He didn't want to get infected and turn into a maniacal cannibal. He didn't want worms writhing in his brain.

If he could live a little longer, he wanted revenge against his ex-girlfriend who had defrauded him with her glib seductive tongue and voluptuous figure. Payback for her leaving him both a pauper and an emotional basket case.

As he swiped the chain saw toward the female ponytailed maniac who reached for him with a choke leash for a dog in her hand, an infected three-hundred-pound maniac wearing a shredded T over his rolls of belly fat and reeking of blood and death lunged at him from behind and tore the nape of his neck out with blood-drenched teeth.

Lying on the pavement on his back, bleeding out, Geiger watched the cloud-dappled blue sky and hoped the choppers would arrive soon and finish him off before the bloodthirsty maniacs devoured pieces of his body while he watched in agonized horror.

Chapter 75

Phoebe rode shotgun, her hands secured behind her back, while Hardy drove his rented black Honda Accord.

Hardy smelled like cedar chips, she realized. Or maybe it was the car. The odor reminded her of a mouse cage lined with cedar chips that she had when she was a child. She felt like a mouse in a cage now. She must find a way to escape.

"You left them there to die," said Phoebe, thinking of Crystal and Geiger.

"They can take care of themselves. They don't need me as their nursemaid."

"At least we could've given them a lift out of the strip mall."

"I have a job to do. It doesn't include rescuing deadbeats."

Phoebe gazed out the windshield. "Where are we going?"

"Somebody wants to see you."

"Maybe I don't want to see them."

"Are you forgetting you're my prisoner?"

"Kidnaping is illegal. You could rot in jail for a long time."

"I don't know if you've noticed, but this city is falling apart at the seams. Fires everywhere, riots breaking out all over town, not to mention the infected maniacs running amok, cannibalizing everybody in sight."

"What's your point?"

"The cops have their hands full. They don't have time to deal with kidnapers or any other kind of crime. Anarchy is open season for criminals."

"Wait till I tell my husband," she said.

"Good old Jason," said Hardy, smiling. "Haven't you heard?"

She eyed him with curiosity.

"He's in a coma," he said.

Phoebe remembered her mother telling her about Jason's coma. She didn't know how Hardy came to know of it.

"He won't be in a coma forever," she said. "When he snaps out of it, he'll take care of you."

Hardy laughed.

"What's so funny?" she said.

"What makes you think he'll come out of it?"

"He will. He's a fighter."

"It was a long way down from his office. And him without a parachute," said Hardy, grinning.

"He survived."

Phoebe didn't know the specifics of the accident.

"There are a lot of questions about his fall," said Hardy. "Haven't the cops contacted you about it?"

"No," she said, wondering if he knew the cops had issued an arrest warrant for her. Was he taking her to the cops?

She scoped out the surroundings through the windshield. They were heading toward the exclusive part of town, Phoebe realized. Not the police station. She felt more or less relieved. But her destination might be worse than the police station, depending on the identity of Hardy's client.

Hardy smiled. "Your mother says hello."

"What?" she said, not paying attention.

"You heard me."

Phoebe stared hard at him. "You don't know my mother."

"A lot you know. I met her a little while ago. We had a nice tête-à-tête about you."

She glared at him. "What are you talking about?"

"I asked her where you were. She didn't want to tell me."

"Good for her."

"No, not good for her. Give her my condolences."

Phoebe's eyes flashed with anger, her heartbeat accelerating.

Hardy smiled. "Don't worry. She's not dead. However . . ."

"However, what?" said Phoebe, hanging on his every word.

"She'll need crutches for the rest of her life or maybe a walker with fluorescent lime tennis balls on its legs." He shrugged. "Or maybe a wheelchair."

"She doesn't need crutches. She can walk fine. You're full of shit."

She was displaying anger, but deep down she felt apprehensive about her mother's health. What was Hardy talking about?

"She could walk fine till I blew out her kneecap," he said.

"What?" cried Phoebe, her face flushing with rage.

Hardy smiled at her. "She wouldn't cooperate. She's stubborn like you. It must run in the family. Let me explain. I kneecapped her. A bullet in the kneecap will shatter it."

"I'm gonna kill you."

Hardy laughed. "How are you gonna do that with your hands tied behind your back?"

"She's a defenseless old woman. Why did you have to shoot her?"

"I told you, she wouldn't tell me where you were. She refused to cooperate."

"She didn't know where I was."

"That's her problem. Do you think they'll fire her from her job if she can't walk?" said Hardy with a wink.

"What are you? Afraid of an old woman. Is that the kind of gutless wonder you are?"

"Shut up," snarled Hardy. One hand on the wheel, he whipped his Beretta out of his jacket pocket. "Or you'll join your mother on sticks for the rest of your life. I'll blow out *both* of your knees, and I'll enjoy the hell out of it. How's that?"

He trained the Beretta on her left kneecap.

Phoebe broke into a sweat.

"Your client wouldn't like it," she said, gambling it was true.

"He doesn't care if you can't walk. All he cares about is if you can talk."

"Are you sure? Nobody likes paying for damaged goods."

Hardy hit the brakes as he almost rear-ended a red Jeep Rubicon halted in front of him at the traffic light.

"Trying to get me into another accident by distracting me, I see," he said. "The rental agency wouldn't be happy."

Shooting her mother was beyond the pale, decided Phoebe. She would make him pay for it. It would have to wait, though. She would have to meet her kidnaper first. She hoped her mother was

OK. She had no way to check on her. Did she get medical help after he shot her?

"She better not be dead," said Phoebe.

"If she is, she is. *Que será, será.* I should have killed her. She can ID me. I'm getting soft in my old age. I might have to go back to her house and finish her off."

She hated the matter-of-fact way he talked about murder and shooting people. He could have been talking about playing dominoes for all the emotion he showed.

"You won't have to worry about getting old," she said. "I'll see to it that your life ends soon."

Hardy guffawed.

"You're starting to sound like me," he said with amusement. "For your information, I plan on leaving the country after this assignment. Nobody will find me. I know how to get lost and stay lost."

"If you can get out of town, you mean."

"I'll get out. I'm not gonna let stupid cop roadblocks get in my way. Nobody can stop me when I set my mind to something."

They parked in front of an expensive high-rise.

Phoebe recognized the building. She let out a gasp.

"Time to see Daddy," said Hardy.

Chapter 76

What did Jason's father want with her? Phoebe wondered as Hardy drove the Honda into an underground parking garage.

Hardy drove down to the lowest level and parked the car in an isolated corner void of vehicles.

"I never park next to another car if I can help it. It's the only way to avoid scratches in the paint," he said.

"You said it's a rental. What do you care about scratches?"

"The agency charges for scratches."

"Then get the insurance."

"It's overpriced."

They piled out of the Honda and made a beeline for the elevator.

When the elevator door opened, he stepped inside with Phoebe and pressed the button for the penthouse floor on the control panel. The door closed, and the elevator shot upward.

"Can you release my wrists?" she said.

"Not yet."

As the elevator door opened, two uniformed, beefy rent-a-cops with stern faces stood in the hallway blocking the way. Their seam-splitting burly bodies looked like they were going to burst out of their tight uniforms any second.

"I'm here to see Jackson Albright," said Hardy.

"Name and ID," said the taller guard with a high fade.

"Declan Hardy. He's expecting me," said Hardy, reaching for his wallet.

High Fade reached for his piece holstered on his waist.

"I'm getting my ID," said Hardy, bringing his hand to a halt.

"Go ahead," said High Fade, drawing his Glock 19 and training it on Hardy.

"Your boss won't be happy if you whack me."

"I don't need your lip. Only your ID."

Hardy withdrew his driver's license from his wallet and showed it to him. High Fade inspected the driver's license and handed it back to Hardy.

"Who's your companion?" said High Fade.

"Don't you recognize her?" said Hardy. "Phoebe Albright."

High Fade looked at her more closely. "Oh, yeah. The mayor's wife. Why's she tied up?"

"I needed to use persuasive measures with her." Hardy released Phoebe's wrists from the zip tie. "She won't try anything here."

Phoebe massaged her sore wrists. She didn't want to come here, but now that she was here she wondered why Jackson had hired a hit man to find her.

"Are you all right, Mrs. Albright?" said High Fade.

She said nothing.

Maybe she could talk Jackson into making Hardy let her go after their meeting, she decided.

"There's a Declan Hardy here to see you, Mr. Albright," High Fade said into his radio strapped to his shoulder.

"He's holding me hostage," Phoebe blurted.

"Mr. Albright wants to see her," said Hardy. "She didn't want to come with me."

Phoebe heard an inaudible voice crackle on the radio in response to High Fade.

"Mr. Albright will see you," said High Fade, stepping away from the elevator door to allow Phoebe and Hardy to enter the carpeted hallway, which reeked of lilac air freshener.

"I knew he would," said Hardy.

"But not yet."

Hardy looked puzzled.

"Both of you need to put on hazmat uniforms before you see Mr. Albright," said High Fade.

"I left mine in my car," said Hardy.

Tilting his head High Fade stared at him, not amused.

"We have uniforms for you," he said. "Come with me."

They entered a dressing room that had hazmat uniforms hanging in a louvered closet.

Phoebe and Hardy rummaged through the white Tyvek uniforms, found sizes that fit, and put them on.

"Is this really necessary?" said Hardy through his face mask.

"The boss insists on it. He doesn't want to catch this new virus going around," said High Fade.

The rent-a-cops ushered Phoebe and Hardy to Albright's penthouse office, buzzed them in, and remained in the hall to guard the door.

Phoebe and Hardy approached Albright's large mahogany desk in front of the floor-to-ceiling window that commanded a striking prospect of the city. Puffs of smoke drifted through the sky, mingling with the sparse clouds.

Sitting behind his desk in a bespoke navy blue suit, wearing a red, watered silk tie, Jackson studied Phoebe and Hardy with his avaricious hawk eyes like his visitors were earthworms writhing out of a hole in the mud after a recent rain.

"Well?" said Jackson, eying Phoebe.

Chapter 77

Phoebe didn't know what he was talking about.

"I don't understand why you had me brought here," she said.

"What happened to Jason?" said Jackson.

"I haven't seen him for a while. I'm not the right person to ask."

"You're his wife. Who else should I ask?"

Looking out through her hazmat face mask, having difficulty breathing in the airtight uniform, Phoebe didn't know what to say.

"How did he fall out his window?" said Jackson. "How did he end up in a coma?"

"Search me. I just found out about it from my mother."

"Are you saying you didn't push him out his office window?"

Phoebe eyed him with shock on her face. "What?"

"How could he fall out his window? It doesn't open. The cops say someone threw a chair through it to break it open."

"You think it was me?" said Phoebe, dumbfounded.

"It's no secret you two were having problems with your marriage—"

"I wasn't anywhere near him when he fell."

"Where were you?"

Phoebe hesitated, not eager to answer. "The Strip."

"The Strip? What were you doing there? You never go there."

"What difference does it make?"

"Can you prove you were there at the time of Jason's 'accident'?" said Jackson, using air quotes.

"I don't have to prove anything."

"You better think up a good answer, because the cops have a warrant for your arrest."

Was that why they wanted her? wondered Phoebe. They thought she had murdered Jason? She didn't believe it. She knew better. They wanted to kill her because she had witnessed cops murdering innocent civilians.

"I was with my friend Meredith on the Strip," she said.

"Will she testify to that?"

Phoebe's heart felt heavy as she recalled the cops murdering Meredith in cold blood on the Strip.

"She can't," she said. "She's . . . dead."

Jackson widened his eyes. "Explain."

She had to tell someone. It might as well be Jackson, she decided. The truth about the cops had to come out.

"The cops shot her," she said.

"Cops?" said Jackson in disbelief.

"They were shooting everybody on the Strip before they torched it."

Jackson's mouth hung open.

"You expect me to believe this?" he said at last.

"It's true." She pointed at Hardy. "He helped me escape. Otherwise, the cops would've killed me."

Jackson turned to Hardy. "Is this true?"

"Cops in choppers blew away infected people on the Strip then napalmed it, torching the corpses and burning the buildings to the ground."

"That's not what I heard on the news. They said an accidental fire burned the Strip."

"It was no accident," said Phoebe.

Jackson tapped his ancient, bony fingers on his desktop.

"What the hell's going on in this city?" he said, lost in thought. "It used to be a beautiful place to live. I was proud to call it home. Now I'm hearing about arson, infected maniac cannibals, murderous cops, looting, and riots. And my son. Somebody tried to kill my son."

"How do you know someone tried to kill him?" said Phoebe.

"Haven't you been listening? Somebody broke his office window and threw him out the hole onto the street. I thought it was you."

"Maybe he's the one who broke the window," said Phoebe, not really believing it, but she didn't see how it could be ruled out.

Jackson stared at her. "Are you saying he tried to commit suicide? My boy. My one and only son. He would never do such a thing. What reason would he have? I gave him everything I had. He lacked for nothing."

"I dunno. It's possible. I know I didn't do it."

"It must be one of his enemies who did it," said Jackson, cutting his eyes back and forth. "A political opponent. Maybe Vitti. He hates Jason because he's scared Jason'll run against him for governor." He focused his gaze on Phoebe. "I'm not convinced it wasn't you. You could've killed Jason and gone to the Strip afterwards. I know you two were having fights."

"I'm not gonna say this again. *It wasn't me.*"

"Vitti could have contracted a hit man, I suppose," said Jackson, thinking out loud.

"There are plenty of them around," said Hardy with a smile.

Jackson changed the subject. "Do you know it's impossible to contact anybody? The phones, the Internet, everything's down."

"Maybe it has to do with the lockdown," said Hardy.

"Why would the authorities jam all comms during a lockdown?"

Hardy shrugged. "There's a ton of shit going down outside. I know that much."

"It has to be Vitti or the feds jamming all comms. They're the only ones with the juice and the capability."

"The city's in chaos."

"The cops want me dead because I witnessed their atrocities," said Phoebe.

Jackson turned to Phoebe. "Do you really believe the cops put out an arrest warrant for you so they would have an excuse to kill you?"

Phoebe nodded yes. "I'm a witness to their crimes. They can't let me go on living."

"I'm not so sure." Jackson paused a beat. "You better not tell anyone about these cop murders you witnessed."

"Why not?" said Phoebe in surprise.

"Think of Jason's career as mayor. The people will blame him if it got around that cops are murdering people."

"He's in a coma. Isn't his career over?"

"He's not gonna be in a coma forever. He'll snap out of it. I'm sure of it."

"His office is near the top of the high-rise. It's a long way down. It would be a miracle if he survives."

"I don't believe in miracles. I do believe in the Albright stock. We're pioneer stock. We're as tough as shagbark hickory," said Albright, puffing out his chest with pride.

"I hope he does recover."

"If he survived the fall, he'll survive the coma," said Jackson, and pounded the desktop with the bottom of his fist to emphasize his words.

Chapter 78

Chief Coffin stood in Jason's hospital room looking at Jason as he lay supine on his bed.

"Who tried to kill you?" said Coffin.

"What?" said Jason, disoriented.

"Who threw you out of your office window?"

Jason's face knotted. "The worms. The worms are eating my brain. Make them stop."

A clipboard in his hand, Zandorf entered the room with an intense expression on his face.

"I don't think he's well enough to be talking to the police," he said, searching Jason's agonized face.

"Is he still hallucinating? What's with these worms he's jabbering about?"

"He must believe he's infected with the virus, even though his CAT scan says he isn't. By the way, we've given a name to the virus."

Coffin wasn't impressed. "Does that make it any less dangerous?"

"There are millions of viruses. We're calling this one Novamors."

"Sounds like something to eat, like smores."

"It means *new death* in Latin."

"Quaint."

"I've done some digging, trying to find the source of Novamors. I found out there was a biolab located on the Strip. I have reason to believe they were studying biological warfare with the intention of developing a viral weapon."

"Don't tell me they had Covid bats imported from Wuhan. Don't these people ever learn?"

"This particular biolab on the Strip was reported to the CDC last year by a whistle-blower who thought the lab was being operated unprofessionally, putting neighbors at risk of infection. The whistle-blower was fired and forgotten. But I remembered reading his report because it had to do with the Strip, where we believe the Novamors virus originated."

"Interesting. How could you do all this digging with comms out?"

"I did it before the communication blackout."

"This blackout is Vitti's work, I bet. He doesn't want anybody to know there's a killer virus in one of his cities. It would jeopardize his reelection."

"I'm convinced the CIA had the whistle-blower fired."

"The CIA? Why would the CIA be involved?"

"Because I found out the CIA owns a shell company that is funding the biolab's research."

"How did you find that out?" said Coffin with wonder.

"With research and friends in the right places, anything is possible."

"You know someone . . . ," said Coffin, nodding.

"I have a friend who works at the CIA. One hand washes the other. He helps me, I help him."

"The CIA wouldn't appreciate this intel getting out."

"What are they doing developing biological weapons? That's what I want to know."

"Aren't bioweapons banned?"

"They were banned after World War I. That hasn't stopped governments from experimenting with them. Look at Covid. A lot of well-informed people think it was developed in a biolab in Wuhan where they were testing viruses carried by bats to see if they could be used as bioweapons."

"So you're saying the CIA is responsible for destroying our city?"

"I'm sure it's not deliberate. The Novamors virus escaped accidentally."

"Make the worms stop eating my brain," cried Jason, convulsing on his bed, the bedsprings creaking.

"Calm down," said Zandorf, holding down Jason. "There aren't any worms."

"They're boring through my brain to exit through my ear," said Jason, his face sweaty.

"There's no blood dripping out of your ears. If the worms were in your brain, your ear canals would be bleeding," said Zandorf, struggling to hold Jason down.

Zandorf pressed a button on the side of the bed, summoning a nurse.

"The pain. I can't stand the pain," cried Jason, shutting his eyes and snapping them open.

Two husky RNs bustled into the room, hurried to either side of Jason, and pinned his arms to the bed. Zandorf backed away from them, letting them do their job.

"I need to know who tried to kill him," Coffin told Zandorf.

"He can't answer your questions in his present incoherent state."

"Why's he keep babbling about worms?"

"He believes Novamors has infected him."

"Why does he believe that?"

"Coma-induced hallucinations," said Zandorf, rubbing his chin in thought. "It's the only explanation I can think of. His test results for the virus are negative."

"Maybe the guy's going nuts."

"I hope not. I have questions I want to ask him and his wife. They might be able to shed some light on how the virus started spreading. Have you made any progress finding Phoebe Albright?"

"My men are so busy fighting riots and virus outbreaks they haven't got time to look for her. And now we got another problem, believe it or not. Rioters blew up city hall."

"What?"

"They fired RPG-7 grenades at it."

"Why?"

"They're protesting the lockdown—like everybody else. We need to get this virus under control. It's tearing apart the city. A civil war is looming."

Zandorf saw Jason was continuing to grimace and thrash around.

"How can he move with so many broken bones and internal injuries?" said Coffin.

"Adrenaline," said Zandorf. "The only pain he's feeling is from the worms boring tunnels in his brain."

"You said there aren't any worms."

"Never underestimate the power of the mind. If he *thinks* the worms are there, in his mind they *are* there, no matter what the truth is." Zandorf turned to the nurses. "Hold his arms down while I give him a sedative."

He reached for a hypo on a metal table near Jason's bed, squirted its contents of methohexital up into the air to make sure there were no air bubbles in the fluid, and administered a shot to Jason in the crook of his elbow.

Chapter 79

"I should kill you now," said Hardy as he exited Jackson's high-rise with Phoebe at his side minus her restraints.

"Jackson won't pay you if you do," said Phoebe, trying to figure out when to make a run for it.

She was relieved they had both removed their hazmat uniforms after they had left Jackson's office. She could breathe much easier without being enveloped in the claustrophobic uniform.

At least they were outside the high-rise instead of in the parking garage, she decided. Here she might be able to make a mad dash for freedom.

"He'll wire the money into my offshore bank account as soon as the Internet is working."

"Are you sure?"

"Of course. I did my job and took you to him. Why wouldn't he pay me?"

"Rich people don't get rich by spending money unnecessarily."

Hardy snorted. "Confucius?" He hung fire. "I'm surprised he didn't tell me to whack you. He seems to think you tried to kill his son."

"I talked him out of that. If he killed me, he'd have a lot of explaining to do to my husband Jason."

"I'm betting he's gonna want you dead soon when he finds out you messed up his son's head."

"I didn't mess up his head. *He* messed up *mine*."

"Maybe you didn't push him out his office window, but you could be what drove him to try to commit suicide on account of your fights. What do you say to that?"

"I say I'm hungry. Let's get something to eat," said Phoebe, casting around for a restaurant and an escape route.

"Your innocent act isn't fooling anyone. You two were going at it hammer and tongs all the time, as I understand it. And I don't blame you."

Phoebe looked at him. "I don't understand."

"Yeah, you do. You found out he was cheating on you. Does Jackson know about his son's cheating? Does he know you knew about Val Lewton and had a motive to murder Jason? Maybe I'll go tell him, and he'll tell me to whack you."

The blood drained from Phoebe's face. She didn't want Jackson to know.

"You don't know what you're talking about," she said.

"Maybe we should pay a return visit to Jackson's penthouse."

"He'll never believe you," she said without conviction.

Sneering, he latched onto her arm. "I really want you dead. Can you tell?"

A Ford-150 pickup tore down the street in front of them and braked to an abrupt, shrieking halt.

"Why did you want me to stop?" said Tex in the driver's seat and craned around to see Rigo, who was standing in the flatbed.

"A bargaining chip," said Rigo, pulling a Ruger LCP .380 semiautomatic from his waistband. He trained the Ruger on Phoebe. "Get in, Mrs. Albright."

"You must be mistaken," said Phoebe, not knowing who the guy was.

"That's not gonna work. Get in or get shot."

"You wouldn't shoot the mayor's wife," said Phoebe, trying to bluff her way out, hoping she sounded sure of herself. "You'd spend the rest of your life in jail."

"The cops'll never find me. They won't even look. They're too busy locking down the city and strangling it to death. I don't have time for this. Get in."

"I don't think she wants to go with you," said Hardy.

"I'm not giving her a choice—if it's any of your business."

"We were going to get a bite to eat—"

"Shut up. You get in too, busybody. And keep your hands where I can see them."

Hardy showed his empty hands to Rigo.

Rigo nodded. "Now get in."

Hardy mounted the tailgate and stepped onto the flatbed as Rigo trained his Ruger on him.

"Now you," Rigo told Phoebe.

Phoebe stepped toward the tailgate.

"Help her up," said Rigo.

Hardy reached down and helped her up onto the flatbed.

"You're gonna regret this," Hardy told Rigo.

"Who are you?" said Rigo, keeping his Ruger trained on Hardy.

"Her CPA."

"Nice threads," said Rigo, admiring Hardy's suit.

"I pay my tailor well."

Rigo patted down Hardy's jacket and was surprised to feel the Beretta wedged inside Hardy's trouser waistband. Rigo yanked the piece out and held it up.

"Did he give you this?" he said, and stuffed the Beretta in his trouser cargo pocket.

He eyed Hardy suspiciously.

"What's the point of kidnaping me?" said Phoebe, who was tired of getting kidnaped.

"You're a valuable bargaining chip with the mayor."

"My husband's in a coma. He can't bargain with anyone."

"Then I'll bargain with the deputy mayor. What's his name? Stress, isn't it? Or Struts? Something like that."

"What is it you want?" said Hardy.

"I want the mayor to reopen our city, Mr. CPA. I'm going out of business. I have mouths to feed in my family. If the mayor doesn't open the city, I'll waste Phoebe and you."

Rigo hammered the top of the cab with his fist.

"Brace yourselves," he said.

Phoebe and Hardy grabbed the side of the pickup as the vehicle peeled away from the curb, the tries squealing.

"RPG-7," said Hardy, picking up on the weapon lying on the flatbed at his feet.

"You're pretty smart for a CPA," said Rigo.

"Expecting to meet a tank?"

Rigo snickered, keeping his Ruger trained on Hardy.

"Maybe I'll hire you to do my taxes."

"You can't afford me," said Hardy.

"Nah, you'll be dead before April 15th."

"We all will," said Phoebe.

"Not if we can get rid of this lockdown. I'm not the only one who's suffering. Everybody in town is. It's time for us to take action."

"According to the experts, if you open the city, the virus will infect everyone."

"I'll take my chances. That's what life is all about. Risk."

"You won't get an argument from me. Their solution to the virus is killing and incinerating all of the infected."

Rigo nodded, his face grim. "I seen their choppers in action. They blew away everybody on the ground then burned their asses. That's their game."

"It's gonna get worse as the virus spreads."

"Another reason to open the city. We don't want to sit around and wait to get infected."

"What the hell is that?" said Hardy.

Phoebe looked in the direction of his gaze. A charred human skeleton was walking down the sidewalk.

"How can that be?" said Phoebe, taken aback.

"Skeletons walking around?" said Rigo. "Are you kidding me?"

"What's it looking for?" said Hardy.

"Food," said Phoebe. "Human flesh."

As the pickup drove by the skeleton, Rigo fired his Ruger in revulsion at the skeleton, trying to kill the abomination. The bullet broke off a rib bone, but the skeleton kept walking.

"How could it reanimate without a brain?" said Phoebe.

"Either you're missing, or your bullets have no effect," Hardy told Rigo.

"Well, I'm not missing. You saw its rib bone fly off."

"It didn't even slow the thing down."

"An RPG-7 would blow that thing back to hell if I had any more grenades for it." Rigo trained his piece on Hardy. "Don't try anything. This mag's not empty."

Hardy smiled with half his mouth and opened his hands to show they were empty.

Chapter 80

Zandorf and Strus were sitting at a table in the hospital cafeteria, eating burgers and fries.

"Novamors is spreading," said Strus. "Our measures to control it aren't working. How are we supposed to stop it from infecting the whole city?"

Zandorf heaved a noisy sigh. "I need to meet Phoebe Albright, so I can see if she's infected or immune to Novamors. She's the only clue we have to go on. She could be the answer if we find she's immune and we can get a sample of her blood."

Strus shook his head in exasperation. "The cops are concentrating on quelling the riots and fighting the infected maniacs. They're not looking for Phoebe."

Zandorf took a bite out of his burger and pulled a face.

"I prefer charbroiled burgers," he said. "They have more flavor."

"That's why I eat cheeseburgers. You can't even taste the burger."

Coffin stalked into the cafeteria, spotted them, and made for their table.

"I have bad news," he told Strus.

"It couldn't get much worse than it is."

"We're getting reports of the skeletons of the infected coming back to life."

"The skeletons?" said Zandorf, appalled. "The burned skeletons?"

"Right."

Zandorf put his burger down and tried to get his mind wrapped around the intel.

"Are you sure?" said Strus.

"We've gotten at least three reports of sightings of skeletons walking," said Coffin.

"Human skeletons?" said Zandorf.

Coffin nodded yes. "We also got a report of a skeleton attacking an old woman and ripping her throat out with its teeth."

"This is insane," said Strus.

"Aren't your men burning the infected corpses like I told them?" Zandorf asked Coffin.

"They're using flamethrowers."

"What kind?"

"What do you mean?" said Coffin, puzzled.

"Commercial or military?"

"Is there a difference?"

"Commercial flamethrowers use gas like propane. The military uses liquid fuel like napalm."

"What difference does it make?"

"The fuel from military flamethrowers burns longer."

"I'm not following you."

"From what you're telling me, it looks like incinerating the cadavers isn't enough to kill the virus. We must also burn the skeletons to ash. For that to happen, the fire has to burn for over two and a half hours at around 2,000 degrees Fahrenheit."

"Can you give it to me in English?"

"The infected cadavers aren't burning long enough and at a high-enough temperature to reduce the bones to ash. Your men should be using military flamethrowers on the infected."

"I don't know what kind of equipment they're using. I'll have to check."

Strus coughed and looked at Zandorf. "Are the fires from the flamethrowers hot enough to dissolve the skeletons?"

"Certain compositions of napalm can provide heat up to 1,800 degrees Fahrenheit," said Zandorf. "Gasoline-based napalm gets up to 1,250 degrees."

"I don't know what my men are using," said Coffin. "I'll have to find out. I don't know what the state police are using either."

"If we really want to be sure, we need to use thermite bombs. Their fires can reach temperatures of 4,500 degrees Fahrenheit. All human bones will be reduced to ash at that temperature."

"How do you know so much about napalm and thermite bombs?"

"I used to work at the DOD," said Zandorf, almost apologetically. "The horrors of war turned me off to the military. I want to help mankind, not obliterate it."

"And yet you're willing to kill victims infected by Novamors?"

Conflicted, Zandorf removed his glasses and rubbed his eyeballs with his thumb and forefinger. He put his glasses back on.

"The safety of the many takes precedence over the safety of a few," he said. "Ideally, we need to find a cure. But we're living in the real world. There might not be a cure. And Novamors spreads like lightning. It has to be stopped dead now. If it spreads beyond this city, the country is doomed. And then the world. We'll have no way to stop it."

"Am I reading you right?" said Coffin. "You want us to start using thermite bombs on our own people?"

"We have to figure from what the chief has said that the skeletons can come back to life and spread the virus. We can't have them walking around, biting and infecting people."

Coffin slapped his forehead. "Walking skeletons. I never thought I'd see the day. Could people be imagining they're seeing these things?"

"If there was just one report, I'd discount it."

"Yeah. Four reports. It's gotta be the real deal."

Zandorf nodded. "I'll ask the president to send us thermite bombs. In the meantime, use military napalm flamethrowers."

"All I know is they're using flamethrowers. I'll have to find out about the composition and the other stuff."

"Make sure your men keep the fires burning for over two and a half hours to turn the infected skeletons to ashes."

"Charbroiled skeletons, huh."

Strus looked at his hamburger and threw it onto his tray with repugnance.

"For some reason I'm not hungry anymore," he said.

Chapter 81

Two uniforms bustled into the cafeteria ushering a handcuffed twentysomething Hispanic guy in jeans and a navy blue tank top with a silkscreen of Marilyn Monroe's face on its chest. His nose had been broken a couple of times when he was younger. He also had an incisor missing.

"This guy says he has urgent news for the mayor," said the lead uniform, who had a brush cut and was about the same age as his prisoner.

"I'm a busy man," said Strus. He turned to Coffin. "Can't you handle this, Chief?"

"He demands to speak to the mayor."

"Out with it," said Coffin, glaring at the prisoner. "Who are you?"

"I'm Luis. I have a message for the mayor from the CDL."

"What the hell is the CDL?"

"Never heard of it," said Strus.

"The Costaguana Defense League," said Luis.

Coffin shook his head in bafflement. "Is that supposed to mean something?"

"We have Phoebe Albright. We will give her to you if you agree to open the city."

Zandorf straightened in his chair, his face lighting up. "Phoebe? You have her?"

"That's right."

"You mean, you kidnaped her," said Coffin. "That's against the law. You're gonna do a shitload of time."

Luis fixed his gaze on Strus. "We'll hand her over to you if you take down the roadblocks on the road leading in and out of the city."

"I need to examine Phoebe," Zandorf told Strus, his tone urgent.

"This explains why we haven't been able to find her," said Coffin. "These CDL terrorists kidnaped her."

"We're not terrorists," said Luis. "We're freedom fighters. We are opponents of the lockdown."

"One man's freedom fighter is another man's terrorist. Since we're the guys in power, you and your CDL gang are terrorists."

Luis said nothing. He kept looking at Strus.

"We don't deal with terrorists," said Strus.

"We're an American patriotic group," said Luis. "We are pro-American and pro-Costaguana."

"I'm not dealing with a flunky. Who's your boss?"

"Is that your answer?"

"Start talking. Or do you want to face kidnaping charges?"

"I'll get him to talk," said Coffin in a menacing tone.

"If I don't return to my boss in an hour, Phoebe will die," said Luis.

"Making threats is another law you broke," said Strus.

"Phoebe's no good to us dead," said Zandorf. "We need her alive."

"I'm not letting the mayor's wife die under my watch," said Coffin.

Strus thought it over. "Luis, you haven't hurt anyone yet. The authorities will go easy on you if you give us Phoebe."

"Not unless you agree to open up the road to and from the city," said Luis.

"Impossible," burst Strus. "That will allow the spread of the most lethal virus the human race has ever faced."

"I have my orders."

Strus scratched the scruff of his neck. "Tell your boss I have to think about it."

"Let me go, and I'll tell him."

Coffin nodded at the uniforms, who allowed Luis to leave the cafeteria.

"Follow him," said Coffin, "but don't let him see you."

"Yes, sir," said Brush Cut, and made tracks for the door with his heavyset partner.

"At least we know Phoebe is alive," said Zandorf. "If she was dead, we would have no hope of finding a vaccine for Novamors."

"If we can believe these CDL terrorists," said Coffin suspiciously. "I'd bet the ranch they're the ones that attacked city hall."

"I think we have to take them at their word," said Strus. "We can't afford to jeopardize Phoebe's life by not making every effort to free her."

Coffin stared at Strus in bewilderment. "Then you're caving in to the terrorist threats?"

"You can't open the city until we have contained Novamors," said Zandorf. "To open it now would be catastrophic for the human race."

Strus clenched his jaw. "I need to talk to the governor."

Chapter 82

Strus exited the hospital and strode onto the sidewalk. He fished out his satphone from his trouser pocket and scoped out the sky to make sure it was clear. Two puffy clouds scudded across the bright blue sky. They wouldn't interfere with his transmission, he decided.

It was getting hot out. He loosened his necktie and felt a little more comfortable.

He phoned Governor Vitti.

"This is Deputy Mayor Strus. We have a situation."

"You got a clusterfuck down there is what you got," said Vitti.

"We're gonna need thermite bombs here. Napalm isn't sufficient to turn the infected skeletons to ash."

"Why do I care about skeletons?"

Strus harrumphed. "This is gonna sound hard to believe, but the skeletons of the infected victims are reanimating."

There was a long pause on the line.

"Is that supposed to be funny?" said Vitti. "You been watching reruns of *Jason and the Argonauts*?"

"No joke. The cops have received numerous reports of skeletons coming back to life and attacking people."

"How do you kill them if they're just bone?"

"That's what I'm trying to explain. Zandorf said the infected corpses have to burn at around two thousand degrees Fahrenheit for over two and a half hours for the skeletons to turn to ash."

"Fine. Do whatever it takes to eradicate the virus."

"There's another problem that needs your attention."

"Let me remind you I'm the governor of a very large state."

"Domestic terrorists are inciting riots in the city. They launched an attack against city hall using an RPG-7."

"Have them arrested. Why tell me?"

"They kidnaped the mayor's daughter Phoebe and are holding her hostage. They said they won't release her until we open the city."

"Do you have the virus contained?"

"Uh, no."

"Then don't knuckle under to the terrorists. Do *not* lift the lockdown until the virus is a hundred percent contained."

"They said they would kill Phoebe."

"Listen to me. Do not lift the lockdown at this time. If you open your city, I'll let everyone know you were the one responsible for infecting California with this devastating virus."

Strus felt like spitting in Vitti's face. The governor had a bad habit of blaming everybody else for his mistakes.

"You're OK with letting Phoebe die at the hands of the terrorists?" said Strus.

"Stop twisting my words. I'm not letting anyone die. That's why we need you to enforce the lockdown."

"Then they'll kill Phoebe."

"Then rescue her. That's why you have a SWAT team."

"Can you at least come here and see what's happening?" said Strus. "There are riots, cannibal attacks, and fires everywhere. Armed mobs are fighting the police and shooting down our choppers."

"You want me to go there and catch that virus? No way. Nobody goes in or out of Costaguana. Anyone who tries will be shot. The CHP have their orders."

"This is why the people are rioting."

"Let 'em riot. If they want to trash their own city, let 'em. If they don't care about the damage the riots are causing, why should I? A bear shits in its cave, it's his problem."

"You wouldn't say that if you could see the mess here—"

"It's your mess. You clean it up. Carpet-bomb the entire city with thermite bombs if you have to."

"Governor—"

"I'm going on vacation to Acapulco."

"Do you think that's appropriate with my city convulsing?" said Strus, ticked off.

"It's mother's milk to me."

"*Costaguana is part of California,*" said Strus, trying to get through to him.

"You're the mayor of Costaguana. It's your baby. Grow a pair and handle it. Am I the only adult in this state?"

"We don't have the resources. We need your help. Let me remind you, it was *your* vaccine that killed five hundred citizens."

"I had nothing to do with that vaccine. Bates signed off on it."

"Wrapping yourself in layers of lies won't protect you—"

"Don't call me again until you've eradicated the virus."

"Governor—"

Vitti hung up.

*The son of a bitch is hanging me out to dry*, thought Strus.

Chapter 83

Lying on his back in his hospital bed, Jason stared into Zandorf's eyes with a mournful expression.

"Doctor, I want you to operate on my brain and remove the worms from it," said Jason.

"There is no reason to operate," said Zandorf, looking down at him.

"You must remove them. I beg you. They are gnawing my brain tissue," said Jason, screwing up his face. "When they're done, my brain will look like a sponge."

"The CAT scan shows there are no worms in your brain. You're imagining them."

"I'm not imagining the pain I'm in," said Jason, a strained rictus carving his face.

Strus flung open the door to Jason's room, apoplectic.

"Vitti's throwing us under the bus," he said.

"He won't help us get Phoebe?" said Zandorf.

"He said the lockdown must remain in place. Nobody leaves or enters our city."

"How can we free Phoebe if we don't obey the terrorists and agree to their demand to open the city? I agree we can't lift the lockdown, but there must be something he can do to help us."

"He could care less about our city."

"Phoebe's our only chance to find a vaccine for Novamors," said Zandorf, scowling.

"If you dig the worms out of my brain, you can dissect them and see what makes them tick," said Jason. "Then you can find a vaccine."

"You need to stop this. There's nothing wrong with your brain."

Jason groaned in pain. "What kind of a doctor are you? Stop the worms from killing me. That's your job. I'll hit you with a malpractice suit so huge you'll have a stroke if you don't operate on me."

"Nobody's suing anybody if we all get infected with Novamors," said Zandorf, fed up with Jason.

"Is this how you treat your patients? By letting them die?"

"Your brain was damaged during your concussion. You're hallucinating. Think about something else."

"How can I think when I'm in agony?"

"Relax."

"When the worms leave through my ear canal, it'll mean they've burrowed a hole all the way through my brain. Can you conceive how much pain I'm in?" said Jason, his eyes red, his face drawn.

"If you don't calm down, I'll have to give you another sedative, or you'll have a heart attack."

The door burst open.

A peroxide blonde Asian teenager wearing a short-sleeve grey sweatshirt charged into the room, foaming at the mouth, a bullet hole in her forehead. Zandorf dodged her by backing away. She lunged for Strus and tried to grab his neck. Strus jerked free of her grip and shoved her away. A security guard bopped into the room, service revolver drawn, and shot her in the head. The teen crumpled.

A frantic intern pushing thirty darted into the room, a silver crucifix dangling from a chain around his neck.

"I thought she was dead," he said. "The EMTs brought her in on a gurney with a bullet hole in her forehead. She had no pulse. Then she jackknifed up and sprinted down the hall, frothing at the mouth. How could she survive a bullet in the brain?"

"A bullet to the brain doesn't kill them apparently," said Zandorf, trying to regain his composure after the attack, smoothing his smock. "The infected skeletons are alive unless they're incinerated at two thousand degrees for two and a half hours."

"But she had no pulse."

"The skeletons are alive."

"Then she's still alive even though he shot her? She looks dead."

Zandorf studied the teen who lay sprawled on the floor.

"She will eventually reanimate," he said. "Her body must be cremated ASAP."

Sweating, the guard continued holding his revolver trained on the motionless teen, his eyes glued on her.

Two interns wheeled a gurney into the room. One of them felt the teen's wrist, trying to detect a pulse. He shook his head. The interns circumspectly loaded the body onto the gurney, half expecting her to start biting them any second.

"Where do we take her?" the lead intern asked Zandorf.

"To a crematorium. Make sure you're wearing gloves. Don't let her bite you."

Terrified, the two interns wheeled the teen out of the room at speed. The guard accompanied them, continuing to train his handgun on the bullet-riddled corpse.

"Jesus," said Strus, smoothing his mussed-up hair with his hand and adjusting his horn-rimmed glasses that sat out of true on the bridge of his nose. "She almost bit me."

Coffin strutted into the room. "What happened to you? You look like you just climbed out of a washing machine."

"An infected maniac tried to kill me."

"I have news about Phoebe Albright."

Chapter 84

"Do you have her?" said Zandorf, pricking up his ears.

"One of my men paid a visit to her mother Lila to find out if she knew where Phoebe is," said Coffin. "He found Lila dead from a gunshot wound to the knee. She was unable to call for help and bled out."

"Who would shoot Phoebe's mother?" said Strus.

"Maybe it was this CDL gang that kidnaped Phoebe," said Zandorf.

"That's what we think," said Coffin. "These terrorists don't fool around. They killed someone at city hall too with their rocket attack. They have no compunction about using violence to get their way."

"Which means they're capable of killing Phoebe," said Zandorf, dispirited. "Not only are they terrorists, they're murderers."

"We don't know for sure that they killed Phoebe's mother, but we *do* know they killed an office worker when they blew up city hall. So, yes, they're murderers. Phoebe's life is at risk."

"We have to assume they'll kill her if the mayor doesn't lift the lockdown."

"The governor says the lockdown stays in place," said Strus. "We have to free Phoebe on our own."

"They don't call him Pass-the-Buck Vitti for nothing," said Coffin.

"Do you have a plan to free Phoebe?"

Coffin changed the subject. "We got another problem. I checked our police arsenal. We don't carry thermite bombs."

"Who does?"

"The military has them. That's for sure."

"Then we go to the feds to get the thermite."

"They must have some at Camp Pendleton in San Diego," said Coffin, stroking the side of his neck.

"It's a good idea to order more napalm as well," said Zandorf.

"I thought you said the napalm didn't burn hot enough," said Strus.

"Thermite is hotter, but the advantage of liquid napalm is it burns for a long time. The longer the fire burns, the more effective it is in reducing the infected skeletons to ash."

"Fine," said Coffin. "I'm sure Camp Pendleton has plenty of napalm."

"That doesn't solve the problem of freeing Phoebe," said Zandorf. "She should be our number one priority."

"We can't free her until we find her," said Strus. "Where is the CDL holding her?"

"We got a tip from a woman who says she witnessed the attack on city hall," said Coffin. "She says she recognized the shooter as her exterminator, Rigo Alvarez."

"Do you think she's reliable?"

"It's worth checking out. I'm sending men to his house to bring him in as a suspect."

"Everything's going sideways," said Zandorf. "I must talk to Phoebe before it's too late. We haven't a minute to spare."

"Too late for what?" said Strus.

"Too late to save this city."

Strus looked nonplussed.

"Have we really reached that point?" said Coffin.

"I'm afraid so," said Zandorf. "We're getting multiple reports of outbreaks of the virus throughout the city. We're not succeeding in containing Novamors."

"What more can we do?" said Strus.

"I will do everything possible to prevent it from spreading beyond city limits," said Zandorf, his face somber. "And I have the full backing of the president in this matter."

A uniform in his early thirties entered the room, chewing gum.

"Chief, we checked Alvarez's house," he said. "He's not there."

"Do you have any leads?" said Coffin.

"One of his neighbors said Alvarez is losing a lot of clients because they're in cities that he can't service because of the lockdown."

284

"I don't like the lockdown any more than anybody else," said Strus, "but Vitti wants it enforced."

"Vitti's right," said Zandorf. "We can't lift the lockdown and release Novamors on the world. We must destroy Novamors."

"Anything else?" Coffin asked the uniform.

"The neighbor said Alvarez spends a lot of time with his friend Tex Clanton. Clanton works for the Department of Transportation as a parking meter revenue collector."

"Good work. Check out Clanton's house and question him about Alvarez. Maybe Clanton knows where he is. Hell, maybe Clanton was driving the Ford pickup that attacked city hall."

The uniform snapped his fingers. "That's what the neighbor said."

"What are you talking about?"

"He said Clanton owns a silver Ford F-150 pickup. The neighbor sees it all the time at Alvarez's."

"Looks like Alvarez and Clanton are working with the CDL," said Coffin. "Get the tag for Clanton's pickup. Put out a BOLO for Alvarez, Clanton, and his pickup." He frowned. "The problem is we don't have enough men. Everybody's on assignment enforcing the lockdown, managing the riots, and containing the virus."

"We don't bargain with terrorists," said Strus.

"Getting and examining Phoebe is our top priority," pointed out Zandorf.

"Everything's our top priority," said Strus, overwhelmed. "That's the problem. I'm not gonna lift the lockdown in exchange for Phoebe's release."

"We'll just have to find her and free her before they kill her," said Coffin.

"This is our last chance to save the city, gentlemen," said Zandorf, his tone ominous.

"I'm not gonna let Alvarez and Clanton dictate orders to us by holding the city hostage with their threats. Their asses are mine."

Chapter 85

Tex drove his pickup to the deserted packing warehouse of a bankrupt clothing company and slotted his truck in the parking lot. He hopped out of the driver's seat.

"What are we gonna do with Phoebe while we wait for the mayor to lift the lockdown?" he said, looking up at Rigo, who stood in the flatbed with Phoebe and Hardy, his pistol trained on them.

"We'll tie these two up in the warehouse," said Rigo. "It shouldn't take long for the mayor to grant our request. He's not gonna risk losing Phoebe."

"Don't count on it," said Phoebe. "My husband isn't the acting mayor anymore."

"We know that. The deputy mayor will do everything he can to protect you. At least he better. Or you won't be with us much longer."

"You're not gonna kill us in cold blood," said Hardy.

"You must not understand how bad it is for the working man in this city with everything locked down, or you wouldn't say that. If I lose my business, I lose my life. Right now my extermination business is going down the drain thanks to the lockdown."

"Do you really want to go to jail for murder?"

"Nobody's going to jail. The mayor will agree to our terms. Nobody's gonna get hurt."

"You're overestimating my importance," said Phoebe.

"I disagree. You're very valuable to them. Why else would they put out a warrant for your arrest?"

"They want me dead."

Rigo did a double take. "You expect me to believe that?"

"It's true." Phoebe decided to go ahead and explain. "I was on the Strip when the cops in the choppers gunned down innocent pedestrians in the street. I saw the whole thing."

"Then you're saying our killing you would be doing them a favor?" said Rigo, flabbergasted.

"It would save them the trouble of killing me themselves."

"That's ridiculous. Cops don't make a rule of shooting innocent people."

"I saw it with my own eyes on the Strip."

"The cops in the choppers are definitely whacking out people," said Tex. "We saw them do it at the bowling alley when we took out their chopper with the Browning."

"Their victims were infected with the virus," said Rigo.

"Even so, do you think the public would be happy if they found out cops were killing the infected instead of trying to cure them?" said Phoebe.

"I don't care what you say. I don't believe the cops want you dead. You're a valuable bargaining chip."

"Listen to me. I saw the cops kill innocent people and napalm the Strip."

"Maybe she's right," said Tex.

"So what if she is?" said Rigo. "I don't believe the mayor wants her dead. He's gonna move heaven and earth to free her. He's gonna open the city for us. Take both of them inside and tie them up."

"No problem."

"Not a good idea," said Hardy.

Rigo waved his pistol at Phoebe and Hardy. "Get out."

Phoebe jumped off the flatbed, followed by Hardy.

Tex withdrew a Ruger Max-9 from his waistband and aimed it at Hardy.

Rigo bounded off the flatbed, gun in hand.

"Let's go," he said. "Put your hands up."

Phoebe and Hardy raised their hands above their heads.

The four of them headed for the warehouse door.

"I hope you're not infected," said Hardy.

"Why would I be infected?" said Rigo. "Maybe you're the one that's infected."

"Could be. If I am, you're gonna be next."

"If you were infected, you'd be acting like a maniac and frothing at the mouth."

"Maybe that's the next stage."

Hardy's words gave Rigo pause. But only for a moment.

"Get going," said Rigo.

They reached the warehouse front door, which was hanging ajar. Cool, musty air wafted out through the doorway.

"Go inside," said Rigo.

Hardy pushed the door open wider and entered.

"Rigo, how do we know they're not infected?" said Tex, frowning with concern.

"Don't you see what he's trying to do?" said Rigo. "He's trying to scare us into letting them go. It's not gonna work. Do you have any plastic zip ties?"

"I got some in the glove compartment of my truck."

"I'll get 'em. You watch them."

As Rigo left through the door, a low-flying jet screamed overhead. Rigo winced at the cacophony.

Tex glanced at Rigo, who didn't look back.

Hardy took the opportunity to reach for the SIG P365 secured in his ankle holster, withdrew the SIG, and drew a bead on Tex, who wheeled toward him, preparing to fire his Ruger.

Hardy double-tapped him in the head. Tex crumpled.

The deafening low-flying jet masked the crack of Hardy's gunshots, preventing Rigo from hearing them.

"I always carry a spare piece," said Hardy.

Phoebe lowered her raised arms. "He'll be back any second."

Hardy bolted toward Tex, crouched over him, searched his trouser pockets, and withdrew the keys to the pickup. He cast around the warehouse and picked up on a rear door.

"Let's go out the back," he said.

He pelted to the back door.

Phoebe debated whether to follow him. She didn't know who was more dangerous. The CDL terrorists or Hardy. She figured she would side with Hardy for the time being. After all, he could have shot her there and then, but he hadn't. She sprinted after him. She knew Rigo would be returning soon with plastic zip ties.

Phoebe followed Hardy as he circled the warehouse to the front. He craned his neck around the corner of the building to see if he could spot Rigo. He saw Rigo enter the warehouse front door.

"Come on," said Hardy, and belted to Tex's pickup.

Phoebe ran after him, deciding she was better off throwing her lot in with Hardy than with the terrorists. She would escape from Hardy as soon as she saw her chance. If she tried to flee him now, he would shoot her.

"Hurry," said Hardy. "I want to be outa here before he comes out of the warehouse."

He flung open the driver's-side door, scooched onto the driver's seat, and jammed the key into the ignition. Phoebe raced around to the other side of the pickup, opened the door, and clambered into the shotgun seat.

Gun in hand, Rigo popped out of the warehouse door, caught sight of Hardy in the pickup, and opened fire.

Hardy returned fire with his SIG. Hardy's bullet flew wide. Rigo sprang back into the warehouse, seeking cover.

Hardy fired the ignition, hung a U-turn in the parking lot, and made tracks for the exit.

Rigo charged out of the warehouse and fired at the pickup. One of his bullets slammed into the rear window, spiderwebbing it.

Hardy ducked. Phoebe followed suit.

Eager to get out of the parking lot and beyond the Ruger's range, Hardy drove over the sidewalk and off the curb onto the road, the pickup and its shocks bouncing as the tires hit the tarmac.

Phoebe felt her head jerk up and down. She braced her arm against the dash. She heard two more gunshots behind her. The passenger-side-view mirror cracked under a bullet's impact..

Hardy floored the gas and rocketed down the street.

"Now where do we go?" said Phoebe as they lengthened the distance between them and Rigo.

"I want out of this goddamn city."

"The cops are blocking all of the roads out of town."

"There's another way out."

"Not unless you know how to fly."

Chapter 86

More citizens were joining the riot at the roadblock on Costaguana's border. In addition to rocks and bottles being hurled at the cops, someone had just thrown a Molotov cocktail at one of the squad cars parked crosswise in the middle of the road. Flames engulfed the black-and-white. The air stank of burning rubber.

The uniforms manning the blockade moved away from the burning car and blasted the charging mob with rubber bullets.

"We need to start using live ammo, Sergeant," said a twentysomething short uniform with a handlebar mustache, his face sweaty. "The rioters are gonna smoke us."

Holding a polycarbonate riot shield in front of him, the fireplug sergeant in his midthirties evaluated the deteriorating situation with narrowed eyes. He had cropped black hair and a square face with a crescent scar accenting his right eye, where he had been pistol-whipped by an armed bank robber when he walked a beat. The sergeant's name was Kwon.

At least a hundred angry rioters were closing in on the cops, screaming obscenities and slinging projectiles.

Kwon didn't want to lose any more of his men. Several had been severely injured by hurtling beer bottles. His orders were to enforce the roadblock no matter what. Nobody must leave town.

"These rubber bullets are a joke," said Handlebar Mustache. "The rioters are laughing at us as they attack. They're gonna break through any minute."

Kwon retreated to his cruiser and pulled out a bullhorn.

"You are violating the law," he announced through the bullhorn, confronting the rioters. "This is the Costaguana Police Department. You are ordered to disperse immediately, or you will be shot."

A rock flew within a foot of his head. He raised his riot shield and ducked. The rock glanced off the shield.

"Fuck you," cried a fortyish rioter with a beer belly wrapped in a sweat-salt-stained black T. "We're taking back our city. Open the roads."

"I am ordering my men to shoot rioters with their service pistols," said Kwon. "They're using live ammunition. Disperse now, or they will fire upon you."

A beer bottle shattered against his riot shield, smearing it with beer.

Pumping their fists with rage, the unruly mob advanced on the cops.

"Open our city," they screamed as they cast bottles at the cops, who were vastly outnumbered.

"Fire live ammo," said Kwon, fearing for his men's lives.

His men opened fire on the mob, felling the front line of attackers, slowing the mob, but they kept coming.

Another Molotov cocktail soared through the air and crashed into a squad car that blocked the road. Flames engulfed the vehicle.

One of the uniforms withdrew an H&K MP5 out of his cruiser and opened fire on the charging mob, cutting down four rioters. The terrifying cries of the wounded suffused the air.

"We can't hold them much longer," said Handlebar Mustache, wiping sweat from his brow with the back of his hand.

"Our orders are to shut down the city," said Kwon, determined to hold the line. "Nobody gets past us."

Handlebar Mustache drilled the chest of an advancing blonde woman pushing thirty. She clutched her blood-soaked ivory blouse and cried out in pain, her face contorted, baring her teeth.

"We need reinforcements," said Handlebar Mustache.

"I radioed for help," said Kwon.

"Where are they?"

"The chief doesn't have the manpower."

"Shit. Are you kidding me?"

"Deal with it."

Kwon shot a tall black, middle-aged guy who had salt-and-pepper hair and a white shaving-brush mustache and was barreling toward him. The guy collapsed, a bullet in his lung. Lying on his back, his chest making a sucking sound, he coughed bright red blood and spat it out.

"This is insane," said Kwon, feeling like puking at the wholesale slaughter, his face drained of blood. "We're killing our own people."

Another Molotov cocktail arced through the sky and hit the tarmac. The bottle shattered and burst into flames the better part of three feet from a cruiser blocking the road.

The rioters were aiming to burn all of the cruisers, decided Kwon. They would firebomb the cruisers then shove the charred chassis out of their way with SUV bull bars. He would do everything in his power to stop the mob, no matter how sick to his stomach it made him to enforce the law by blowing away townsfolk. When the chief said do it, Kwon did it. Nobody ever said he had an easy job.

A guy over six feet tall in his thirties wearing a red Angels baseball cap backward wielded a baseball bat as he attacked a squad car.

"They're killing us," he yelled. "The vaccines are toxic. Everyone vaccinated died. They're poisoning us."

Livid with rage, he bashed in the squad car's windshield with his bat.

"Stop or I'll shoot," said Kwon, training his Glock on the batter.

"It's a conspiracy," cried the batter. "The government's trying to kill us. The cops are in on it. Doctors. Everyone. They're all in on it."

The guy took another furious swing at the windshield, bursting it.

The vandal might be infected, decided Kwon. No sense in taking chances. His life was at stake. Despite lingering doubts and reservations, he drew a bead on the batter and blew his head apart.

Chapter 87

A grumbling, rambunctious mob was gathering outside the entrance of St. Luke's Hospital.

From Jason's hospital room Zandorf could see them milling with disgruntled faces on the cement concourse in front of the lobby five stories down.

"What's going on outside?" he said, peering out the open window.

"The crowd's getting ugly down there," said Strus, approaching Zandorf.

"It's the worms," screamed Jason in horror, lying on his back in bed. "I'm not gonna have a brain left. Can't somebody help me?"

"Is he still hallucinating?" said Strus, giving Jason a black look.

"They're killing us," hollered a member of the mob below, shaking his fist at the entrance to the hospital lobby. "The vaccines are poison. Everybody died from them. The doctors want us all to die."

"How did they find out about the vaccines?" said Zandorf. "I told everybody to put a lid on it."

"People talk," said Strus. "Relatives of the deceased probably spread the word. You can't keep something like this under wraps forever."

A bare-chested teenager smoking a cigarette, a tat of a fire-breathing dragon decorating his abdomen, hurled an empty beer bottle at one of the entrance's plate-glass doors and shattered it.

"Are they gonna storm the hospital?" said Zandorf. "Where's Coffin?"

"Are they all infected?" said Strus.

"I don't think so. They're infuriated, but they're not foaming at the mouth. They don't seem to have superhuman strength either. They're rioters. Granted, sometimes it's hard to tell the difference."

Zandorf picked up on a police cruiser with its red and blue lights flashing pulling up in the semicircle in front of the lobby where the mob was gathering. Two uniforms sprang out onto the sidewalk.

"Break it up," said the young, dark-haired cop with high cheekbones. "Time to disperse. Go back to your homes."

"The doctors are killing us," said the teenager, his face red, holding his cigarette between his fingers. "They killed my mother with one of their poison vaccines."

"What's your name, son?"

"John."

"John, this is an illegal assembly. You are ordered to disperse and go home."

"First, they lock down our city and take away our jobs. Now they're killing us with toxic vaccines."

Another protester hurled a full beer bottle at a plate-glass door. The door disintegrated into green shards. Foaming beer soaked the cement floor.

"Stop it and go home this minute," said the cop.

"You're part of the conspiracy to kill us," said John.

"You need to calm down and leave before you do something you regret."

"It's going around town that cops in choppers are killing us too," John told the other protesters. "We need to make our voices heard."

"You got that right," said a middle-aged waitress, smoothing her brown and yellow fast-food uniform. "If we don't pipe up, they're gonna keep killing us."

"You're all upset because of the virus," said the cop. "I understand your pain, but you can't let it get to you. You don't want to break the law. Once you cross the line, there's no turning back."

"You can't bust all of us," said John, flexing his biceps.

"I don't want to arrest anyone. Just go home and chill out. We're all in this together."

"This is getting ugly," said Zandorf as if to himself as he watched from the window above. "I need to talk to the president."

"How can the president help us?" said Strus.

"Decisions have to be made. We can't go on like this. The city is at a boiling point. There are too many rioters. It's only a matter of time before one of them breaks through the roadblocks quarantining the city and spreads Novamors."

"I don't see what the president can do."

"He can issue orders to save the country."

"How?" said Strus, at the end of his rope.

"At this point, there's only one solution," said Zandorf, his voice sobering.

"Kill the doctors," cried John on the concourse, pumping his fist with ire, unable to hear Zandorf or Strus.

The mob cheered.

"They'll kill us if we don't kill them first," said John.

"Kill," several rioters cried. "Kill. Kill. Death to the doctors."

"Inciting to riot is illegal," yelled the cop. "Death threats are illegal. Stop mouthing off and go home. Or you're all gonna sleep it off in the joint."

"You're outmanned, cop."

The cop whipped out his holstered Glock and fired a warning shot into the air.

"Disperse this minute," he said.

The mob grumbled, not sure what to do, discomfited by the gun report.

"It's hot out here," said the cop. "Let's all go home and cool off."

"Let's kill the killer doctors," cried John. "We want Zandorf."

"It's you they want," Strus told Zandorf as they watched the donnybrook.

"They don't know what they want," said Zandorf, sweat beading over his upper lip. "They're out of their minds with panic. No telling what they'll do. We need more cops here."

"Where's Coffin?"

Zandorf watched the mob below with misgivings.

The mob commenced chanting, "We want Zandorf. Give us Zandorf."

"He vaccinated my mother," said John, shaking his raised fist, unaware that Zandorf was watching him from above. "He killed her. He's killing us. Give us Zandorf, the murderer."

He tossed his cigarette onto the concourse and bolted for the lobby entrance.

"Shit," said the cop, and opened fire on him, downing him.

John lay face down on the concrete. He didn't move, a bullet lodged in his spine.

"He shot the kid," said a beefy rioter wearing a yellow hard hat and a dirty fluorescent yellow vest, outraged.

He sucker-punched the cop, knocking him senseless, snagged the cop's Glock. He shot the cop's partner in the chest. The partner reeled backward, reaching for his pistol in vain. Jacked up, Hard Hat charged the entrance, gun in hand. Emboldened, the rioters stormed after him.

"Give us Zandorf," they yelled.

"Jesus," said Zandorf from the window above, his eyes wide. "We're under assault. I need to tell the president right now."

He dashed out of the hospital room.

Rooted to the spot, Strus gazed out the window at the frenzied mob, his face pale as the daytime moon.

The cop wounded in the chest tried to stand up. He crumpled on the sidewalk, writhing in pain.

"I need a drink," muttered Strus, unable to tear his eyes away from the mayhem unfolding below, overwhelmed by the urge to vomit.

Chapter 88

Hardy floored the gas in the Ford pickup.

"Where are we going?" said Phoebe, riding shotgun.

"You'll see. And don't try cutting the steering wheel like you did when you totaled my car. Or I'll blow your head off."

"You're gonna kill me anyway. What's the difference when you do it?"

"Maybe not. I haven't made up my mind. Your filthy rich father-in-law might be willing to pony up more shekels for your safe return."

Hardy picked up on a motorcycle cop in the rearview mirror. He was advancing on the pickup tailgate.

"We got a friend on our tail," he said.

The helmeted motorcycle cop flashed his blue and red lights and pulled ahead of Hardy, motioning him to pull over.

"Must be a BOLO on Tex's pickup," said Hardy.

He pulled over to the side of the road.

"If they get me, they're gonna kill me," said Phoebe, her heartbeat racing.

"*I'll* kill you if you try anything. Don't say a word."

Hardy withdrew his SIG from his waistband.

"Maybe I was just driving too fast," he said, keeping his piece out of view, watching the cop park his motorcycle and make for the pickup. Hardy cut his eyes toward Phoebe. "Don't look so worried. Relax."

Hardy wanted to kill her and so did the cop, decided Phoebe. How was she supposed to relax?

The cop stood barely five eight, even wearing his glossy black jackboots with their inch-high heels. His white helmet gleamed like bone bleached by the desert sun.

Hardy secreted his SIG under his thigh. He smiled briefly at the motorcycle cop, even though he couldn't see the cop's face thanks to the black-tinted visor shielding it.

He powered his window down, looking respectful of the cop.

The cop reminded Phoebe of an astronaut floating on thermals toward them with his helmet on. She wished she was in outer space, instead of here. She imagined she heard David Bowie singing "Space Oddity." The sound of cop jackboots crunching gravel on the tarmac as he approached brought her back to reality.

He came to a halt next to the driver's-side window.

The helmet faced Hardy.

"Yes, Officer?"

"You were doing over fifty in a twenty-five-mile-an-hour zone, sir. Your tags are expired too."

"I—uh—um—just got them in the mail. I haven't had time to stick them on the plate."

"And . . ."

"There's more?" said Hardy, all innocence.

"Can you explain the bullet hole in your back window?"

One of Rigo's bullets, decided Phoebe. How was Hardy going to explain his way out of this? Maybe getting busted was the best possible outcome. The cop would take them to the station. She would explain she had been kidnaped—except the cops were going to kill her when they found out who she was. Maybe the motorcycle cop himself would blow her brains out. Getting busted wasn't the answer. No matter what happened, she was screwed.

"My son," said Hardy. "He shot his BB gun at the back window. I'm gonna take it out of his allowance. Teach him a lesson."

"Kind of a big hole for a BB to make," said the cop, glancing back at the perforated back window.

"Cheap glass, I guess."

Phoebe couldn't see the cop's face through his black visor. His voice continued in a monotone, giving nothing away.

"Let me see your driver's license and your car registration, sir," he said.

"Of course," said Hardy.

Instead of reaching for the glove compartment, Hardy whipped out his SIG and shot the cop twice in the visor, penetrating and cracking it, and, in case it was bulletproof, a third time in the throat, shredding the jugular. Blood jetted from his mutilated throat. The cop dropped on the tarmac in a heap. He didn't move.

Phoebe widened her eyes. "You didn't have to shoot him."

"My license doesn't match the name on the truck registration. He would've busted me for jacking the pickup."

Hardy fired the ignition and peeled away from the shoulder.

The pickup roared down the road, a rooster tail of dust in its wake.

"Is that all the thanks I get for saving your bacon from the killer cops?" he said.

"Out of the frying pan into the fire," she said, her face impassive.

Hardy laughed. "That's pretty good. I like your sense of humor. Maybe I'll keep you alive a little longer if you tell me more jokes."

Phoebe wasn't amused. Instead of telling stories like Scheherazade, all she had to do was crack jokes to stay alive one more day. The idea sent a chill down her spine. She could be one joke away from death.

"I hope you know where you're going," she said. "The only road out of town is blocked."

"I'm going the only way out."

"There is no way out."

"That's what you think. Stick with me, baby. We got a ticket to ride."

Chapter 89

Zandorf stood out on the balcony of the hospital administrator's office on the top floor and extended the antenna on his satphone.

He had a direct line to the president.

"Mr. President, we have a critical meltdown here."

"Novamors?"

"Yes, sir. We cannot contain it. It's spreading all over the city. The vaccines we got from Cobygenex were laced with lethal doses of fentanyl and killed all recipients."

"Dear God."

Grimacing, Zandorf tugged at his collar. He could hear rioters at street level yelling, "Death to Zandorf."

He took a deep breath, knowing the end was near. No options remained.

"We need to greenlight the Armageddon Option," he said.

The president sucked air. "Are you certain?"

"Positive."

"You know what this means?"

Zandorf knew what it meant. It meant he would die in the inferno, along with everybody else in Costaguana. He was signing his own death warrant by initiating the Armageddon Option. But it was the only way to contain Novamors.

Zandorf gulped. He was sacrificing his life to save humanity. It couldn't be helped. Everyone in Costaguana had to be considered infected by Novamors. Total destruction of the city and everyone in it was the only certain method of eradicating the virus.

"How do we proceed?" said the president.

"Firebomb the city, using thermite bombs and napalm. The city has to burn hot and burn long."

"Why firebombs? I don't understand."

"Intense fire is the only way to kill Novamors. The skeletons of the infected must burn for at least two and a half hours at preferably two thousand degrees Fahrenheit so they are reduced to ash. Otherwise, the skeletons will reanimate and kill everyone they contact."

"I thought a bullet to the brain and cremation were sufficient."

"That's what we thought at first, but we had to change our minds. The skeletons must be reduced to ash to kill Novamors. The virus can continue to live in the bones."

Zandorf could hear rioters yelling his name in the hallway. There was no way he would let them take him alive. In the berserk mood they were in they would tear him to pieces. In any case, they would all die in the firestorm ignited by the president. Nobody in Costaguana would survive.

Zandorf pulled a Glock 17 from a pocket in his smock. He had got it from Coffin for self-protection.

"I can send choppers loaded with thermite bombs and napalm to you from Camp Pendleton," said the president.

"Yes, sir."

The voices in the hallway sounded louder, decided Zandorf. They were coming for him.

"I appreciate the sacrifice you're making for our great country, Vincent," said the president. "I know how difficult this decision must be for you."

"Yes, sir."

"I'll tell your family you sacrificed your life for your country."

"Thank you, sir," said Zandorf, thinking of his wife Mary and their two teenage daughters with remorse.

He wished he could have done more for them. At least they were safe from Novamors in their home in Bethesda, Maryland. He could think about how unfair life was, but he knew it was a waste of time.

"I have a question," said the president.

"Yes, sir."

"Did Costaguana vote for me in the last election?"

"Uh—I—uh believe they did."

"Damn. I need every vote I can get. Are you sure this is the only solution?"

"Positive."

The klaxon blared in the hallway as somebody had sounded the alarm at last. Not that it would do any good, Zandorf knew. The cops—if there were any cops available—would never get here in time to stop the bloodthirsty mob.

For him it was either a bullet to the head, death at the hands of the incensed mob who wanted his blood, or death by immolation when the choppers firebombed the city.

He heard the door to the administrator's office kicked open and a bloodcurdling whoop of triumph from the first rioter who entered the room and clapped eyes on Zandorf.

"The killer doctor's here."

Zandorf gaped, inserted the Glock's muzzle between his lips, and aimed at the roof of his mouth.

Chapter 90

Hardy drove the pickup to the railroad station, where a train sat on the tracks.

A black-and-white was parked in front of it, straddling the steel rails that bracketed the ballast beneath them.

Phoebe saw a cop wearing aviator shades sitting behind the steering wheel.

Hardy parked ten feet away and trained his SIG on the cop's head. The cop didn't budge.

"Why do you have to kill him?" said Phoebe.

"He's in our way. The train's our ticket outa here."

"Tell him to move."

Hardy laughed. "Yeah, that'll work."

He shot the cop in the head. The cop's head exploded, cracked open. Shards flew all over the front seat.

"A fucking dummy," said Hardy, surprised at the broken plastic dummy head. He lowered his SIG. "I'll be. They don't have enough manpower to cover all exits out of town, so they're using dummies. This is gonna be easier than I thought."

"You really think the engineer is gonna drive us out? I'm sure he has orders not to leave the station."

"I don't need an engineer. I'm a professional fixer. To be a fixer you have to know how to do a lot of things. I can drive that thing."

It was Phoebe's turn to laugh. "Piece of cake. Sure."

"What are you laughing at? That's an EMU. An Electric Multiple Unit train. Those things practically drive themselves. It's all computers. Turn the thing on and go. Starting it isn't a problem. Stopping it—well, that's another matter. Brakes can be tricky on trains." He shrugged. "What the hell. We can always jump off if we can't stop it."

They piled out of the pickup and approached the train.

"The front unit is the driving car, or cab car," he said.

"What about the choppers?" said Phoebe, scanning the sky. "They'll never let us leave."

Hardy scoped out the sky. "I don't see any."

"Not yet."

"Funny they'd leave the door open," he said, noticing the cab car's door hung ajar. "You first," he said, waving his SIG at her and pointing at the door

"Scared?" she said.

"I don't want you running away. Get your ass in gear. Unless you can tell me a good joke. If you do, I'll enter first."

Phoebe thought fast. The door brought a joke to mind.

"When's a door not a door?" she said.

"I dunno."

"When it's ajar."

Hardy's face remained impassive.

"That sucks," he said. "Get going."

Phoebe climbed the metal steps to the door.

A fiftyish bald guy with fringes of grey hair sprouting from his temples like steel wool soap pads stuck his head out the door. Clad in an engineer's uniform, he charged out at her, foaming at the mouth, his face knotted with unbridled wrath. Terrified, she lost her footing and fell off the steps onto the ground, banging her knees. The infected maniac barreled down the steps, his hands stretched out toward Hardy.

Hardy fired his SIG at the maniac, hit him in the throat. Blood fountained out. The maniac engineer kept coming, gnashing his teeth, growling. He pounced on Hardy, knocked him to the ground. Hardy kept hold of his gun, lying on his back. The engineer stood over him, blood pouring down his ripped throat.

Momentarily stunned by his fall, Hardy recovered his wits and trained his piece on the engineer as the guy threw himself on top of him and opened his jaws wide, preparing to take a bite out of Hardy's face. Hardy blew the engineer's head apart with two slugs to the forehead, which split in half and jerked back. Part of his brains slid out his skull like yolk out of a cracked eggshell.

Hardy shoved the slobbering engineer off him and shot him again in the head for good measure. The engineer rolled in the dirt once and lay motionless on his back. His milky gaze stared into space. Snake eyes.

"Craps," said Hardy. "You lose."

Seizing her chance Phoebe started to take a powder. Before she completed two steps she heard Hardy behind her.

"Don't," he said, drawing a bead on her with his piece as he lay on his back. "I'm not done with you. Get into the cab."

"There could be another one of those things in there," said Phoebe, sweating with anxiety as she came to a halt and faced him.

Hardy got to his feet, his SIG pointed at her.

"I don't see any more of them coming out," he said, glancing at the cab interior.

"I didn't see that guy till I was halfway up the steps," she said, leering at the engineer who lay immobile on the ground with a split head.

"If you see one, let me know. Move. We don't have time for this. The cops might send a real cop here any second to take the place of that dummy."

Phoebe balked.

"Move your ass or die," said Hardy. "Up to you."

"Your gunshot will bring the cops."

Hardy snorted a derisive laugh. "I already fired four shots. Where are the cops?"

Phoebe relented.

Apprehensively, she climbed the steps into the cab car, scoping out the interior to make sure another infected maniac wasn't lurking inside.

Hardy followed her.

The cabin was empty.

"Now let's get out of this hellhole," he said, and inspected the control panel.

Phoebe made a move he didn't like. He turned his SIG on her.

"Tell me a joke and I'll let you live a little longer," he said. "It better be good. Not like the last one."

Phoebe had trouble recalling jokes. Half the time she told the joke backwards and got the punchline mixed up with the setup. She struggled to think of a joke, breaking into a sweat, knowing her life depended on it. She recalled one she had heard in grade school.

"What do dentists call their X-rays?" she said.

"I dunno."

"Tooth pics."

Hardy groaned. "You'll have to do better than that."

"What does a house wear?"

"I dunno."

"Address."

"Come on. You gotta do better than that."

"Uh—it was really cold in DC today . . ."

"How cold was it?" said Hardy, playing along.

"It was so cold I saw a politician with his hands in his own pockets."

"My trigger finger is itchy."

Phoebe thought frantically of another joke.

"What's the difference between a dead politician in the road and a dead skunk in the road?" she said.

"I dunno."

"The dead skunk has skid marks in front of it."

Hardy coughed a laugh and lowered his piece. "Not bad. Stay away from the door. Run, you die."

"How are we getting past that squad car on the tracks?"

"Easy-peasy. We shove it off with the train."

Phoebe heard choppers whump-whumping in the distance. She looked out the windshield into the sky and saw twenty-odd choppers heading in this direction.

Hardy followed her gaze.

"Reinforcements for the killer cops," he said. "Time for us to get moving."

He studied the control panel.

"I thought you said you could drive this thing," said Phoebe.

"Don't worry about it. Worry about telling me another joke."

Phoebe felt like she was suffocating. She was out of jokes.

Chapter 91

Strus turned away from the window in Jason's hospital room and eyed Jason, who lay in bed on his back.

"We're under attack," said Strus, his face haggard.

"Who? What?" said Jason, befuddled.

"More and more rioters are storming the building."

"Can you get the worms out of my brain?" said Jason, his eyes bugged out, his hands trembling.

"Worms are the least of our worries. There's a hysterical mob out for blood, rampaging through the hospital. We're not safe here."

"You don't understand. The Novamors worms are eating my brain." Jason grimaced. "I can feel them digging holes in it. *The pain. The pain.* Can't you help me?"

"I'm not a doctor. Look at me. I'm the acting mayor."

"*I'm* the mayor. You must do as I say."

"You're in no condition to assume your duties. Don't you recognize me?"

Jason squinted at Strus. "It's hard for me to see through the waves of pain. I hear people yelling."

"Those are the rioters. They're here to kill the doctors, because the vaccines were laced with fentanyl and killed everyone who got one. They want revenge."

"I am the mayor. I order you to remove the worms from my brain."

Ignoring him, Strus made for the door, worried the rioters might go after him as the acting mayor who had ordered the lockdown. Beyond the closed door he heard people bellowing angrily. He couldn't tell which floor they were on.

"Maybe we should bug out," he said, disconcerted. "They're out of their minds with hate. There's no telling what they'll do to us."

"How can I run? I can barely move." Jason winced. "The worms. Somebody, make the pain stop. It's like red-hot fire irons impaling my head. My melting brains are gonna start leaking out my nose."

Strus nudged open the door and peeked into the hall. He didn't see any rioters.

"I'll see if I can get security to help us," he said.

He bolted out the door.

"Come back and take the worms out of my brain," cried Jason, his face flushed. "I can't stand the pain."

He struggled to sit upright, yanking tubes out of his arms, his internal injuries aching. Every time he moved he suffered shooting pain. But no pain was more insupportable than that of the worms gnawing his brain. Half-blinded with pain, he gazed at the open window, watching the blinds stir in the breeze.

Groaning, he tried to stand. The pain was excruciating. It was all over his body. His legs, his ribs, his spine. Gnashing his teeth, he managed to stand on the broken bones in his legs. He felt lightheaded. He had to reach the window before he passed out. The worms must be destroyed, he decided.

He halted toward the window, which seemed like a mile away. He could barely move his legs constricted by the bandages swathing them. He had to be careful he didn't fall. If he fell, he would never be able to get up. It was difficult to concentrate because the worms were eating his brain. There must have been hundreds or even thousands of them feeding on him. Phoebe had sicced the worms on him. She was getting revenge for his cheating on her with Val.

He had to reach the window. He edged closer. He could do it if he set his mind to it. He felt like he was losing his balance. He told himself to settle down. He had a strong will. He hadn't become mayor on account of a weak will. Weaklings never succeeded in politics. It was a matter of determination as well as maintaining a carefully crafted image. He had to overcome the pain and proceed.

He could feel the breeze from the window caressing his flesh as he stood in his johnny.

His life was on a downward spiral ever since he had met Val Lewton on the Strip. She had infected him with Novamors. Even though his doctors had said he wasn't infected, he knew the truth.

He knew the Novamors worms were burrowing into his brain. He could feel them. The doctors could take all the CAT scans of his brain they wanted and tell him he wasn't infected. The X-rays proved nothing. He knew the truth.

The advance of medical technology was a wonderful thing, but technology wasn't infallible. It hadn't detected the worms infesting his brain, driving him mad with pain.

He had to keep walking.

He was getting closer inch by agonizing inch. Every inch was a struggle. The closer he got to the window, the farther away it seemed. Maybe Xeno's dichotomy paradox was true: that he would never reach the window if he kept cutting the distance to it in half. *Bullshit*. This was reality, not an abstract math problem. If he kept advancing, he would reach the window.

The breeze became more forceful as he neared the open window. Which proved he must be getting closer. Xeno be damned.

He felt himself wobbling. No, no, he told himself. *Don't fall*. It was like surfing. A matter of keeping his balance. The last thing he needed now was a wipeout.

He felt a worm slither out of the pupil of his eye and tumble to the linoleum floor. A blood-streaked white worm squirmed at his feet. Worms were squirming throughout his head. He had to hurry to the window before they incapacitated him. Did the worms know he was heading for the window? Were they trying to prevent him from reaching it? They didn't want to lose their meal ticket.

Revolted, he kicked the worm on the floor out of his way.

He edged his foot forward, keeping his balance.

He was so close he could reach out and touch the window. He heard the mob screaming below.

"Kill the doctors," they screamed. "Kill the doctors."

He kept shambling forward and reached out for the steel window jamb.

The breeze hit him full in the face. A blood-smeared white worm writhed out of his nostril and caromed off his johnny's chest. Two other bloody worms crawled out of his mouth. He coughed to clear his throat, expelling three more worms. Were the worms going to smother him? Was that their plan? He gagged.

He cheered in triumph upon reaching the window. He would cheat the worms of their victory.

He saw scores of choppers raising a ruckus as they infested the sky. He had never seen so many helos together—almost enough to blot out the sky with a steel canopy of fuselages and churning rotor blades.

He poked his head out the window and peered at the concrete concourse below, where rioters milled, pumping their fists, their faces masks of rage.

Streaks of fire fell to shooting out of the chopper cockpits at the hospital lobby and the agitated rioters.

Nerve-shredding screams of pain and outrage rang out from the mob as rioters burst into flames.

The rioters must be infected with Novamors, decided Jason.

There was only one way to kill the worms and save himself from their feeding frenzy, he knew.

He hauled himself onto the steel sill and managed to straddle it, one broken, bandaged leg hanging outside the lobby facade. He gazed at the concourse directly beneath him. It was a long way down. He experienced vertigo as he balanced precariously on the sill. His heartbeat raced as he knew what he must do. It was the only solution.

He tipped over and toppled out the window.

"Stinking worms," he cried, and plummeted to his death on the concourse below.

Chapter 92

Phoebe heard a noise in the passenger car behind the cab car.
"What was that?" she said.
"I didn't hear anything," said Hardy.
"In the next car."
The choppers had flown past them, the sky limpid.
"We're good to go," said Hardy.
He fired the engine. The train advanced, crashing into the cruiser that blocked its path. The train rammed the vehicle out of the way and picked up speed.
"Toodle-loo, hellhole," he said, waving back at the city.
"I heard something back there," said Phoebe, eying the passenger car behind them.
"I didn't."
"How do I open the door?"
"Everything's electric. I'll open the door on the control console."
Phoebe walked to the passenger car door, the railroad's wooden crossties blurring underneath her as the train sped over them. She peered through the steel door's window.
"What was it?" said Hardy.
Phoebe saw rows of empty passenger seats.
"I don't see anything," she said.
She tried to open the door. It didn't budge.
"How do I open the door?"
Hardy searched the control panel. He pressed a button.
"Now try it," he said.
She managed to slide open the door with a whoosh.
She scoped out the passenger car interior. Nothing but rows of empty seats. She didn't see anything rolling around loose on the floor, which might have caused the knocking sound she had heard.
"What was it?" said Hardy.
"The car's vacant."
"I told you it was nothing."

Which was when somebody walked into the aisle from a seat in the rear. It was a little girl, not yet ten years old, in a pink dress. She wore powder blue sneakers. She had long hair with blonde curls that cascaded over her shoulders.

"It's a little girl," said Phoebe.

The girl had a grin on her face. No, it wasn't a grin, more like a rictus, decided Phoebe.

The girl gripped a hammer in her hand.

Phoebe realized the window next to the girl's seat was broken. The girl had been hammering the window. Trapped in the passenger car, she had been trying to escape.

"You poor thing," said Phoebe, feeling the train accelerate and bracing herself in the doorway as the vibrating train gently swayed.

Phoebe could see flecks of foam stippling the girl's grimacing mouth.

The girl raised the hammer over her head. Screaming, she bolted toward Phoebe.

Terrified, her heart pumping out of control, Phoebe tried to close the door. It wouldn't budge.

"Close the door," she screamed over her shoulder at Hardy. "It won't move."

As the train shot away from the railroad station, deafening explosions from thermite bombs rocked the earth and turned Costaguana into a forest of raging, jagged flames that reached for the clouds, consuming everything in their path.

"The goddamn idiots went and did it," said Hardy with equal parts rage and awe. "They're firebombing the city."

"She's infected. Close the fucking door."

Bathed in sweat, Phoebe continued to struggle to shut the electronic door.

Another child sidled from behind a row of seats into the passenger car aisle. He was a snarling blond boy waving a meat cleaver above his head. A brunette girl with a ponytail sprang out of the row of seats behind him. Frothing at the mouth, pulling a face, she brandished a hatchet. Another infected child bounded into the aisle. And another. And another.

"Help," cried Phoebe, unable to close the door. "The car's full of them."

The train barreled forward, picking up momentum.

Behind the last car, a pall of black smoke suffused with whirling smuts buried the graveyard pyre of Costaguana under the bloodred sun flanked by knots of scudding carmine clouds torn from the pits of hell.

## ABOUT THE AUTHOR

Multi-award-winning author Bryan Cassiday writes horror fiction and thrillers. His postapocalyptic horror thriller *Horde (Zombie Apocalypse: The Chad Halverson Series Book 6)* won both the Independent Press Award for Best Horror Novel 2022 and the American Fiction Award for Best Horror Novel 2021. His Scott Brody thriller *Threads* won the Independent Press Award for Best Thriller Novel 2023 and the American Fiction Award for Best Hard-Boiled Crime Novel 2022. He lives in Southern California.